PRAISE FOR *CAGE*

'A simply fabulous conclusion t[...] penetrating Reykjavik Noir Tri[...]g ensured I devoured this read, from the first word through to an ending that completely and beautifully hit the spot ... With shocks and surprises in store, and that oh-so satisfying end, *Cage* provoked, chilled, and thrilled me' LoveReading

'An electrifying read, packed with emotion and touching moments that grab the reader, but it also leaves them feeling the creeping Icelandic chill that gets under their skin and has them desperate for more books from this author!' The Quiet Knitter

'It's an intriguing story that builds up to an amazing climax ... high drama and intrigue' Mac's Book Reviews

'Lilja is a master of keeping you in the dark just long enough to sweeten the enlightenment when it comes. She is also a master puzzle maker and of dropping little clues everywhere. There was a great main storyline and great tributaries ... which all flowed into the main story' Mrs Loves To Read

'I devoured this in just a few hours. If you've read the first two books in this series and loved them like I did, then you won't be disappointed with this one! The evolution of the characters, the fast-paced storyline and wonderful ending made for a fantastic read!' Laura Rash

'For a relatively short novel, there's a whole lot of Icelandic intrigue packed in! Get the other two instalments and read in order for maximum effect' The Book Trail

'Suspenseful ... takes full advantage of its fresh setting and is a worthy addition to the icy-cold crime genre popularised by Scandinavian noir novels' *Foreword Reviews*

'A pacey, tense read with an underlying layer of humanity and the messiness of life' Mystery Scene

'The characters are so fascinating and the writing is mesmerising' Steph's Book Blog

'A cold, chilling and beautifully intricate plot ... the best Icelandic noir has to offer' Chocolate 'n' Waffles

'An addictive and thrilling read, perfect for crime fiction fans looking to branch out into other sub genres of crime fiction' Murder and Moore

'Fresh and original – the plot is dark, exciting and I absolutely recommend it!' Keeper of Pages

'Original, very well written and full of twists that will leave the reader totally engaged from the first page, a must read!' Varietats

'A superb thriller and deserves to be on the reading list of all book lovers, not just thriller aficionados. Character and plot wise it works on all levels' Books Are My Cwtches

'Hugely compelling and addictive ... Lilja Sigurðardóttir has a real talent and manages to weave some fantastically complex plots together without losing any of the momentum' Mumbling About

'Tense, very cleverly put together and I can guarantee you will fly through the pages of this book!' Rae Reads

'The tension escalated throughout the book, culminating in a thrilling, heart-stopping conclusion' Off-the-Shelf Books

'A rather fascinating and brilliantly edgy look at contemporary Icelandic society' Live and Deadly

'Complex and surprisingly witty and I thoroughly enjoyed reading Lilja Sigurðardóttir's intelligent and original novel' Hair Past a Freckle

'A satisfying and tense novel. But this book has an emotional punch too – a whole flurry of punches coming at the reader from all directions' Blue Book Balloon

'Exhilarating, intense and compelling' Novel Gossip

'Uniquely involving with a strong plot and I loved every page. Highly recommended' My Chestnut Reading Tree

'A pleasant, unique read which kept me thoroughly entertained – I enjoyed stepping out of my comfort zone with this one!' The Writing Garnet

ABOUT THE AUTHOR

Icelandic crime-writer Lilja Sigurðardóttir was born in the town of Akranes in 1972 and raised in Mexico, Sweden, Spain and Iceland. An award-winning playwright, Lilja has written four crime novels, with *Snare*, the first in the Reykjavík Noir series, hitting bestseller lists worldwide. *Trap* was published in 2018, and was a Guardian Book of the Year. In 2018, *Cage* won Icelandic Crime Novel of the Year. The film rights for the series have been bought by Palomar Pictures in California. Lilja lives in Reykjavík with her partner.

Follow Lilja:
Twitter: *@lilja1972*
Instagram: *www.instagram.com/sigurdardottirlilja/*
Facebook: *www.facebook.com/sigurdardottir.lilja*
Website: *www.liljawriter.com*

ABOUT THE TRANSLATOR

Quentin Bates escaped English suburbia as a teenager, jumping at the chance of a gap year working in Iceland. For a variety of reasons, the gap year stretched to a gap decade, during which time he went native in the north of Iceland, acquiring a new language, a new profession as a seaman, and a family, before decamping en masse to England. He worked as a truck driver, teacher, netmaker and trawlerman at various times before falling into journalism, largely by accident. He is the author of a series of crime novels set in present-day Iceland (*Frozen Out, Cold Steal, Chilled to the Bone, Winterlude, Cold Comfort* and *Thin Ice*) which have been published worldwide. He has translated all of Ragnar Jónasson's Dark Iceland series. Visit him on Twitter *@graskeggur* or on his website: *graskeggur.com*

Cage

Lilja Sigurðardóttir

Translated by Quentin Bates

**ORENDA
BOOKS**

Orenda Books
16 Carson Road
West Dulwich
London SE21 8HU
www.orendabooks.co.uk

First published in Icelandic as *Búrið* by Forlagid in 2017
First published in English by Orenda Books in 2019
Copyright © Lilja Sigurðardóttir, 2017
English translation copyright © Quentin Bates, 2019

A catalogue record for this book is available from the British Library.

ISBN 978-1-912374-49-6
eISBN 978-1-912374-50-2

The publication of this translation has been made
possible through the financial support of

 ICELANDIC LITERATURE CENTER

Co-funded by the
Creative Europe Programme
of the European Union

Typeset in Garamond by MacGuru Ltd

Printed and bound by CPI Group (UK) Ltd, Croydon CRO 4YY

For sales and distribution, please contact
info@orendabooks.co.uk or visit *www.orendabooks.co.uk*.

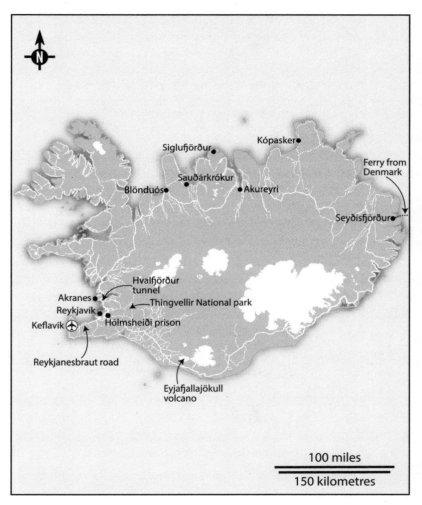

Iceland

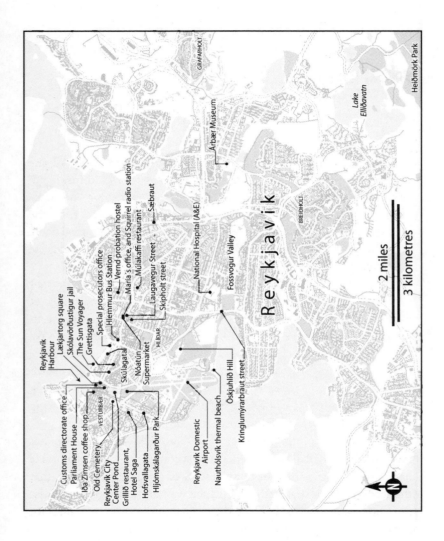

Reykjavik

Reykjavik Harbour
Lækjartorg square
Skólavörðustigur jail
The Sun Voyager
Grettisgata
Special prosecutors office
Hlemmur Bus Station
Vernd probation hostel
Maria´s office, and Squirrel radio station
Múlakaff restaurant
Laugavegur Street
Skipholt street
Sæbraut
National Hospital (A&E)
Fossvogur Valley
Árbær Museum

Customs directorate office
Parliament House
Iða Zimsen coffee shop
Old Cemetery
Reykjavik City Center Pond
Grillið restaurant,
Hotel Saga
Hofsvallagata
Hljómskálagarður Park
Reykjavik Domestic Airport
Nauthólsvik thermal beach
Öskjuhlíð Hill
Kringlumýrarbraut street

Skúlagata
Nóatún
Supermarket

GRAFARHOLT
Lake Elliðavatn
Heiðmörk Park
BREIÐHOLT
HLÍÐAR
VESTURBÆR

2 miles
3 kilometres

N

April 2017

1

The cell door shut behind Agla's back with a smooth click. All the doors and walls in the new Hólmsheiði Prison were sound-insulated, so the women's wing was quiet in the evenings. There was no slamming, and no calls or mutter of televisions carried through from the cells of the other women serving their sentences there. Instead there was a heavy silence, which seemed to engulf her like water – and she was sinking slowly and gently to the bottom.

She had known that being locked up wasn't going to be a pleasant experience. A few years earlier she had been on remand for a couple of days while the market-manipulation case against her was being investigated, so she had been expecting something similar. But this was unlike anything she had anticipated. It was one thing to spend two or three days in a cell, at the end of which her lawyer had appeared like a guardian angel, sweeping her away to dinner; it was quite another to walk into this building that still smelled of damp cement and filler, knowing that it would be her world for the next year.

Now she had a month to go before she was eligible for parole. In her mind she had divided her sentence into sections: she had to complete half of her time and then the rest would be on probation. But now that the second section was within sight, she was consumed with trepidation. Somehow she had become the animal in the zoo that dared not leave its cage for fear of looking freedom in the eye.

As her time in prison had passed, she had found the cage an increasingly comfortable place to be; to the point where she was numbed by it. There was now something reassuring about having all her power taken away from her. The more she had complained about the hard mattress and the piss-warm shower, the more a simple fact had filtered through into her consciousness: whatever she did or said in here made no difference. Her own will was of no consequence.

She had the impression that life was progressing evermore slowly, and she was finding it increasingly difficult to make decisions. The warders would often suggest she played games or did some handiwork, or brought her books from the library; but she could no longer be bothered to play, work or read. The same seemed to apply to the other women. She'd seen those whose sentences had begun after hers turn up furious and bristling with pain, just as she had; but after three months all their fury had dried up, and now they hardly even spoke to each other.

Two of the Icelandic prisoners had arrived at the same time as Agla. With the justice system overloaded, like Agla and many others convicted of non-violent offences, they had had to wait a long time before they could start serving their sentences. Another woman had come here from a prison in the north, and one had joined them some time later. The foreign women were on the other corridor, so they had come and gone without Agla noticing. All of them had been mules – young women from Eastern Europe, dressed in track suits, with dyed hair and poor English. Like the Icelandic prisoners, they kept to their own corridor, but somehow their community seemed to be livelier, although the gales of laughter and the songs could sometimes turn into screams and fights.

At the beginning of her sentence, Agla had made daily visits to the fitness room, accepted interviews with the prison chaplain – if only to have someone to talk to – and made an effort when it was her turn to cook. Now, though, she no longer had the energy for any of this, and her fellow prisoners were lucky to get rice pudding and meat soup, as she couldn't summon the energy to cook anything more demanding. Not that they complained; they had probably stopped tasting any flavour in the food long ago.

She took the nail clippers from her vanity bag, then used them to pick tiny holes in a sheet, so that she could tear it into strips. Two strips would definitely be needed, twisted together so they were strong enough. She had planned this a long time ago – when she had been informed that her probation was coming up, but she hadn't made a decision about a precise day. Earlier, though, just after the evening news on TV, she had had the feeling that it was now time. Her decision was accompanied by neither sorrow nor fear, but instead by a kind of epiphany, as if a fog in her mind had lifted and for the first time in many months she could clearly see that this was the right thing to do.

It took longer than she had expected to rip up the sheet, and when she wound the two strips together, they lost half of their length, and became a short piece of rope. She looked around and immediately saw the solution, as if, now that the moment was near, new possibilities were appearing that she had not seen before. She unplugged the power cable for the TV and unwound it from its coil at the back of the set. It would work fine; it wouldn't fail.

She made the sheet rope into a loop that would tighten around her neck, and then tied the loop to the cable. She got to her feet and went over to the radiator on the wall by the door. It was just about the only thing in her cell that anything could be tied to. Agla hoped it was high enough up the wall. She tied the cable to the top of the radiator and pulled at it – gingerly at first, afraid that the makeshift noose would give way, and then with all her strength. It seemed secure. She hoped that her body would not let her down at the last moment, responding with some self-preservation instinct and trying to keep her on her feet.

For a second the silence was broken by a blackbird's song, as it made its nest somewhere nearby. The thick walls were not able to stifle the cheerful birdsong, and it triggered in Agla an immediate desire to step outside into the fresh air and inhale the scent of the blossoming birch trees. But this urge disappeared the second the birdsong came to an end, and images of her mother and Sonja passed through her mind.

The pain and the regret that came with these thoughts were so bitter, her heart ached; but at the same time she felt a sense of relief that this would be the very last time she would be tormented like this. Never again would she be outside these walls, having to stand alone, wondering why Sonja had abandoned her. Never again would she have to face the endless choices that freedom offered, and that, up to now, had mainly brought her misfortune. It came as a relief that her life was over.

She stood with her back to the radiator, pulled a plastic bag over her head and looped the noose about her neck. The moment she had tightened the noose, she sighed once, with satisfaction, and then sat down.

2

The chill evening breeze left Anton shivering. He zipped up his coat and checked the time on his phone. Eight minutes had passed since Gunnar had taken the moped they had brought to where they had decided to hide it. The only reason he had brought Gunnar in was because of his moped. At one point he had considered taking his dad's car, because he could drive just fine, even if he was only fifteen and didn't even have a provisional licence yet. But taking the car would have been risky – especially if they were pulled over by the police – and if anyone was about, a car would be more noticeable than a moped with no lights.

He heard quick footsteps approaching him from behind, and he spun around. It was Gunnar, running towards him with his white helmet on his head like a giant mushroom. They had agreed to wear helmets the whole time, both to reduce the likelihood of the police stopping them and so that any security cameras wouldn't pick up images of their faces. Fortunately, though, there didn't appear to be any cameras here. He had been checking the area out over the past few days, and knew that the roadworks guys used a diesel generator for the lights and heating in their shed. But now everything was dark – so dark that the green hue of the northern lights dancing in the eastern sky was unusually bright.

Anton shouldered the backpack containing their tools, and they hurried on quiet feet over to the fence, where Gunnar took the wire cutters from the bag and started making a hole big enough for them to crawl through.

'That's just a catflap,' Anton said. 'The hole has to be bigger. We need to get back through it with full backpacks.'

'OK,' Gunnar agreed, snipping a few more wires, but he was obviously tired already, so Anton took the cutters from his hand and continued the work. Even though these were decent cutters, brand new and sharp, the mesh was still unbelievably hard to cut. He had to use all his strength to break each strand.

To begin with they had planned to go over the fence, but the coils of razor wire at the top put an end to that idea – they would have had to cut through that anyway, so it was as well to forget climbing and make a hole down here. It was also safer, as there was less chance of them being seen at ground level.

'Give it a pull now,' Anton said.

Gunnar twisted the tongue of mesh upwards so that Anton could crawl through, then Gunnar followed behind him. They jogged past the workmen's cabin to the storage shed behind it. Anton shook off his backpack, and they took out the head torches and fixed them to their helmets. He was pleased with this idea; they could see what they were doing without having to hold torches or a lamp.

'OK,' he said. 'Let's do it.'

Gunnar did not need to be told twice. He took out a hammer and began battering the padlock, while Anton set to work with a screwdriver, trying to unscrew the hinges. This was one aspect of the job they had not agreed on. They had spent time lying in the scrub, looking down on the place with a pair of binoculars, watching to see how the shed was closed and arguing about the best way to open it. It didn't seem to be a proper door, more a homemade job with a sheet of plywood that had been cut to fit the opening and fixed with hinges on the outside. After racking their brains for a while, they decided on both approaches; they'd see which was the one that got them inside the shed first. Anton knew that the method didn't matter. It was the objective that was important. But Gunnar seemed to think there was a principle at stake, and insisted on smashing open the padlock, so Anton had accepted this compromise.

'There!' Gunnar whooped as the first of the three padlocks gave way and hung open.

'Cool,' Anton grunted, concentrating on the screws. He had removed them all from one hinge and was almost there with the second.

As he pulled out the last screw, Gunnar was still getting his breath back after the battle with the padlock.

Anton took the hammer from him, slid the claw into the opening and put his weight behind it. The door dropped out of the frame and hung on the remaining two locks on the other side.

'Yesss!' Gunnar crowed, his excitement obvious. 'You win. Ice cream on me after. You're the meanest gangster in town, man.'

He was clearly enjoying every moment.

Anton, on the other hand, was surprised at how calm he felt. He had been sure he would be more nervous. But now a warm feeling of achievement swept through him as he stepped inside the shed and the light on his helmet flickered over the boxes.

This was the first step towards his objective. He knelt down and opened the first box and began stacking sticks of dynamite in his backpack.

3

'I'm on the visitor list,' María said, her resentment growing deeper and stronger the longer she spent talking to the prison officer responsible for dealing with visitors.

She had booked this visit a good few days before, and refused to believe that Agla had now taken her off the list. As far as María was aware, she was the only visitor Agla ever had. Yes, the visits did seem to trouble Agla, but each one always lasted the full allotted time, even though it invariably descended into arguments and quibbling. And yes, María always had a long list of questions, which Agla usually avoided answering, but her visits had to be about the only variation in the routine of being locked up. At least, María assumed that this was why Agla had put her name on the visitor list in the first place. It seemed to her highly unlikely that Agla had now changed her mind.

'You can call tomorrow to book another visit,' the prison officer said, tugging his shirt down over his paunch and stuffing it into his waistband. 'Agla can't have visitors today.'

'Why not?' María asked, leaning forwards, elbows on the table, driving home the point that she wasn't about to leave.

'She's indisposed,' the prison officer said, peering at the visitor list and scribbling a note on it.

'I want to know why,' María said. 'Or let me call her myself, so she can tell me in person that she doesn't want a visit.'

The prison officer sighed deeply.

'Agla can't see any visitors today. Try calling tomorrow.'

'I'm an investigative journalist and I demand to know why prisoner Agla Margeirsdóttir isn't available for a previously agreed visit. If I don't get an explanation then I'll have no choice but to take this to the Prison and Probation Administration.'

The prison officer sighed again, deeper this time, and his eyes rolled towards the ceiling.

'Sweetheart, this isn't Guantanamo Bay. We have a duty of confidentiality regarding the health of inmates, so all I can tell you is that Agla is unwell today, and that you can call tomorrow and book another visit.'

Now it was María's turn to sigh. This was as far as she was going to get for the moment. There was no point in taking out her frustration on the prison officer. In reality, she didn't suspect there was anything untoward about Agla's absence; she was simply impatient. This time the questions on her list were all unusually urgent – she wanted to know about Agla's links to Ingimar Magnússon and William Tedd, the Paris-based markets guru. She had come across both names during her investigation into Agla back when she had worked on economic crime for the special prosecutor. That had been in a previous life, before Agla had, indirectly, caused her to be sacked.

María let her thoughts wander as she made her way back to her car. Although the days had begun to lengthen, the April sun was still low in the sky, and she squinted into the brightness. It would be more pleasant when these knife-edged, blue-white rays gave way to mild spring sunshine. In this light everything seemed to be grey and forlorn after the harshness of winter. There was no sign yet of any growth and the sunshine beat down mercilessly on the dry moorland that replaced the bare earth as she left the prison behind her. Not that the time of year made any difference. She wouldn't be taking a summer holiday to enjoy the weather. She couldn't afford one. Her online news service, The Squirrel, just about made ends meet, but only because of the income from the handful of advertisements she had been able to secure. So far she hadn't been able to sell her material to any of the larger media outlets. Now, though, she suspected she was on the trail of something juicy. Just the names Ingimar Magnússon and William Tedd were enough to tell her she was on the right track.

María sat behind the wheel. Her heart skipped a beat when she noticed, hanging from the mirror, the little crystal angel that Maggi had given her. That had been a year before he had left her, saying that she wasn't the person he thought he had married. If she were to trace everything back to its origins, then the divorce could also be laid at Agla's door. Her whole life had been wrecked when she had been sacked by the special prosecutor, and for many months she had been in a kind of angry, disbelieving limbo. Finally Maggi had given up, saying that he no longer recognised her. If she were completely honest, she no longer recognised herself either.

It didn't do to think too much about Maggi – it would wreck her day completely. If she didn't take care and let herself drift too far, she would end up in tears on the steps outside his place. The worst of it was that, although she couldn't help hoping that he would ask her in and then would hold her tight, she knew full well that he would actually just look at her with a mixture of disgust and pity, before shutting the door in her face.

She started the engine and wondered whether she ought to rip the angel from the mirror and throw it out onto the moor. But she couldn't bring herself to do it. Maybe she would do it tomorrow. In the morning she would call the prison and book another visit. And since she wasn't able to ask Agla her questions right away, she would have to start on Ingimar.

4

She had been more heavy-handed than usual today – to Ingimar's satisfaction. He was exhausted after being whipped, and he had needed her help to reach the bed afterwards. This was the best part of it, exactly why he came to her; the hour he spent in her bed on the borderline between sleep and wakefulness, overwhelmed by the adrenaline that his body automatically pumped into his bloodstream as the first lash of the whip burned into his back, and the endorphins that accumulated the longer the treatment lasted, leaving him in a daze.

In his younger years he had believed that what he craved was the humiliation – of being tied, manacled, hung from a hook and whipped; of being completely in her power. But now he knew better. The key to it was the vulnerability that came afterwards; his defencelessness as she helped him, sobbing and bruised, to the bed, where she would apply a soothing balm to his back, tuck him in and whisper sweet words that were both calming and encouraging, just like a mother with her child. This was when he felt he was truly loved; he revelled in lying in bed without having had to do anything to deserve it, not one single thing.

'You're a good boy,' she whispered, kissing the top of his head and leaving the room as he began to doze. He lay there in a dreamless state for a while, he had no idea how long, until his thoughts were again clear and linear, and he felt there was no longer any need to lie still. The time for rest was over. He got to his feet, pulled on his trousers and took his shirt with him to the kitchen where she was waiting for him with a smile.

'Let's take a look at you,' she said, examining his back. 'You're fine,' she added, handing him his singlet and helping him into it. It stung like hell, but he liked that. He would feel the pain for the next few days, every time he dressed, took a shower or leaned back in a chair, and that was the way he wanted it. This reminder was something he needed; the reminder that he was human. It was the same as the Roman emperors who had a slave walking behind them, whispering 'remember you are mortal, remember you are mortal'.

'I'll make a transfer to your account,' he said as he buttoned his shirt.

She stepped closer and helped him with the top button and knotted his tie for him.

'Not too much,' she said. 'You always pay me too much.'

'I'm grateful,' he said.

'You're still in a state when you make the transfer, so you make it too much.'

'It's no more than you deserve,' he said, kissing her cheek.

'Now you be a good little worm and do as you're told.' She smiled and winked as she teased him. 'Otherwise you'll feel it...'

He gave her an exaggerated bow.

'Yes, madame!'

They understood each other instinctively. She knew precisely when it was safe to inject a little humour into the game they played, and when things had to be kept serious as it was crucial to not lose the momentum.

'Call me whenever you want,' she said, holding the front door open for him.

He blew her a kiss on his way down the steps, and as was so often the case, he was astonished at the change he'd undergone since he had turned up here a couple of hours ago. He had walked in tense with stress and with his mind in overdrive, but now he was relaxed and his thoughts had clarified, as if his soul had been cleansed.

He started his car and turned up the heater. It wasn't particularly cold, but a whipping always left him with a chill that lasted a few hours. His phone showed one missed call and two text messages, all from the same number. He opened the first message. It was a long one, from an investigative journalist called María. He sighed. He knew who María was: a former investigator at the special prosecutor's office who had fallen badly out of favour and who now ran her own online news outlet, an effort driven forwards more by determination than ability. She was the type who saw conspiracy everywhere she looked and who could make the most innocent thing look suspicious. The message was a series of questions concerning himself and Agla, and any business connections they might have.

That was something he could answer easily. Right now there were none. They had ended their joint business affairs some years before and since then had taken care to avoid each other.

He opened the second message and the flood of questions continued. This demonstrated an incredible optimism on her part. Surely she didn't expect him to answer all these questions by text message? Normally he kept clear of journalists and wouldn't have hesitated to delete these messages right away.

But the last question in the series troubled him:

What is the nature of the business conducted by yourself and William Tedd with Icelandic aluminium producers?

5

If she had imagined during the weeks before she'd sat down in front of the radiator with the noose around her neck that she couldn't possibly have felt worse, she was wrong. Those days had been a walk in the park compared to waking up after trying to kill herself.

The pain of renewing her acquaintance with life, having already waved it a final goodbye, was so unreal, she wasn't even able to feel angry with herself for making a mess of it. She opened her eyes and saw that everything around her was white, which told her she had to be in hospital. She closed her eyes again and hoped that she might slip back into unconsciousness. But it was hopeless. She was awake and a prison officer she knew was called Guðrún was in a chair at her side, leafing through a magazine.

'How are you feeling?' Guðrún asked, ringing a bell.

Under the circumstances, this was a bizarre question, and there was only one possible reply: bad. Agla tried to form the word but all that came out of her throat was an indistinct growl that could have been made by a wild animal. That would have to be a wounded, angry animal.

A woman in white scrubs came in and looked her over.

'Don't try to talk,' she said. 'Just rest and drink cold water. Your throat is still swollen and you've not long come off the ventilator, which will have left your throat sore as well. I'll get you some water and painkillers, and the doctor will be along to talk to you.'

She looked into Agla's eyes, and laid a hand on her arm, squeezing it briefly. Then she smiled and left the room. This tiny sign of human warmth was like a punch to the stomach, and Agla could feel tears flowing from her eyes and down onto the pillow. Self-pity wasn't something she made a habit of, regardless of how tough things might be, but somehow this was pushing humiliation to a new level. A screwed-up attempt at death had become the perfect summation of a screwed-up life.

The nurse returned with a painkiller that she pumped through the cannula in the back of Agla's hand. Then she spooned up an ice cube from the water glass at Agla's side and lifted it to her lips. Agla opened her mouth like an obedient child and took the ice cube just as she felt the morphine take over. In a second, everything became a little better. The tears stopped flowing from her eyes, and she felt there was a security in having Guðrún at her side, again deep in a magazine.

Agla came round to the sound of the doctor's deep voice, which somehow had seemed to grow louder inside the void of her unconsciousness. Maybe he had been standing there talking for a while.

'You were lucky,' he said. 'You were extremely fortunate that the rope stretched almost enough to let you sit; it meant your bodyweight wasn't concentrated entirely on your neck. Otherwise you'd have broken it, and damaged your spinal cord too. But as the rope stretched and you weren't hanging there for long, we're only looking at damage to your airway, and some swelling and bruises. Even your larynx is in pretty good condition. So you'll be in here overnight and then you should be able to go home tomorrow,' he said. Then he glanced at Guðrún, who coughed gently. 'I mean, you can be discharged tomorrow.'

Agla blinked slowly instead of trying to nod her head, as her neck was still too stiff.

The doctor turned to leave.

'There'll be a psychiatrist coming to see you later today. That's the rule when this kind of thing happens,' he added from the doorway.

When this kind of thing happens, Agla thought to herself. Why doesn't he just say *when people try to kill themselves*?

6

Júlía tiptoed up to the school steps, where Anton stood with his back to her, and slipped her little finger into his hand. He responded by twisting his little finger around hers. This was their special thing, an expression of what passed between them and their main physical connection. Anything further had been forbidden, which in itself had been unbelievably embarrassing, but hadn't actually changed things much. They could still spend all the time they wanted together, her father had said when he had visited Anton's father to 'talk things over', and they could go to each other's houses and see each other, just as long as their bedroom doors remained open.

Anton had seen how his father had been taken by surprise by this visit, and how he had tried to hide it. To begin with he had used small talk, and had filled the old man with coffee and biscuits to stifle any serious conversation. Then, much to Anton's surprise, he had agreed with Júlía's father. Anton had expected him to go along with what his son was doing without saying a word. But instead he had announced to Anton in his grave voice that if he was serious about the girl, then he could wait. And Anton *could* wait. Everyone at school knew they were together, so none of the other boys dared go anywhere near her, which meant that he could be sure she was his; the prettiest girl in the school. In fact, she was easily the prettiest girl he had ever seen. Of course they broke the rules; they kissed and cuddled when nobody could see them, but it wasn't often, as he could sense that she was uncomfortable with disobeying her father, and he didn't want to pressure her. As his father had spelled out to him, if he wanted to hold on to the girl, then he would have to behave in a way that made her feel safe around him.

So he tried to do everything he possibly could to make sure that she had a feeling of security when she was near him.

He gently squeezed her little finger and turned his head towards her. She smiled.

'Shall we go to the pictures tomorrow?' she asked.

'Dinner and a movie?' he suggested with a wink. That had to mean a burger or a kebab, followed by a bus ride to the cinema. It would be her birthday soon, and he had decided he would take her out somewhere smart, a shirt-and-tie place, and he'd have to do a deal with his father to cover transport and some extra finance.

By then he would also have given her the birthday present. This was what he had dreamed of for so many weeks. He was certain that it would be the best moment of their whole lives.

'Talk to you this evening,' she said as Gunnar cruised up to the school steps on his moped, which was still muddy from the night before.

'Talk to you this evening,' Anton said, squeezing her little finger again. There was no need to say it, as they talked every evening and sent each other endless messages and chatted online. As well as being the prettiest, she was the most fun girl he had ever met.

He hopped onto the moped and held on tight to Gunnar's coat as he set off. They had agreed to meet after school to find a better place to store the dynamite, and to think over the problem of detonators. He had been sure that they would find detonators in the shed as well, but there hadn't been any. They had searched everywhere to be certain. They would just have to find some other way to set the dynamite off.

7

'If you get a call from a journalist called María, phoning from Iceland, then don't give her any chance to ask you anything,' Ingimar said once he and William had exchanged the usual greetings.

The background music he could hear down the line told him that William was out enjoying himself somewhere. The man was a well-known party animal who never let a celebration or a gathering pass him by. He reminded Ingimar of a younger version of himself. Back in his younger days he had the same kind of energy that allowed him to spend a night on the town and be awake and ready for a tough day's work after only three hours' sleep. As far as he was concerned, that was now all in the past. But the same didn't apply to William.

'I'm at a friend's birthday party,' he said, his strong American accent coming across clearly. 'You'd have had a great time.'

Ingimar knew what that meant: fine wines and fine women. He leaned forwards and used the car's mirror to inspect the grey in his hair. For a second he felt a touch of regret for that life – but in fact he did not miss it. These days he could knock back wine at whatever time of the day he wanted to without feeling it, and he had pretty much given up chasing women. *She* didn't count. That wasn't chasing skirt. That was something different.

'Everything looks good,' Ingimar said. 'This María is just fishing, but I wanted to warn you anyway. She's one of those annoying people who doesn't understand when to lay off. She's trying to connect Agla with our project, and we need to be careful, we don't want her getting mixed up in this.'

'Why? Don't you like Agla?' William laughed, and, as if to under-score the glamour of his party, an up-tempo salsa number struck up in the background.

'It's not that I don't like Agla. Quite the opposite. It's just that if she gets the slightest inkling of what we're up to, before we know it half the profits will end up in her pocket,' he said.

William roared with laughter.

'That's her, right enough,' he said. 'Now get yourself to Paris, *mon cher* Ingimar. I'm on the trail of a sweet little thing here who has a twin sister. So we could be up for a memorable double date!'

Ingimar smiled to himself. He enjoyed William's zest for life. Americans were so delightfully shameless about their pursuit of pleasure.

'Speak soon,' he said, and ended the call.

He would certainly have enjoyed a trip to Paris, where he could have had William entertain him. But over the last few years it was as if life itself had tracked him down, and responsibility, which was something he had never worried much about, had become an increasing burden. Anton needed him close by, especially considering what his mother was like.

He took a deep breath and got out of the car. As he walked up to the house, his feet seemed unusually heavy. He slipped the key into the lock and opened the door silently. Inside there was silence, and all of his senses seemed to detect the stale aura of unhappiness that filled the house.

8

María felt the same stab of shame every time she entered the building where The Squirrel had its office, because on the other side of the corridor was her landlord, the nationalistically inclined Radio Edda, which played bad Icelandic music and appeared, according to the quality of its discussion programmes, to place a particular emphasis on removing rights for minorities. She would have preferred to locate The Squirrel somewhere else, but she couldn't afford it. The rent at Radio Edda was well below the market rate for this central area of the city, but being here saved her a great deal of driving compared to an office somewhere on the outskirts. Still, even though it was cheap, she always felt the urge to hide her face every time she entered or left the building. Over the doorway hung the station's slogan: *Iceland for Icelanders*.

She was hardly inside the office when Marteinn came hurrying in behind her.

'Brown envelopes, María. Brown envelopes, stuffed with cash that change hands at Freemasons' meetings. Freemasons, María!'

She stared at him questioningly. He had that peculiar glint in his eyes that made him look like a startled horse and that indicated he was heading for a psychotic episode.

'My dear Marteinn,' she said. 'Don't you think you ought to be on your way to the doctor?'

'No,' he said, sitting at his desk.

It would have been an exaggeration to say that Marteinn was her colleague. He was more like an adopted pet who came and went, always on his own terms. She let him write a daily column in The Squirrel with the title 'The Voice of Truth', and in between he helped by digging out information. When his health was in good shape, he was remarkably skilled at searching out all kinds of oddities on the internet, although María suspected that he occasionally hacked into secure computer systems to get what he wanted. She had long since given up trying to manage him. He wasn't exactly staff, as he never asked to be paid. Having someone on board who made an effort without invoicing for it was a real positive, though he wrote pleasantly barbed articles that often attracted attention, and it made a difference to not be a completely solo operation. It was almost like having a proper job when she sat down and had a cup of coffee with him while they talked over his latest conspiracy theory.

'Don't you think you ought to get your medication checked?' she said now. 'Shouldn't you go to the clinic before they close for the day?'

'No,' he said with determination, hunching over the computer that sat among the piles of junk on his desk like a fledgling in a nest. 'I need to write this article first.'

'You've already given me enough for the whole of next week,' she said.

'But this is about the bribes that are paid to ensure that the pollution readings around the smelter are always within limits. This is what happens when the Freemasons meet, María. And people need to know about it!'

She sighed. He seemed to come up with a new conspiracy theory twice a day, most of them involving the Freemasons in some way or other. She had to admit that most of the time she enjoyed his presence, and occasionally he would pick up something that wasn't too far-fetched and that sparked her interest enough to make it worth checking out. But the sources of his theories weren't always the most reliable.

'Where did you hear about it?' she asked.

'What?' He looked up and stared at her, his eyes blank. 'Hear about what?'

'Brown envelopes changing hands to ensure that pollution readings are always acceptable.'

'Oh, that,' he said, turning back to the computer, his fingers hammering the keys. 'I had a dream about it.'

María groaned. She stood up and went out into the corridor to go to the toilet, promising herself that today she would count how many times she needed to go. It wasn't normal how frequently she needed to pee, and how quickly the urge to go would grow. Only a minute or so had passed since she knew she had to go, and now she was so desperate that she was afraid she might wet herself, particularly as this damned metal door wouldn't shut behind her. She kicked it so that it settled into its frame and then squatted on the toilet with relief.

Marteinn was a worry. If he didn't agree to go to the mental health clinic by himself, then she would have to take him. It wouldn't be the first time. More than once she had spent a day trying to keep him calm in the waiting room until it was his turn to see the doctor. It would be worthwhile trying to get him to go before he became even more of a mess, suspecting everyone and everything around him, her included.

9

'Oh, Agla,' said Ewa, the prison officer with the Polish roots, when Agla appeared in the reception suite accompanied by Guðrún, who was carrying the bag of medication Agla was supposed to take.

Guðrún handed the bag to Ewa to deal with, but Agla was still finding it difficult to speak, so she just nodded to Ewa and looked away. She was consumed by a sudden desire to apologise to Ewa, as if she owed her a debt for the friendliness she had shown her since she had started work at the prison, but she was still in too much of a daze. Ewa took her arm and led Agla – cautiously, as if she were fragile – along to the female corridor.

'Let me know if you need anything,' she said in a low voice. 'Whatever it is. There's nothing so big or so small that I can't try and fix it.'

Agla smiled weakly. Although Ewa was always ready to help, she couldn't give her back her life, take those bad decisions back, neatly tie up the loose ends, or rewind a couple of decades. And she couldn't assuage the pain of losing Sonja, which still only left her for a few moments at a time.

More than four years had passed since Sonja had vanished from her life, leaving only a short text message that simply stated that she couldn't do this any longer. Agla had sat numb on the unopened boxes in the huge house she had bought for them and replayed their every conversation over and over in her mind as she searched for an explanation. Now, all these years later, she still had no understanding of why Sonja had left her, and the rejection still seared.

Ewa squeezed her arm gently as she left her at the entrance to the female wing. Agla went straight to her cell. The door stood open, and she was panicked by a thought: would the noose still be hanging from the radiator? But then she saw someone lying in her bed.

'Hæ,' the girl said, sitting up. 'You're supposed to be on suicide watch, so you're in the security cell and I'm in here now.'

Agla stared at her and her eyes scanned the cell. It was as if she was in a dream – reality had been shoved to one side and twisted. She recognised the place, but didn't. There were clothes all over the floor, a suitcase was open on the desk and the girl on the bed was surrounded by scattered sweet wrappers.

'Did you try and top yourself?' she asked, putting a piece of chocolate in her mouth. 'Sorry, I was in rehab right after I was sent home from Holland to finish my sentence here, and now I'm completely hooked on sugar.'

Agla opened her mouth to ask who she was, but stopped. There was still no sound coming from her larynx, and it was even painful to whisper. It was no business of hers who this skinny, scruffy bitch who had stolen her cell might be. She turned in the doorway and went to the cell at the end, next to the door to the communal area, and there she found her things. One of the warders had laid out her personal stuff on the shelf in the bathroom and stacked her books on the table, but her clothes were still folded up in a cardboard box.

Agla let herself fall back on the bed and stared up at the all-seeing eye of the security camera that glinted in its glass dome in the middle of the ceiling. There seemed to be no end to this fuck-up. For the coming days and weeks, she would have to put up with being streamed live.

10

Ingimar sat for a long while at Rebekka's bedside, watching her sleep. She was lying just as she had been the night before when he had come to check on her – on her left side with her right hand under her cheek, her left hand oddly stretched out and resting on the bedside table. The wedding ring had twisted around on her finger so that the diamonds were on the palm side. This was not what he had foreseen eighteen years before, when he slipped that ring onto her finger. But that's the problem with passion; it blinds you to what would actually be better for you. It would have been better for him to have remained unmarried.

There would undoubtedly be several hours before she would emerge from her drugged mist, and it was just as likely that she would reach out for the box of tablets on the bedside table and go back to sleep instead of getting up. With one finger he steered a stray lock of hair from her face and let it rest behind her ear. She did not stir, but muttered something unintelligible, and a thin bead of saliva leaked from her mouth into the pillow.

Ingimar stood up and went to his own bathroom, which had originally been a guest bathroom, until they had started to sleep separately. There had been no decision to sleep in different rooms, but he had not been able to sleep next to her when she was so heavily drugged. It seemed as if her complete immobility woke him repeatedly during the night, and every time, when he saw that she had not moved at all, he was struck by a deep discomfort. Before he could go back to sleep, he felt he had to put an ear to her mouth to be sure that she was still breathing. This feeling of unease ultimately became something he could no longer tolerate.

One night he had moved to the divan in the guest bedroom and had slept like a log, as if her shallow breaths in the next room were no longer any business of his. Within a few weeks the divan had been replaced by a bed. So the guest bedroom had become his bedroom, and the guest bathroom had become his personal space. Not that it mattered, as they no longer ever had guests.

He went downstairs, switched on the coffee machine and then made cocoa for Anton, carried it upstairs and sat by his bedside until he began to stir. Since he had entered his teens the boy seemed able to sleep around the clock. Ingimar had never needed much sleep; all his life he had been a morning person, awake and active. But people are different. He reflected that at Anton's age, he had already been a fisherman.

Once Anton was sitting up in bed, Ingimar went to the bathroom and turned the shower on, lathering his face with shaving soap as the hot water began to run. As always, he shaved as he stood under the flow of water. The skin on his back stung under the heat of the water, so he finished with a blast of water so cold it made him gasp.

He dressed and said goodbye to Anton, then went into the kitchen and poured coffee into a paper cup to take with him. He put on his overcoat and looped his scarf around his neck, closing the door behind him on his way out. There was something special about taking a breath of the fresh outdoor air, and for a moment he felt as if he had surfaced from a long dive underwater, lungs thirsty for oxygen. He felt a new lightness now that he was out under the open sky.

What was so peculiar was that around the time of the financial crash, his life had also fallen apart. It hadn't been the collapsing banks that had hurt; the opposite was the case, as there were more business opportunities than ever before, and the profits were in excess of anything he could have dreamed of. There had been a crisis of another kind. An inner one. In the wake of this turmoil, he had found himself caught up in woman trouble, having made the mistake of sleeping with the same girl several times, in the process becoming captivated by her. He had taken the decision to ask for a divorce, but it became clear to him that there could be no such thing. He could not part with Rebekka now that she was in the state that he, admittedly indirectly, had got her into. And he couldn't leave Anton behind. Although Anton didn't conceal his disdain for his mother from her, Ingimar knew that if it came to the crunch, the boy would rather live with her than with him. Anton was in the same position as Ingimar, not daring to leave Rebekka on her own.

Ingimar walked with steady strides, but slowed his pace when he heard his phone buzz in his coat pocket. He took it out, glanced at the screen, and saw that this wretched journalist woman wasn't going to give up. Now her questions were about how high the bribes had been to ensure that the pollution readings for the smelter remained within acceptable limits. He smiled. This was a weird kind of journalism; it was as if the woman was churning out endless conspiracy theories in the hope that one day she might accidentally hit on a true one.

11

Anton always heard his father going downstairs in the mornings, but there was something so comforting about getting to spend a little longer in a warm bed. He lay still, pretended to be asleep, and waited for the cocoa to arrive. The routine was always the same. First he heard the clack of the letterbox as his father fetched the newspaper, then there would be the sound of running water and that would soon be followed by the muttering of the coffee machine. Once the microwave had pinged, it wouldn't be long before there were footsteps on the stairs. Then the door would open, his father would place the mug of cocoa at his side and would perch by his feet on the bed.

'Good morning, young man,' he would say. He always said the same thing: *Good morning, young man*, and then he'd massage his shins. After a moment, he'd tell him the time.

'Time you were on your feet,' he would say, still with his hand on the boy's shin, as if there was nothing to hurry for.

Sometimes Anton greeted his father with a *hæ*, but if he was lazy, which was most of the time, he'd silently extend the other foot from under the duvet to be massaged as well. Then his father would quickly pat his shoulder, still wrapped in the duvet, and would go to his own room. A moment later there would be the sound of the shower running, and then he would reach for the mug of cocoa.

It was always his father who woke him in the mornings – for as far back as he could recall, at least. He had a few fragments of memories about playing with his mother in his pyjamas back when he had been small, but her waking hours seemed to have become increasingly fewer as she had grown older. Last night she had been miserable over dinner – which had in fact just been pizza – and gave him a roasting for his bad grammar. He would certainly like to improve it, but he hadn't understood what was wrong with what he had said. Shortly after that she had gone up to bed and was unlikely to emerge before midday. Her day had shortened to just a few hours, while the night had become longer and longer as the darkness within her grew.

It took Anton as long to drink his cocoa as it took his father to shower, shave and dress. Just as he was stretching his tongue into the mug, trying to reach the sweet, thick residue at the bottom, his father appeared in the doorway, looking at him as he knotted his tie.

'Have a good day,' he said.

'And you,' Anton replied, swinging his legs out of bed. He knew it would be better to say 'you too', but he enjoyed the fact that his father never corrected his grammar. That was something only his mother ever took the trouble to do.

He lifted his hands high above his head and stretched. Today he was going to go down to the cellar to look at the dynamite for a moment before going to school. He wanted to see if the strange feeling that had come over him the previous day would return. The feeling that he could do anything; that he alone was capable of changing the world.

12

'I knew I was a kind of decoy, y'know. But I didn't dare disobey the Boss. In this business you just do what you're told. I had a little less than a hundred grams of some cut gear taped up in my crotch. Nothing much at all. I reckon I was supposed to be pulled. There must've been another mule on the same flight with a kilo or more that was properly hidden, and in all the fuss they were making when they pulled me, he walked straight through.'

The girl sat and talked while the other women sat in a daze, listening to her chatter. Agla squeezed past the table to the cupboards to fetch herself a cup for her morning coffee. She liked it black. She didn't bother eating breakfast, even though her fellow prisoners and the warders constantly reminded her how unhealthy that was.

'I could have ditched the package at the airport in Panama and tried to disappear there, but that didn't have a hope of working out.'

As the girl continued to talk, Agla sat at the far end of the table with her coffee and tried to concentrate on the book she had brought with her.

'I heard about one guy who tried to make a run for it like that,' the girl said, 'but he came to a bad end. A stretch in prison's better than being chopped up for dog food!'

The other women muttered their agreement, and two of them stood up, saying that they were going to the laundry to work. There were no cars to be polished today, so the bookkeeper from up north, who for some reason preferred washing cars to doing laundry, stayed where she was. Normally there was at least one car a day to be washed, but now that spring was coming and there was no salt on the roads, people found it easier to give their car a wash themselves. For much of April the prison officers had taken turns bringing in their own cars to be washed and polished, so that there was some activity, but now that well had run dry. It would have been ridiculous for the staff to bring in cars so clean they sparkled and have them washed again.

The new girl, who so far still hadn't seen a reason to apply a brush to her mop of hair, stood up, then planted herself in a chair next to Agla; she was uncomfortably close.

'What do you want?' Agla whispered without looking up.

'I want to sit next to someone who smells nice,' the girl whispered back, as if whispering was some kind of game and not a necessity for someone with a damaged larynx. 'You smell nice. The bookkeeper's Chanel stink was suffocating me. What year is it? Nineteen sixty-five? There are more modern fragrances, y'know.'

The girl giggled to herself. Agla sipped her coffee. This person's over-familiar attitude was seriously starting to irritate her. She inched her chair closer to Agla all the time. Agla shifted her chair in the opposite direction, a signal that enough was enough. But the girl apparently failed to notice.

'What did you do?' she asked, as if that was a perfectly normal question to ask in a prison.

Agla had used her computer time to search for the other women on the internet, trying to find out about their backgrounds, but none of them had actually asked her anything. Maybe that was because they all knew who she was. The fact that this girl knew nothing about her told its own tale; she couldn't have read any newspapers or followed the news.

'Nothing,' Agla hissed.

'Sure,' the girl giggled. 'Just like everyone else in here.'

She'd taken her impertinence a step too far.

'I worked in finance, like plenty of other people,' Agla snapped, louder than her sore vocal cords could manage, so that she had to gulp, then dissolved into a bout of coughing.

'And I smuggled dope, just like loads of other people,' the girl said with a broad smile.

Agla quickly got to her feet and left the kitchen. She had no intention of allowing herself to be compared to a drug smuggler. Coffee could wait until later.

She had only just entered her cell when the girl appeared in the doorway.

'Sorry! I didn't mean to piss you off. I just wanted to talk. I'm still so happy to have people to talk to in Icelandic. Dutch just sounds so weird.'

The smile had disappeared from the girl's face, and now she stared at Agla with her eyes wide open, her expression apparently sincere.

'Hmm,' Agla grunted, not knowing what to say. Her anger had now left her, and she stood awkwardly and stared at the girl.

She wasn't as young as she had first appeared; she had to be somewhere close to thirty. Her hair was no less of a mess than it had been when she got up that morning.

'Have you never seen a comb?' Agla said in a lame attempt at an insult.

The girl simply laughed.

'It's supposed to look like that,' she said. 'It's a style. By the way, my name's Elísa.'

'Agla,' she muttered in return.

She was struggling to come up with something else to say to this odd person when one of the prison officers appeared, reminding her that she had a visit booked.

13

'Yes, I know him,' Agla had said two weeks ago, and she had signed the visit request, even though she had never heard of this man before. Her curiosity had been sparked by the email in which he requested a visit. He had stated that there was an important business matter they should meet to discuss. She had forgotten about it until now.

Although she was in no mood for a visit, she grabbed the opportunity to escape from the girl, who still stood and stared at her with such irritating curiosity.

When the man she had never heard of appeared behind the glass screen in the visiting room, she hoped he wasn't yet another journalist who had sneaked in under a false flag. So far only journalists had shown any interest in visiting her.

'George Beck,' he said in introduction. He was a middle-aged man – an American, going by his accent – in a black suit and with a bundle of papers under one arm. 'I apologise for being late,' he added. 'But they found it necessary to search me twice, even though I don't have anything but paperwork with me and I'm behind this glass screen.'

He smiled and Agla returned it, knowing that a visit to Hólmsheiði was always an experience. First the weapons search, then the X-ray, occasionally the sniffer dog and finally the glass cage.

'The first two visits are always behind glass,' Agla explained. Not that she needed to; this man was hardly likely to become a regular visitor.

'As we don't have a great deal of time, I'll get straight to the point,' he said. 'I represent a major drinks manufacturer and I have an offer to make.'

He stood up and held his business card up to the glass. She could see a little picture of him in one corner, under the company's logo. Agla raised an eyebrow. International companies didn't make a habit of searching out convicts in Icelandic prisons to offer them work. She pointed to her throat under her roll-neck sweater.

'I'm sorry, but I have a sore throat. Could you explain?'

'Of course,' George laughed and sat down again. 'This may sound strange, but we're interested in certain connections that you may have.' He took a slim plastic folder from the stack of papers and held it up to the glass as he had the card. 'On this first page the graph shows the world market price for aluminium over the last few years.'

Agla glanced at it. The line showed a gradually increasing price.

'The next page shows what my company has had to pay for aluminium for its cans over the same period.'

He pressed this against the glass and Agla compared the two graphs. 'You're paying way over the market price,' she said.

'That's right,' George agreed. 'The problem is that there's no aluminium to be had at the world market price, but there's plenty on the open market, which is where we've had to buy it these last few years. We've had no choice.'

'I'm not familiar with the metals business, so you'll have to tell me where this is going,' she whispered, forgetting her surroundings for the first time in longer than she could remember, and without even thinking to ask what it was that this man wanted from her. George leaned forwards, lowering his voice, as if he thought they were having a confidential conversation here in the Hólmsheiði prison's glass cage.

'The situation is this,' he said. 'There are two aluminium markets; registered and unregistered. LME, the London Metals Exchange, handles all the business with registered aluminium worldwide, and it sets a market price based on production volumes. But they don't register all aluminium production, as part of it is sold on the open market, outside the system. Normally large buyers, as we are, don't buy on the open market as there's enough available on the registered world market. But over the last three years there has been practically no registered aluminium available, so the price of aluminium on the unregistered, open market has been shooting up.'

'I assume that you or your company have complained to LME?' Agla said.

'Frequently,' George replied. 'But they can't do anything. They tell us that worldwide aluminium production is in balance, and that there's more than enough produced. But they say they can't interfere with who buys it.'

'And who is buying all the registered aluminium?'

'That's what we don't know. There's a complete wall of silence around the whole thing,' he said. 'That's where you come in.'

Agla lifted a questioning eyebrow and waited for him to continue.

'We're co-operating with several other major aluminium consumers and we want to offer you – what should we call it? – a consulting role.

We'd like you to check things out for us and pull a few strings. Find out who is buying all the LME-registered production. You have links with a gentleman who has brokered deals for those purchasing this massively expensive, unregistered aluminium that we have also had to buy. He organises direct sales from aluminium producers in Iceland, Norway and Russia. So he ought to know what's happening to all the LME-registered production from the same smelters.'

'Ah.'

Agla knew instantly who he was referring to. There was only one man who could fit such a description. Ingimar.

14

'Politicians, the media and police forces across Europe have closed their eyes to the fact that radical Muslim groups have been able to establish themselves here, and it's a question of when and not if they take action,' the voice on the radio said. 'And what are we going to do about this? Are we just going to sit and wait until it's too late?' the voice demanded.

A meaningful look passed between Anton and Gunnar.

'This guy's a high-school teacher,' Gunnar said.

'And there was some lawyer on there yesterday being interviewed and saying the same thing,' Anton replied. 'He said that people need to wake up and do something.' He could feel the return of the disquiet, the feeling that had plagued him ever since he had promised Júlía's father that he would take care of her. 'Shit,' he said. 'Someone's got to take a stand against these bastards.'

'Yep,' Gunnar agreed, switching off the radio. 'But how are we going to do it?'

Anton looked at the stack of dynamite they had placed in a black sack on the floor of the basement room his parents referred to as the boiler room. It had once housed a cylinder that had been part of some ancient heating system, but now it was just a storage space.

Gunnar was impatient. He didn't want to spend time listening to Radio Edda or talking things over. He was desperate to try setting off some explosions. Anton was starting to doubt that he was part of this because of deeply held convictions, instead suspecting that for Gunnar it was more about the excitement.

'We need to see what we can use as detonators,' Anton said.

'How about a little petrol bomb in the middle that sets the dynamite off?'

'Hmm,' Anton hummed, indicating that he was thinking seriously about it. 'But then we can't control the explosion,' he added, and Gunnar stared at him with blank eyes. He clearly didn't have any better ideas.

'We could Google it?' he suggested, and Anton had to agree that this was their best strategy. There had to be videos on the internet that would show them how to make real explosions – and not just in Minecraft. It was just a question of coming up with the right search terms.

'Yeah. Good idea,' he said, getting to his feet.

'Let's go upstairs and look it up on your computer. But first we need to take a look at Big Boob Babes on Pornhub,' Gunnar said.

Anton laughed.

'Not now. I'm going to the cinema with Júlía.'

'Shit, you're so pussy-whipped,' Gunnar said.

Anton punched his shoulder.

'Shut the fuck up,' he said with a grin.

He knew that Gunnar was jealous and that he would give anything for the opportunity to go to the movies with Júlía.

15

They were offering a ridiculous amount of money for her to check things out for them. For that price, they could have employed an army of private investigators to find out far more easily what was happening to all the aluminium. She was well aware, however, what the term *consulting*, as the man had put it, meant for a company like this. They intended her to become involved. For the same reason, she would be paid by a sub-contractor to a sub-contractor to the big drinks company – making the trail harder for any interested party to follow.

She accepted the offer instantly. She snatched at it as if it were a lifeline thrown to a drowning man, because she could feel her interest spark as she thought how she would get to grips with this. Behind such a situation there had to be a tangle of threads, and at the back of such a tangle there was always a big bank; and if anyone could see past the surface of the banking business, it was her. That was exactly why she was right here, sitting out a sentence for financial crimes. It wasn't because she had made mistakes. Just the opposite: she had done extremely well. She had actually admitted to a few minor misdemeanours so as to distract the prosecutor from other, much larger ones. Her former partners from the bank were sitting out much longer sentences at the white-collar prison at Kvíabryggja, whereas she seemed to have landed on her feet, like a cat. Taking into consideration her unsuccessful suicide attempt, it looked as if she might have a few extra lives as well.

An unusual aroma was coming from the kitchen. Agla frowned in surprise; she was expecting the mince Vigdís usually cooked when it was her turn.

'I swapped with Vigdís,' announced the new girl, Elísa, as Agla made her appearance in the kitchen. 'I just felt like cooking for everyone.'

Vigdís, Gunna and Bogga were sitting at the dining table, staring at Elísa as if mesmerised. Agla sat with them and looked her up and down. Elísa had now encountered a hairbrush, parting her dark hair on one side and tucking it behind her ear. She wore dark make-up around her eyes and a pair of skull earrings. Agla had to admit that the girl had good looks, despite her peculiar style. She wore a singlet underneath the apron; Agla could see a screed of reading material tattooed on her slim arms.

'There you go!' she announced in triumph, placing the pan on the table next to a bowl of rice. 'Pad-ped – genuine Thai street food.'

Vigdís left the room to fetch the bookkeeper, who had a habit of arriving for dinner on the dot of seven, while the time was now only just six-thirty. They all sat a little shyly around the table as Elísa heaped food onto their plates as if they were children.

'Are you going to tell us the rest of the story?' Vigdís asked as she took her seat. This humble request confirmed Agla's feeling that they were just small children who had been placed in a home, and Elísa was the exciting new kid in the group.

'Where was I? Sure, that's right. Well, I was on another job before and I'd swallowed around fifty bags and I thought I was going to burst! It's true, I looked down at my belly and thought I had to be pregnant. There was this massive bump there. Then I started retching and crying, and the Boss said I had to get down another ten. That was way too much for me. I suppose I'm too small to carry that much, cos some of it went right through me and ended up in the toilet on the plane. I couldn't bring myself to hook it out, wash it off and swallow it again, like we'd been told to, so I just flushed it away. The Boss wasn't impressed with that.'

'Is this something we should be talking about at a meal time?' Agla asked. Her voice was hoarse and low, but it was enough to stop Elísa's tale.

'Don't ruin the story!' Vigdís said.

'No, don't stop,' Gunna echoed.

The bookkeeper and Bogga said nothing, but glared at Agla. She was well on the way to ruining the most excitement they had experienced for a long time.

'Anyway,' Elísa continued, 'I reckon that was when they decided I could be sacrificed. At any rate, that last time they sent me with not very much, and with it packed really badly, from Panama to Holland.'

She fell silent and ate silently for a while, and Agla regretted having snapped at her.

'I'll wash up,' Agla said, as a way of making amends.

Elísa looked up at her in surprise.

'Thanks,' she said with a smile, and somehow Agla found herself wincing at the sight of the smile and the look that accompanied it.

Long after Agla had finished washing up and was back in her cell, she still felt the heat in her face. It was either due to the food, which had been as spicy as proper Thai food should be, or because of the awkwardness with Elísa. The others had disappeared after dinner, leaving the two of them to clear up the kitchen. Elísa seemed almost in awe of her, while Agla cursed herself for criticising the girl.

'What, are you some kind of bankster?' she had asked as Agla dried the last of the plates.

'You can call it what you like,' she said, placidly. But then her temper caught up with her. 'And you? What are you? A junkie?'

Elísa giggled quietly, almost apologetically.

'Yeah, I suppose so. But I've been through rehab. Again. I think ... or let's say I hope I can stay straight this time. I'm free of the Boss and all that smuggling crowd now, and I hardly owe them anything anymore. I'm taking it a day at a time, and all that. But then I'm so easily tempted, I'm not sure I'll be able to stay straight once I'm out of here.'

Her sincerity triggered Agla's regret a second time, and she muttered something along the lines of, sure, things would work out for her this time, and then she left the kitchen.

She was back in her cell, her face flushed, when she realised that she had forgotten to thank Elísa for the meal. This young woman aroused some strange emotions in her, a longing to either hit her, or else crush her in her arms. It had been a few years since she had wanted to hug anyone. There had been nobody she had wanted to embrace since Sonja's departure. She growled to herself over her own ineptness. Tomorrow she would make it up; she would make time to talk to her, thank her for the meal and apologise for calling her a junkie.

In the bathroom she splashed cold water on her hot face and as she peered at herself, she noticed her perfume. Chanel. She picked it up and dropped it in the bin; 1965 was indeed a long time ago.

16

Hunger forced María out of The Squirrel's office as the normal working day was coming to an end. Marteinn hadn't been seen all day, and she hoped that he had done as she had told him and gone to the clinic to make sure his prescription was correct.

The day had been spent prioritising the unpaid bills and calling a few companies, begging them to place advertisements with The Squirrel. After that she had got lost in the internet, feeling like she was in an aimless daze, which was maybe no bad thing. It was better than being miserable and thinking about Maggi all day long, and then being caught up in studying his Facebook page in fine detail, as she had done right after the divorce.

'Just the person I wanted to see!' announced the voice of Radio Edda's producer, appearing in the corridor that separated their offices just as María was on her way out. 'I read your last article about disability and I'd really like to get you on to the morning programme for an interview,' he said, his voice slightly slurred.

'I don't do radio,' María said. 'The written word is my thing.'

That was her standard response to the man's endless behests to join him for an interview. He seemed certain that, because she rented office space from them, she had to agree with their standpoint, despite the wealth of material published in The Squirrel that should have made the opposite plain.

'We're working towards a common aim,' he said, moving closer, as if to corner her, so that she would be unable to escape his booze-laden breath as he blathered on about everything they had in common. María knew his tactics and made smartly for the door, holding it open for him with an amiable smile. This was not the time for listening to the old guy holding forth.

'No,' she said. 'I'd say that our social outlooks are polar opposites. You are on the far right and I'm on the far left.'

The producer navigated his way out through the doors, which were barely wide enough for a man of his generous build.

'Left and right are obsolete concepts,' he gasped as he set off towards the door of the shop next door. 'These days it's all about north and south.'

María had been on the way to the same shop to pick up a ready meal, but when she saw the old boy go in there, she decided she had no desire to stand in a queue, listening to him going on about how the government was stealing from the disabled so that it could provide luxuries for Islamic immigrants instead.

She got in her car and was about to start the engine when her phone pinged an alert. She had received an email. She had to read the message a couple of times to make sure that Agla was genuinely asking her to pay her a visit.

I have important business to discuss with you, the message read.

María opened a new message to the visits co-ordinator to confirm the date and time.

17

Júlía stood up when their number was called and went to fetch their kebabs, while Anton worked his way through the process of buying cinema tickets on his phone. She had wanted to see a romantic comedy, which he wasn't excited about, but he said nothing. She had gone with him to see action movies that he knew she didn't much enjoy, so naturally he should show her the same consideration.

With the tickets paid for, he looked up to see what was keeping Júlía, and his heart lurched. She was standing in conversation with the cook, who was still holding their food. What was so special about a kebab that it called for a discussion? Júlía had her back to him, but he saw the long hair hanging down her back shiver as she laughed. What could this burger-flipping cook in a stained apron have to say that was so funny? The man had black hair and there was a dark, Arab look about him, something that applied to practically all the staff in this place. He had to be a Muslim.

Anton felt the anger swell inside him and rush to his head as he marched over to the counter.

'Are we going to eat this before it gets cold?' he demanded, snatching the baskets from the man's hands and turning to bang them down on the table.

Júlía followed and took her time sitting down, taking off her coat and hanging it over the back of her chair.

'Are you all right?' she asked, giving him a searching look.

Anton stuffed a handful of chips into his mouth, chewed but then struggled to swallow as his throat had suddenly gone dry. He took a gulp of his drink to help it down, almost choked, and finally managed to swallow, by which time she had been waiting for an answer for a while.

'What's the matter, Anton?'

'Why were you talking to the cook?' he demanded.

'Because I know him a bit.'

Júlía pulled her basket closer and began salting her food. She always salted before tasting.

'And how do you know him?' he asked.

'He's a friend of a friend,' she said and smiled.

Anton was in no mood to smile back.

'And what was so funny?'

'What?'

'What was so funny that he made you laugh so much?'

'Nothing special. Just chat, y'know,' she said, her eyes questioning.

He could no longer hold back.

'No, I don't know what you could have been talking to that guy about. How old is he, anyway?'

There was a stronger note of accusation in Anton's voice than he had intended.

Júlía pushed her food from her and folded her arms.

'How should I know how old he is? Twenty-something, probably.'

'And where's he from?'

'He's from Syria.'

'I knew it,' Anton hissed. 'You'll end up married to some Muslim.'

He could hear that his voice sounded angry, furious, even, but in reality he was struggling to hold back tears. Júlía stood up, took her coat from the back of the chair and walked out. Anton sat still for a moment, took a couple of deep breaths, and leaped to his feet to hurry out after her.

'I'm sorry, Júlía,' he said as he caught her up. 'Sorry, sorry, sorry.'

She walked in silence, staring straight ahead. He reached for her hand, but she didn't do it – didn't give him her little finger to hook into. Instead she pulled her hand away and wrapped her coat more tightly around her.

'Let's just go see the film and forget this, OK?'

His voice was wheedling.

She stopped and faced him.

'You're going to have to stop this,' she said as tears streamed from both eyes, down her cheeks and onto her upper lip. She wiped them away with a swipe of her coat sleeve. 'Stop going on about me ending up married to a Muslim. I don't know who I'll get married to. In any case, it won't be you if you behave like this.'

Anton felt his heart melt inside him as he was consumed by regret. He couldn't stand it when she cried.

'Sorry, sorry,' he mumbled, and could feel tears on his own cheeks. 'Let's go see the movie,' he said. 'I'll buy loads of sweets.'

Now Júlía's face broke into a smile and he laughed with relief. She extended her hand with the little finger cocked at an angle to hook it into his.

18

'Look at the dog,' Agla said, leaning forwards to speak, as her voice still felt strange, as if she had a throat infection. 'Back in the past the dog and the wolf were cousins who were starving because man was catching all their prey. The wolf continued to compete with man, trying to beat him to the best food. But the dog decided to join with man, to follow him and get the bones when man had finished with them. Gradually, the dog started helping the man hunt, and was rewarded with better pieces of meat, and now he gets fed and petted, and sleeps at the man's feet. Wolves are dying out all over the world while the dog is the evolutionary winner as there have never been as many dogs as there are now.'

María had sat and listened to Agla's speech in silence, and now she stared at her with eyes wide.

'And you're comparing me to the dog?'

'Not at all,' Agla said calmly. 'I'm comparing you to the wolf.'

'Meaning that I and those like me are dying out?'

'I'm pointing out that in this instance, it might be more to your advantage for us to be on the same side.'

María smiled bitterly. Now all that remained for her was to become Agla's ally. This was the Agla who had prompted the disaster that had engulfed her. This was the Agla she had dreamed of nailing, the Agla who deserved to spend the next hundred years behind prison walls but who would undoubtedly waltz out of here in a few weeks with an ankle tag, leaving her free to go back to her usual tricks.

'You could get an explosive story out of this. I'll pay all the costs and whatever you ask for on top.'

Under normal circumstances María would have stood up and walked out, ignoring the temptation. It wasn't the offer of cash that triggered her curiosity, more the hint of supplication in the last sentence. After that arrogant lecture about the animal kingdom, it was as if all the wind had been taken from Agla's sails, leaving her adrift. There was a vulnerability in her eyes that María had never seen before and the hand that held the paper coffee cup trembled slightly.

Agla was wearing a blue-grey cashmere sweater that María had seen before and been envious of; this time she wore it over a roll-neck top and tracksuit bottoms, and the sweater was creased and stretched, as if it had been slept in.

'I'm looking for information,' Agla said. 'Information that could be useful to both of us.'

'Information that you want me to get hold of illegally,' María said firmly.

'You must still have contacts at the special prosecutor's office,' Agla said. 'All I'm talking about is someone doing you a small favour by getting hold of data that's partly in the public domain already.'

'I'm not interested in hearing more unless you tell me honestly why you need to know this,' María said.

'That should be obvious,' Agla said. 'I'm in prison. So my ability to find out what I need to know is limited.'

'I mean, what are you going to do with this information? It surely doesn't happen that all of a sudden, up here in Hólmsheiði, you decide that you need information about the financial status of particular companies.'

Agla sighed and stared searchingly at her for a moment. María could tell from the look in her eyes that she was turning things over in her mind.

Eventually Agla sighed again and sat up straight in her chair.

'You have to give me your word that you won't publish anything until I give the word. And you have to keep my name completely separate from any media coverage of all this. OK?'

'Then this has to be something juicy,' María said. It would have to be something big to make up for sacrificing an opportunity to write about Agla.

Agla looked her in the eye, and María saw a smile appearing a little at a time on her face, until it reached her eyes.

'Believe me,' she said, giving María a conspiratorial wink. 'This is as juicy as it gets.'

19

'This is fucking ace!' Gunnar crowed in delight at the sight of the boy's stock of fireworks.

They had sneaked out of gym class to meet the boy who called himself Mr Firecracker online, and who seemed to stock up on fireworks around New Year and then sell them at triple the price over the subsequent months. He was a head shorter than either of them and at least a year younger. He must attend another school as Anton had never seen him before.

'What school do you go to?' Anton asked.

The little guy shook his head.

'No names,' he said gruffly and folded his arms. 'I don't ask for names or which school you go to, and you don't ask me.'

Anton wasn't sure whether to laugh or let his temper show. The boy kept the fireworks in a shed in a garden in the Hlíðar district, so Anton guessed that he lived in the house in front of them, and went to school somewhere close by. The boy was just playing at being the big man.

'It's brilliant, isn't it?' Gunnar said, weighing a large cherry bomb in his hand.

Anton grunted without answering. He couldn't see why Gunnar was so excited about a few fireworks when the dynamite in his basement at home easily had a thousand times more explosive power.

'It's too big,' he said, taking the cherry bomb from Gunnar's hand and showing him an ordinary rocket. 'We need a few of these.' Gunnar's excitement dried up as he picked up a few similar rockets.

'Would you like a bag?' the boy asked, as if he was serving in a shop.

Anton shook his head, laid the rockets out in his backpack and handed the boy the money.

'Special celebration?' the boy asked cheerfully, stuffing the bundle of notes into a back pocket without bothering to count them.

'We're going to use them as—' Gunnar began.

Anton quickly interrupted him.

'My girlfriend's birthday,' he said and Gunnar immediately nodded in agreement, as this was in fact true. The explosion was supposed to be a birthday present for Júlía.

'Where next?' Gunnar asked on the pavement outside as he started the moped.

'A builders' merchant,' Anton said, taking his place behind him. 'Or an electrical place.'

This was the serious stuff. He had watched a few videos on the internet that showed how to make a detonator. He needed some wire and other components. This fireworks business was just indulging Gunnar, who really thought that it would be cool to set off the dynamite using a firework. They would do a few trial runs to figure out what the best method would be, and they would only have to sacrifice a few sticks of dynamite doing tests. There would be more than enough left for a powerful explosion; a seriously big bang.

20

Presumably, George Beck and his associates expected her to go straight to Ingimar. But that would have been precisely the wrong approach. Ingimar would do everything in his power to keep her away from this. She needed a clearer picture of what was going on before going anywhere near him. She needed more background. Maybe it hadn't been all that clever to come over all David Attenborough on María, but that TV programme about the development of species had sprung into her mind as she watched María in the visitor's room, howling like a wolf about the world's corruption. So it was a good comparison.

'You're working?' asked Elísa, who all of a sudden appeared in the library with a questioning look on her face.

'Yes. I can work through the computer.'

The girl's eyebrows rose in surprise.

'So you get unlimited computer time? On the net?'

'Yes. Or rather, no. I have an exemption: I can have a couple of hours a day. But they track all my online traffic so I can't go on Facebook and things like that.'

Agla didn't understand why she felt she needed to be apologetic; maybe it was because of the endless debate in the media about financial criminals getting better treatment in prison than other convicts.

'Too posh for the laundry, are you?'

Elísa had undoubtedly heard the same debate at some point.

'I work for an accountancy firm, completing tax returns for individuals and small companies. Just tax returns. It's not exactly exciting.'

'Hey, then you can do my tax return!'

Agla shook her head in surprise. In a matter of seconds this person could go from downright accusatory to amiable. She couldn't figure her out. Perhaps she was simply the kind of person who came out with the first thing that entered her head.

'I could do that,' Agla said. 'But then you'd have to be nice to me.'

A broad grin spread across Elísa's face and she leaned against the bookshelf, tugged her T-shirt free of her waistband and lifted it to reveal a strip of bare belly, rocking her hips provocatively.

'Mmm,' she said, fluttering her eyelashes. 'How nice do you want?'

Agla shot to her feet, hurried to the door and rang the bell repeatedly.

After the warder had come to take Elísa back to the female wing, Agla sat back down at the computer, wracked with sobs. Somehow Elísa's joke had hit her badly, like a punch to an already sore belly. Thoughts that she had long kept in check flew through her mind in a series of flashing images – all showing a tangle of sorrow and suppressed desires. Underneath it all, like a deep bass note, was the hollow, echoing emptiness that had filled her heart ever since the day she sat on a box in the empty house, trying to understand Sonja's message.

I'm sorry. I can't do this <3.

After the numbness of the first few days had come the disbelief that made her want to laugh the whole thing off; laugh at her own foolishness in buying a house for them; laugh at the joy she had allowed to grow in her heart; and laugh coldly and cruelly at her own stupidity. Then there had been the time when the heart Sonja had tacked onto the end of her message – a clumsy left arrow and a three – began to take on new meaning. Agla had begun to wonder if one day Sonja would call her from the airport, as she had once done, begging to be fetched. Then there had been the time when Agla searched for Sonja. It had ended with the terrible moment when she found her in London.

Elísa's provocative joke had stirred up this emotional turmoil, and her thoughts again turned to the noose.

The computer pinged an alert to let her know that a message had arrived in her inbox. Agla wiped her face with her sleeve and took a couple of deep breaths to bring her sobs to an end. The email was from María, and Agla felt relief as she read it, as well as the spark of excitement that always took root inside her when she had a complex piece of work ahead. María agreed to her offer to co-operate. So maybe there were alternatives to the noose – other ways to free herself from this misery.

21

Ingimar relished taking Jón, the smelter's financial director, to places outside his comfort zone. Kaffivagninn had long been one of Ingimar's favourites, with its view over the Reykjavík harbourside, small fishing boats at the pontoons, the city skyline beyond, and the fishermen around the tables sipping coffee through lumps of hard sugar brought back pleasant memories. Jón looked thoroughly ill at ease in these surroundings, however. He ran a finger along the back of a chair, as if checking it was clean before he laid his neatly folded overcoat over it. Ingimar got to his feet and pointed to the counter, and Jón followed hesitatingly.

While he wasn't exactly hungry and didn't make a habit of eating at this time of day, Ingimar couldn't resist treating himself to an open shrimp sandwich, if only to see Jón's reaction. This vulgar Icelandic version of a Danish *smørrebrød* appeared to upset this bony man's sensibilities to such an extent that he could hardly bring himself to look at the sandwich, instead glancing at it occasionally from the corner of an eye, seeming to be deciding what to say.

'That's a mountain of mayonnaise,' he observed.

Ingimar reached for the pepper, shaking it generously over the contents of his plate. Jón ordered an espresso from the new machine that looked to have been installed more for tourists than locals. Ingimar would also have liked a stronger brew, but he helped himself to filter coffee from the urn just to get a reaction from Jón.

Ingimar made a start on his sandwich as soon as they had taken their seats, sipping grey coffee from a mug between mouthfuls.

'What's new on the aluminium front?' he asked, slicing off a piece of the canned pineapple that graced the pile of shrimp and popping it into his mouth.

'Much as usual,' Jón replied, lifting his espresso cautiously to his lips. The tiny cup was somehow perfectly in keeping with his slim fingers, while the heavy mug almost disappeared in Ingimar's fist. They were complete opposites and Ingimar's thoughts somehow strayed to dogs. Jón was a chihuahua, no question at all, and while he would have liked to have seen himself as some kind of slim greyhound, he was probably more of a bulldog. He was solidly built, and getting thicker as the years passed. A lump of a man, as Rebekka never got tired of calling him.

'Anything special going on?' Ingimar asked. They didn't meet often, so there had to be something behind Jón's suggestion that they get together over coffee. For security reasons, they made a point of not speaking on the phone. If there was something that needed to be discussed, they'd meet in person.

'There's this Squirrel website,' Jón said.

'Yeah.' Ingimar pushed the plate and the remains of his sandwich away. There was a third of it left, but there was too much, and the mayonnaise was too thick. It was more than he could manage, even though he was enjoying seeing Jón shudder. 'María doesn't change, does she?'

'She's been calling our press officer constantly, and sends emails with all kinds of questions.'

'That's nothing new.'

'No. But just to be sure, it might be worth seeing her credibility damaged a little.'

'That would be sensible,' Ingimar said, wiping his mouth with a serviette. 'Especially if she keeps this up.'

'It shouldn't be difficult,' Jón said.

Ingimar nodded his agreement. He could easily update Wikipedia, adding an entry about her departure from the special prosecutor's office, and including a link to the media speculation at the time.

Then there was the guy on the journalistic ethics committee who owed him a favour. Knocking holes in María's credibility would be almost too easy. She was just one of the puppets on a stage, and he was the master.

Ingimar finished his coffee and pressed himself back into his chair, feeling the pain in his back.

Remember you are mortal, the heat in his scourged back told him. *Remember you are mortal.*

22

What surprised María the most was that Agla appeared to be telling her the truth. Although there was something unreal about a drinks giant, an aircraft factory and a computer manufacturer joining forces to offer a convict in an Icelandic prison a massively well-paid consultancy, there was something about Agla's demeanour that convinced her it was all true. Having interviewed the woman at least twenty times while she was working for the special prosecutor and having made endless failed attempts to interview her since turning to journalism, María felt she knew Agla well. She had become familiar with the arrogance, the evasions and the tricks, and also the rare moments when Agla would drop her defences and tell the truth. On top of that, she had badgered the right people and been allowed access to Agla's visiting schedule, and there she found George Beck's name. A Google search had confirmed that he worked for a drinks manufacturer, just as Agla had said.

What tipped the balance of her decision was the electricity at The Squirrel's office going off. It had been quite a few months since she had last paid a bill and now the power company had cut off the supply. If she didn't bring in some cash soon, the same would happen at home before long. All her doubts were pushed aside, and within a few minutes she had persuaded herself that the best thing to do was join Agla's team – for the moment at least; she would be able to nail her later on. The ease with which she made this decision shocked her slightly; but she realised it was chiefly because like most people, when cornered, she looked for the simplest solution.

But if she was going to be in the pay of the devil, it would be as well to make it worthwhile. Using the torch on her phone, she sifted through the pile of bills, adding up what she owed – something she had not dared to do before for fear of learning the overall picture. Then she doubled the total and emailed Agla.

Agla's reply arrived before any doubts had time to take root in María's mind. Agla apparently did not see María's fee as large, so María got to her feet and felt her way to the door in the darkness. The decision had been taken. She had let the establishment lead her by the hand, had sold her credibility and had become a stereotype – a tool of big business. On the other hand, Agla seemed to be looking into something that did arouse María's interest. What's more they seemed to be hoping for the same outcome: she was also hoping to get enough material to frighten the aluminium giants; the ones who were robbing Iceland.

Twenty minutes later she was standing on Finnur's front steps. She had deliberately not called her former colleague from the special prosecutor's office to warn him, preferring not to give him an opportunity to hide himself away. The expression on his face when he saw her confirmed her suspicion.

'A rare white raven,' he said, gesturing for her to step inside.

She shook her head.

'This isn't a courtesy call,' she said. 'I need some information.'

He sighed.

'You of all people should be able to appreciate my position,' he said. 'It's not easy to speak to the press, and I can't do so without specific permission.'

'I don't need to talk to you,' María said. 'I need a list from the Central Bank. It's a list you can easily request and you don't have to justify asking.'

'My dear María—' Finnur began in an avuncular tone, before she interrupted him.

'I could say the same to you,' she said. 'You of all people should be able to appreciate my position, considering you initiated a certain investigation that resulted in me losing my job.'

She had expected him to protest more vigorously, had assumed she would have to apply more pressure, but instead he hung his head and nodded. There was no doubt that he was plagued with guilt over her situation.

'What do you need?'

23

It no longer became properly dark in the evenings, but as dusk stretched into a colourless grey, it was still difficult to see in the boiler room. Anton switched on his head torch, and Gunnar did the same. They had put together a few different versions of detonator and fastened each one to a stick of dynamite. Gunnar had made three little bombs by binding the rockets they had bought with tape to dynamite sticks, and Anton had prepared rather more sophisticated ignition systems using batteries, lengths of wire and the heads of matches to provide the spark. His detonator worked – he had tried it out a couple of times without any dynamite, but there was no telling how it would work when they tried it for real; and they couldn't watch it as they would have to run some distance away before the explosion.

Between them they had made a bomb using the ignition from a gas refrigerator. That was the closest they had been able to get to a remote control, but Anton was sure that the problem would be solved if they could figure out how to connect this to a clock. First they would have to test this version of the detonator to be sure that it would light the fuse.

'What about Molotov cocktails?' Gunnar asked, holding the petrol can that Anton had finally agreed to buy, hoping to satisfy Gunnar, who seemed to think that petrol was the solution they were looking for.

'I reckon we shouldn't make those until later; on the spot,' Anton said. 'We can take the can and the bottles with us, and make them up just before we set the explosion off.'

'Isn't it better to have them ready?' Gunnar said, already tearing an old T-shirt into strips to stuff into the necks of the bottles.

'I don't want to be messing around with petrol in here,' Anton said. 'My dad's upstairs.'

Gunnar gave in.

'All right,' he said. 'But if we have everything ready for the cocktails then we can go straight after school tomorrow.'

Anton nodded. He had to admit to himself that he was looking forward to trying out the explosives, even though he wasn't nearly as excited as Gunnar was. He switched off his head torch and turned up the radio. An MP he hadn't heard of before was being interviewed on Radio Edda.

'The problem is that radical Islam has knocked on our door. It's already here in our countries, and it has little if anything to do with any kind of faith,' the politician said. 'Islam isn't just a religion, it's an all-encompassing philosophy of human relations that takes in everything – law, social affairs and not least how people relate to each other.'

'We need to remind ourselves why we're doing this,' Anton said, and Gunnar nodded so energetically that the light on his head danced in the gloom.

24

'But where's your income?' Agla asked in bewilderment as she peered at the computer screen. She had decided not to let Elísa find any chinks in her armour. Instead she would act as if nothing had happened, so she had appeared in the common room before dinner and suggested they get her tax return out of the way. She had already arranged it with the prison officer on duty, who took them to the library and switched on the wifi with the strict instruction that they were only to work on

Elísa's tax return, and Agla wasn't to let her anywhere near anything else on the internet.

'There,' Elísa said, pointing at the income column.

'Do you have any unearned income?'

'Like what?'

'From associations or limited companies?'

'What?'

'Profits, then? Where did you get money from?'

'Just from the fish plant I worked in for a few months last year. And from the Boss, you know. Not that I'm going to declare that to the taxman!'

'Are you telling me that this is the only income you had for the whole year?'

The girl was clearly in a mess, and her declared income for the year was less than half of what Agla paid herself monthly. Judging by Elísa's online bank account, there were a few debts to payday lenders already in arrears and in recovery, so the earnings from the Boss could hardly have been large.

'If you like I can transfer a small amount to you so you can pay off all these debts and start afresh,' Agla said. It irritated her to see these recovery notices over amounts that were hardly more than pocket money.

'Are you so rich you don't know what to do with your money?' Elísa asked.

'These aren't big amounts,' Agla replied.

Elísa seemed to realise that she wasn't joking.

'No,' she said, smiling awkwardly and dropping her eyes. 'Don't do it. I'd only go wild when I get out of here and blow it all on dope. But thanks, all the same.'

'These small loans are all in recovery now, so they're only going to get legal costs and interest piled up on top of them. You know that?' Agla said, and made a mental note to herself to dispose of her shares in a payday lender. That particular investment, while low-risk and profitable, had suddenly given her a sour taste in her mouth.

'I try not to think about it,' Elísa said and shrugged.

Agla looked at her carefully and tried to work out what she might be thinking, but didn't get the impression that she was thinking about anything at all. In any case, she seemed to see no urgency to resolve her financial woes. A lock of tousled hair fell over Elísa's forehead. Agla was filled with a sudden desire to reach out and tuck it behind her ear. There was something about that wild hair that made her long to tame it, comb it, make it follow some rules. Instead, she copied the numbers of the financial demands, opened her own online account and paid them all off in one fell swoop.

'What are you doing?' Elísa asked, peering at the screen with a blank look on her face. This girl had a personality all of her own, but was far from the sharpest intellect Agla had encountered.

'I paid off your debts,' Agla said. 'I can afford it and you can't go on racking up interest while you're in here and can't pay anything off.'

'Oh.'

A single tear straggled down Elísa's cheek, and that, combined with the untamed lock of hair, put Agla suddenly at a loss. It wasn't the kind of amount worth shedding tears over; but then she had never been able to grasp why women were so sensitive about money. It had been the same with Sonja: she'd never let Agla pay for a single thing. And when Agla had bought the house – that was when she had freaked out and left her.

'Don't cry,' she whispered. 'It just annoys me, seeing that interest piling up.'

'I'll never have the money to pay you back,' Elísa said and wiped away the tear from her cheek, much to Agla's relief.

She was about to tell her that it didn't matter – which was entirely true – when she felt Elísa's hot hand on her leg, too high up her leg.

Once more, Agla felt as if she had been punched; in fact this time it felt more like a stab. How could she have been so stupid as to try and help this person? She never seemed to fail to wreck any friendly overtures with some clumsy response.

'I don't know what the hell you think I am!' she rasped, then got to her feet and sounded the buzzer. It had been months since all these locked doors had got on her nerves, but since this girl's arrival, she'd truly felt like a prisoner – constantly prevented from escaping Elísa's attentions.

25

María was shredding the back page of the *Fréttablaðið* freesheet newspaper into little strips. There was no real point to this activity, it was just an outlet for the frustration that had welled up inside her when she saw the news item stating that the ethics committee of the journalists' union had censured her for The Squirrel's misreporting of a story. She had been certain that this had been forgotten long ago. It was true; she had jumped the gun, running a story before it was confirmed. But she had then deleted the post and apologised to all those concerned. She knew that someone had notified the ethics committee, but had no idea that they had examined the case. It came as a complete surprise to see this surfacing now, more than a year later.

She got to her feet, went to the bathroom and turned on the shower, realising as she did so that Maggi would see the news item. He always made a point of reading *Fréttablaðið*. He would be sitting over his organic porridge somewhere, reflecting on how much of a disappointment she had been to him. As she stared at her own tired face in the mirror, she had, once again, the nagging feeling that she had also disappointed herself.

She had once been so sure about her own qualities: her sense and determination; the fact that she didn't let anyone pull the wool over her eyes. Ahead of her she'd thought she had a bright future in the justice system, plus a long, contented marriage with Maggi, and maybe two or three children.

She was gripped by a sudden longing to call Maggi, to try and work out from his tone of voice whether or not he had read the item about her, but she managed to control the urge to pick up the phone. He had asked her to stop calling him. He couldn't stand hearing any more tearful apologies, and in reality she understood his position completely. When she wallowed in self-pity, she couldn't stand herself either.

In the shower she opened her mouth wide, let it fill with water and screamed with all her might so that water spurted out in hot gushes. She had perfected being able to scream underwater, into a pillow and even into her elbow, ridding herself of all the tension and disappointment without scaring the neighbours witless. It was better to scream than to cry, and it was a sign of recovery that these days she screamed more than she wept.

Out of the shower, she wrapped herself in a dressing gown, sat on the sofa with her laptop and checked her emails. Her despondency instantly vanished when she saw a message from an unknown sender. It was from a Gmail address made up of a series of numbers, but when she saw the document from the Central Bank in the attachments she knew right away who the sender was. She forwarded the list to Agla, got up and went over to her desk and plugged the printer in.

In the bedroom she rooted through the pile of clean clothes, found jeans and a T-shirt, and decided that she could buy socks somewhere during the day and could get by without underwear, as she often did now. Her laundry system suited her perfectly, but would have shocked Maggi to the core. There were two piles on the floor – one of dirty stuff on its way to the washing machine, and the other of clean clothes that had come out of the dryer. The result was a circular flow of clothes; at some point, they spent time on her body as they transitioned from the clean to the dirty pile, like a hard-working official working his way through stacks of documents.

The system didn't extend to underwear, though. She hadn't managed to keep that side of things under control and resorted to frequent purchases of economy packs of pink or light-blue knickers, which cost a fraction of what she had paid for the classy lingerie she had worn while she and Maggi had been married. Socks had become disposable items. There was no way that she could be bothered to pair them up.

The printer had churned out the Central Bank's list by the time she returned. The coffee left in the jug was cool, but she poured it into a mug anyway and sat down on the sofa with the printout.

26

Agla could make neither head nor tail of the Central Bank list that María had emailed her. She had repeatedly compared it to the data from the London Metal Exchange, and on the surface it seemed that the Icelandic smelter exported a healthy amount of registered aluminium through the LME system. The price level for these sales, however, was less than a third of what it should have been on the world market. The smelter's revenues had therefore halved in size over the last three years. At the same time, though, large invoices were presented every month to the smelter by a company called Meteorite Metals, and the smelter paid them punctually.

She looked up Meteorite Metals and found that it offered storage facilities for metals. She then went to the smelter's annual report for the previous year and saw that practically all of that year's aluminium pro-duction was recorded as an asset – it hadn't been sold. This was looking highly suspicious. Agla's conclusion was that the Icelandic smelter was producing aluminium but then simply shipping it overseas for storage.

Agla clicked on a folder on her desktop marked Filed Invoices, which was where she hid the Tor browser, which she used when she didn't want the prison authorities to know what she was doing. She keyed in her password, sent María a message on the Bleep app and waited for a moment to find out if she was online.

Agla: *There's no sense in producing aluminium for years and leaving
    it in storage.*
María: *Isn't it a known business strategy to sit on assets to push the
    price up?*
Agla: *Sure. But the price hasn't risen.*
María: *Weird.*
Agla: *Yep.*
María: *You saw Meteorite? What's that?*
Agla: *Seems to be for metal storage.*
María: *Have you Googled it?*

Agla: *Yes. Nice front page, but probably not much behind it.*
María: *You mean it's a fake company?*
Agla: *Could be. Could you fly over and take a look?*
María: *WTF? What would I do?*
Agla: *Go there. Check that the company exists. Just keep all your receipts.*

There was a long pause before María replied.

María: *OK.*

Agla wondered whether María would find out anything interesting. It was very likely that Meteorite Metals didn't actually exist and was just a brass-plate company used to hide a trail of money. Agla was familiar with how all this worked; she even owned a few brass-plate companies herself. She suspected that the scheme had been designed so that all the costs of producing the aluminium were borne by the smelter in Iceland, while the revenue went direct to a parent company overseas – which therefore paid zero tax in Iceland. She knew the kinds of tricks that could be played to make this happen. Whatever really lay behind all this, the scheme bore all Ingimar's hallmarks.

Elísa met her as she returned to the women's wing.

'Hey, I'm really sorry about last night,' she said, following Agla to her cell.

Agla's only response was to shut her cell door behind her, but as soon as she turned round, the door opened again and Elísa put her head inside.

'A closed door means that someone prefers to be alone,' Agla said drily.

'Yeah, I know. House rules and all that. I just...' Elísa fell silent and slipped further inside. 'I just wanted to explain, y'see, I'm not used to people doing anything for me without wanting something in return.'

Agla sighed. Her own experience was much the same. Everyone wanted something for their efforts.

'All I want is to be left alone,' she said. 'Shut the door as you leave.'

'But, listen, I was only joking when I did what I did. I must've got the wrong end of the stick – I thought you were like me.'

'Like you how?'

'You know. Queer,' Elísa said and giggled as if it were funny.

Agla felt the anger growing inside her.

'It's none of your fucking business what I'm like or why I'm here, or anything else! Just stop being so nosy and leave me in peace!'

27

The north wind was so cold that they were both left with red faces and running noses by the time they took the turning off Hafravatnsvegur and set off along the track up the slope. Gunnar killed the moped's engine and Anton gingerly dismounted. On the way it had occurred to him that if they came off the moped for some reason, they would be in real trouble – all the explosives they had prepared were in the pack on his back and there was a full can of petrol jammed between them on the seat. It wouldn't need much of a spark to blow them sky high.

They walked side by side up the slope, to where the moorland petered out and the undergrowth became so thick they had to go in single file. Gunnar went in front with the petrol can in his hand, Anton behind with the pack on his back. The birches were still leafless, but the buds were starting to show, indicating that before long the woodland would take on the green hue of spring. The air was too cold to carry any scent of the woods, but Anton still felt that he sensed an aroma of spring. It reminded him of his childhood, and an image appeared in his mind of his father by a lake with a fishing rod, and somewhere close at hand his mother sitting on a blanket with their picnic at her side. In between them ran a younger version of himself, small and happy. His mother hadn't always hated his father. He had memories of them kissing, laughing, dancing cheek to cheek in the living room.

But somewhere, at some time, something had gone wrong, and the suspicion that it was his fault gnawed at his conscience.

'Right!' Gunnar said, once they were over the ridge and into the valley, out of sight of the road. 'What shall we start with?'

Anton delicately removed the pack from his shoulders and looked around. This was a good place. There was stony ground on the slope, so there was no chance that they would set fire to any peat or heather. Not far away was a cliff face, and in front of it were a few respectable boulders behind which they could take shelter.

'Let's start with the Molotov cocktails,' Anton said, knowing this would make Gunnar happy. He would be relieved to have the petrol out of the way so he could concentrate on the serious stuff without an overexcited Gunnar constantly prodding him.

Anton pulled out the four vodka bottles he had taken from under the kitchen sink – his mother no longer bothered taking the empties down to the basement to the recycling box – and unscrewed the caps. He held the funnel and Gunnar poured the petrol. With the bottles filled, they stuffed rag strips into each one.

'Ready?' Gunnar asked, clicking the lighter in his hand.

'Hold on!' Anton said. 'This is how we do it; you light one and throw it as far as you can, and we go behind those boulders up by the cliff. All right?'

'OK,' Gunnar agreed as he lit the first rag.

Soaked in petrol, it burned fast.

'Shit, shit, shit!' Anton muttered, as he ran for the rocks. He hadn't expected Gunnar to be in quite such a hurry.

There was a clatter of breaking glass followed by the rush and roar of the petrol igniting. He just managed to throw himself behind the rock, a hand over his head. He was considerably more frightened than he had expected to be.

'Woohoo!' Gunnar whooped, performing a joyous war dance a few metres away. He hadn't got behind a rock, but had turned to see the explosion. 'It rained sand, man!' he crowed. The grin on his face stretched from ear to ear. 'Did you see that?'

Anton had to admit that he hadn't seen the explosion, so, to make amends for his own fear, he picked up the next bottle and took his lighter from his pocket.

'We throw two at once,' he said. 'One, two, three!'

They lit the rags and threw the bombs together. Anton had to call on all his willpower to stand and watch the explosion and not to run away. The bang was twice as loud this time, as the bottles smashed one after the other and dissolved into a firestorm, which subsided as a black cloud rose into the air. It was more impressive than he had imagined. He felt his face burn with shame as he thought how he had run as fast as his legs would carry him away from the first explosion. Gunnar, on the other hand, appeared to be in his element. He picked up the last bottle, lit it and hurled it.

It had just gone off with a bang when an angry voice rasped behind them.

'What the hell do you think you're doing?'

There was a furious expression on the man's face. Again Anton had the urge to run and hide.

'We're just messing about,' he said apologetically, reaching for his backpack and shouldering it.

'Get the hell out of here, you and your racket,' the man growled. 'We're trying to enjoy our meal in peace and quiet.'

He waved a hand towards the cliff face, where a whole group of people sat around a red blanket. Anton couldn't understand how he had managed to miss them when he and Gunnar came down the slope. His only explanation was that they hadn't been there then. But now he saw they were in the middle of their meal, and had even brought their best china with them. The blanket was as loaded with delicacies as the table at home was when his mother was in the mood for entertaining.

The pack on Anton's back shook as they jogged in silence further down the valley. Once they were out of sight of the group of people, they looked at each other and burst out laughing.

'Shit! That was a surprise!' Gunnar gasped. 'I thought it was the cops at first.'

Anton slipped the pack from his shoulders and dropped breathlessly to the ground.

'Who has a picnic when it's this cold,' he puffed through his laughter.

He felt a sense of relief. At first he had thought the man had to be a policeman, or a county sheriff or something, because he was wearing a coat with two rows of silver buttons and his voice was imperious, as if he owned the valley.

'It looked like they were drinking out of little trophy cups,' Gunnar laughed. 'What a weirdo! This tourist boom just gets crazier all the time. They're really taking the piss if they're taking tourists out for that kind of weirdness.'

'It must be some kind of a role-playing club,' Anton said. 'No tourists dress like that.'

May 2017

28

'Please, let me out.'

Sonja stood with the keys in her hand and looked at the man in the cage. The smell coming off him was so strong she could hardly breathe, but at least he was no longer shivering and sweating. He grasped the bars with both hands and wept. Sonja knew from experience that having spent days in there, he would have trouble standing upright when she finally released him. She had sometimes wondered whether she ought to replace the cage with one that was taller and more suitable for humans, but that would probably make imprisonment less effective. And anyway, everyone knew about the tiger that had once lived in the cage and what its role had been, which meant that it carried a certain notoriety, and evoked a certain fear.

She drew the tablets from her trouser pocket and handed them to him.

'Take these, Thorgeir. When they've started to work and you've calmed down, I'll come and let you out,' she said.

He snatched the pills and gulped them down with a mouthful of water from the bottle at his side.

'Please, don't close it,' he pleaded, his voice shrill, as she shut the door to the store room.

She would give him thirty or forty minutes, and by then he would be in a decent enough state to take a shower and get dressed. This was a day too early, and she knew it, but she had to clear the house and have everything ready. Tomorrow Tómas would come home to the rambling mansion that had once belonged to Mr José and Nati, the Mexican drug kingpins who had each come to a violent end right here in the living room, before being fed piece by piece to the tiger that had been the cage's previous occupant.

She shivered with anticipation as she thought of Tómas, and immediately the knot of trepidation tightened in her belly. She still had to organise the trip home, and that was always a headache. The route couldn't be too easy to anticipate, but neither could it be so long and complex that Tómas would become exasperated.

'How is he?' Alex asked as she appeared in the living room.

'He's past the cold-turkey stage,' Sonja replied. 'But he'll still need to deal with all the mental stuff. He just cries and cries. He needs a little more time, really, but I have to get him out of here. It would be great if you could clean the cage before you go.'

'OK, I'll do that,' Alex said.

'Then there's the journey home,' she said. 'I've planned a route for you – Switzerland via Amsterdam. There'll be a hire car waiting for you in Zürich to drive to the school.'

'And then?'

'When you've picked Tómas up, drive to Lucerne and take a domestic flight back to Zürich, then come back here via Copenhagen.'

Alex nodded. He knew better than to protest or grumble. He was aware that she could easily change the itinerary tomorrow, and again after that. To begin with he had complained about all this fuss, saying that these complex routes to bring Tómas home from school were unnecessary. He had tried to convince Sonja that his experience as a bodyguard was such that he would sense if they were being followed. But then, two years ago, he had saved her life by throwing himself between her and an armed killer sent by a competitor. This incident had convinced him that the dangers were real.

29

María jammed the water bottle between her thighs and unscrewed the cap. The car was hot, so the water was already warm. She was already regretting not having gone to a more reputable car-hire firm. She could have gone for a top-class 4×4, or even a basic car that had aircon, as Agla was covering everything, but somehow she had fallen back on her habit of keeping costs to a minimum, and found a small, cheap company. The car demonstrated why the rental was so low.

She had driven round and round the vast warehouse, which seemed as big as a sports stadium, with a goods-in entrance on one side and a goods-out exit on the other. She had seen a few trucks disappear into the front of the building and reappear at the far end, so there had to be something going on, even though there were only eight cars in the staff car park, each one with a couple of empty spaces around it, as if the owners wanted to make the most of having more than enough room.

Sitting in the car, María sent Agla a short email to say that the metal storage unit existed, and that it was a large building emblazoned with the Meteorite Metals logo, and not just the brass-plate company Agla had suggested. Then she drove into the empty car park marked *VISI-TORS* and pulled up, the hand brake squealing in protest as she yanked it hard to be sure the car wouldn't roll away.

When she got out, she found that the temperature was the same outside as it had been in the car, but now she could feel her skin burning in the sun's glare. She had never been able to tolerate too much sunshine, unlike Maggi, who would happily spend days outside in the garden, becoming nicely tanned. She just burned red in the sun. She shook off thoughts of Maggi's naked body, and pushed open the door marked *OFFICE*, coughing deliberately.

'Hello, darling,' the receptionist said in an amiable, almost musical voice. 'What can I do for you?'

She had a stately hairdo piled on top of her head, and for a moment María wanted to ask whether it was a wig or had the woman put a lot of effort into dyeing and curling real hair. Instead María introduced herself and showed her press card.

The friendly smile instantly became a suspicious scowl.

'I'll call the manager,' the woman said, picking up the phone and putting it to her ear without taking her eyes off María. She waited for a moment, then told the person on the other end of the line to send Donald down. 'There's a journalist here at reception,' she said, although her tone of voice and the expression on her face suggested she was announcing that there was a rat down here with her.

The Donald in question seemed to have much the same feeling; hardly a minute had passed before he burst through a side door into the reception area.

'What do you want here?' he said aggressively.

This hostile reception took María by surprise, and she coughed again and began her speech, explaining that she was a journalist from Iceland and ran a small online news outlet.

But Donald interrupted her before she'd finish her sentence.

'We don't talk to journalists here.'

'I'm just looking for some background information about aluminium trading—' she began, before Donald again firmly interrupted her.

'You can leave now.'

'I'd really like to talk to the manager of this company,' she said.

'Then you need to talk to Meteorite Metals International. We don't talk to journalists here.'

'And your name is, Donald ... what?'

'Call security,' Donald snapped at the receptionist, placing his feet wide apart and folding his arms in a clear indication that he had nothing more to say.

It was obvious that this was as far as she was going to get. María decided that this probably wasn't the moment to ask if she could use the toilet. She'd just have to hold it in.

'I can find my own way out,' she said, just as two security guards appeared, each taking her by an arm and escorting her through the car park to her car.

She got in stiffly, relieved to be out of their hands, and reversed out of the space. The two guards walked behind the car all the way to the gate, where they stopped and watched as she drove away.

As soon as she was out of sight, María stopped by the side of the road and got out of the car, where she pulled down her jeans and pissed into the roadside dust. Her breaths were coming fast, and she could feel her heart thumping in her chest. The dramatic reaction to her arrival confirmed Agla's suspicion that there was something strange about this metal storage unit. There was something very strange about the whole thing.

30

Elísa's bank statements offered an insight into her life – the further Agla dug back into them, the clearer her mental picture of the young woman became. Now that she had access to her online banking details, having completed her tax return for her, Agla hadn't been able to resist the temptation to check through her card transactions. What was clear was that Elísa was hooked on ice cream, and had seemed to buy some every evening, often after paying for a meal at some fast-food place.

Looking at her, there was no indication that these were her preferred eating habits – endless pizzas, noodles, burgers and all kinds of junk food. Most evenings seemed to end at a cinema, where Agla guessed Elísa shovelled down sweets, as there were usually two or three transactions made at the snack bar.

Then there was a long period with no transactions, followed by the single large payment she had made herself, and shortly after that a transfer to a woman called Katrín who, according to her personal ID, was twenty-five years old and whose legal residence was abroad. It seemed that whenever Elísa came into some money, she gave it to this woman. The same pattern had been repeated for more than two years, right up until Elísa had been jailed in Holland a few months previously.

Agla thought over everything she'd discovered, and however much she tried not to let it prey on her mind, the question kept coming up: who was this Katrín and why did Elísa give her almost all her money? Surely she had to be a dealer.

The warder appeared, ready to take her back to the kitchen for lunch. Elísa sat there, as usual telling the other women a story.

'It all started when I got a loan,' Agla heard her say as soon as she entered the kitchen.

'All problems start that way,' the bookkeeper said.

Agla stopped herself from snorting in derision. She had found out all about the bookkeeper and knew she had embezzled money belonging to the shipping company she had worked for. It had started with a few small amounts, according to the court documents Agla had found online.

'I knew that this guy was well dodgy,' Elísa continued. 'But I was completely skint. I didn't know what to do, and they were about to throw me out of the room I was renting. I'd already been to the guy who'd paid me pretty well to fuck me before, but he'd found someone else. So I ended up hunting through garbage bins for bottles to sell so I could buy cat food – the cat was wailing, it was so hungry, you see. Then, when I'd scraped together enough for a tin, he just turned his nose up at it and walked away. That was when I lay down and cried.'

'And?'

To Agla's ears it sounded as if both the bookkeeper and Vigdís demanded the answer at the same moment. They seemed captivated by Elísa's tales of woe.

'Well, I met this guy at a party that evening and asked if he could lend me a hundred thousand krónur. He said "yeah, no problem", and we went back to his place and he just got the money out of a drawer and handed it to me.'

So back then she hadn't yet figured out that nobody does anything for nothing? Agla thought, but said nothing.

'And I was going to pay the rent and buy cat food and all that stuff, but the next day the money was all gone.'

'How on earth did that happen?' Agla heard herself say, surprised at her own reproachful tone of voice. She was standing at the worktop with the butter knife in her hand, staring at Elísa, who had a look of satisfaction on her face. Maybe she was just pleased that Agla had spoken to her for the first time in days.

'Like you said,' she said with an apologetic smile. 'I'm a junkie. And junkies need junk.'

Agla wanted to bite her own tongue. She had not meant to speak to Elísa or any of the others. Her plan had been to take her sandwich and cup of coffee to the common room to eat there, as she had made a habit of doing since that awkward evening when Elísa's attitude had upset her so deeply.

'Of course,' she muttered, still surprised at her own sudden need to express her opinions on this young woman. It was as if an inner bitchiness had welled up, and before she knew it, she had spat out something she had had no intention of allowing to be heard.

'All the same, it's called alcoholism these days,' Elísa said. 'I'm an alcoholic. If I didn't drink, then I wouldn't do dope. I do dope simply so I can drink more.'

Agla had to admit this was a tendency she was familiar with. In the past she had made a habit of snorting coke, just so she wouldn't get too drunk. But her circumstances were very different to those of this slip of a girl.

She returned to the library, and even though the lunch hour wasn't over, Ewa let her in, and she sat down at the computer. She shut down the window with Elísa's bank account, and shook her head at her own behaviour. She couldn't understand why she had been digging into this woman's life; it wasn't just that it was none of her business, but on top of that Elísa had a talent for being annoying.

She opened another of the Meteorite Metals annual reports and hadn't scrolled far through it when she came across what she had been half expecting to find, sooner or later: the relocation of the company's headquarters from Indiana in the US to Paris three years before.

Her heart beat a little faster as her suspicions grew, and it skipped a beat when she saw which bank handled the company's business in France. This was what she had instinctively thought right from the start. Ingimar had a hand in this, and what was more, so did William Tedd.

And it wasn't just that the bank William worked for in Paris handled Meteorite Metals' business. It also owned the company.

31

Ingimar was almost at the bridge when his phone rang. He generally ran around the lake in a clockwise direction one day and anticlock-wise the next. He tried to alternate the routes, but often the wind was what made the decision for him; he'd start by running with the wind behind him so he wouldn't have to run against it until he had warmed up. He always jogged slowly and could feel that every step was taking a toll on his knees, but this was the nearest thing to an exercise routine he was able to keep to. He had set himself the target of jogging every day, and in his mind this was still what he aimed for. However, the fact of the matter was that he only found time to run around once a week.

He fished the phone from his pocket and put it to his ear, only managing to catch the second half of William's agitated greeting.

'Slow down, man,' he said. 'I didn't hear what you said.'

'A journalist from Iceland turned up at the warehouse today and tried to push her way inside. A woman called María.'

'At the warehouse in Indiana?'

'Yes. That's why I'm concerned. Didn't you say she was nothing worth worrying about?'

'That's right.'

'Then what's she doing in the States? She must be on to something if she's made the effort to travel there in person to ask about aluminium in storage.'

Ingimar's knees were suddenly even more sore, and he slowed his pace so that he was ambling along. He was a few metres from the bench with the statue of Tómas Guðmundsson, the Reykjavík poet, so he limped over to sit next to him. This particular run had now been ruined.

'I'll check her out. It's the same woman who has been calling me constantly with all kinds of crazy conspiracy theories. She's also been pestering the smelter with these half-arsed theories. Don't lose any sleep over it.'

'I'm not that concerned, but it's best if we keep this to ourselves and a few others – the way it's been up to now. It's awkward if there's some journalist sticking her nose in and asking all sorts of questions.'

'I agree completely,' Ingimar said. 'I'll check her out.'

'Excellent,' William said. 'And now I'm about to pull the cork from a rather wonderful Leroy I was given. You should have been here to share it.'

'Bye for now,' Ingimar said, standing up.

He would have had nothing against tasting a fine wine, his body fragrant and oiled after an hour at the Turkish baths he always made a habit of visiting when he was in Paris. Instead he was here, in the Reykjavík drizzle, limping home to cook fish for Anton's dinner.

32

'Are you in a bad mood, my lad?' his father asked as he put the fish on the kitchen table.

'No,' Anton said, reaching for the butter. If there was something you couldn't have boiled fish without, it was butter. His father melted some rendered lamb fat to pour on his fish, while he preferred butter that he mashed into his food as if he was still a child.

'Everything all right with you and Júlía?'

'Sure,' Anton replied.

It was true. They were fine. He had been at her house for dinner the day before and her father had clapped him amicably on the shoulder, and they talked about handball for a while before they all watched the TV together. Júlía found the customary time in front of the television after dinner a trial, but Anton enjoyed sitting there, squeezed between Júlía and her mother on the sofa, munching popcorn. There was something about it that gave him a warm feeling. When he grew up, he would have evenings like this with his own family. He had every intention of being the kind of dad who made popcorn and shepherded the whole family onto the sofa to watch lousy television, simply so they could all be together.

Evenings at his own house were pretty tragic: once his mother was in bed and his father was glued to the computer or out somewhere, he was left to watch TV by himself.

'Did you think about finding me a job on a boat?'

Anton looked at his father.

'What's this obsession with seafaring, Anton? There are plenty of jobs out there that are less dirty and dangerous.'

'You said you'd think it over,' Anton reminded him.

His father nodded.

'Are you short of money?' he asked, as he always did when he was tired of whatever they were discussing and wanted to change the subject.

'No,' Anton replied. 'Not now. But it's Júlía's birthday soon, and I was wondering if you could let me have a decent amount so I could take her out somewhere smart for dinner.'

'Not a problem, my lad.'

His father sat up straight in his chair and looked across at him with interest. 'Did you have a particular place in mind?'

'I haven't decided,' Anton said. 'I was hoping you could help me find some quality place with good food, and y'know, waiters and table-cloths. And maybe someone playing the violin. Or ... y'know.'

His father grinned.

'I know. You're looking for somewhere that's romantic and classy.'

His father looked him up and down, and Anton had the impression the old man was proud of him.

'My little boy's becoming a grown man,' he said, slapping him once on the arm with a heavy hand. 'I'll think it over and find a smart place for the two of you.'

Anton nodded and helped himself to more fish from the dish on the table; and to please his father he picked up the little pot of rendered fat and spooned some of it onto his fish, but keeping clear of the brown stuff at the bottom that the old man liked so much.

'And a birthday present?' his father asked. 'Have you thought about that?'

'Yes,' Anton said and felt his heart beat faster.

The birthday present; that wasn't something he was worried about, although he couldn't tell his father that. He still had to figure out how to fit a timing switch to the bomb because he didn't want to be running from falling debris as it went off. He was also finding it hard to work out just how much explosive he was going to need. There was nothing on the internet that told him how much to use to rip apart steel, smash glass and destroy concrete. It was difficult to work out how much dynamite was needed to change the world.

33

It was dusk by the time María returned to the spot where she had parked the car – between some trees not far from the road. Although she had done her best to stay in the shade, the day had left her sunburnt, and now that darkness was about to fall, mosquitoes buzzed in clouds around her and their bites already itched. All the same, she thought the day had been productive. She had counted ten fully loaded trucks driving into the warehouse, and the same ten trucks driving out the other side, still fully loaded, she was sure. She'd watched carefully as the drivers eased their vehicles over the speed bumps to spare their shock absorbers; such caution had to mean the trucks were carrying a lot of weight – what other reason could there be? The trucks were all the same size, and were all clearly marked with the Meteorite Metals logo. The theory that had been taking shape in her mind as she'd sat on a log on the hillside above the factory was now fully developed. Her thinking was that the warehouse was empty. The trucks driving in and out again were purely for show, just to make it look as if there was some traffic in aluminium here, and it could be registered somewhere and used to play the market. This was all about smoke and mirrors, ensuring a profit for someone who could bypass regulations somewhere, cashing in on deals and swindling the community in the process. She wasn't sure how the trick worked, but this was her theory. Now she just needed to confirm that the warehouse was empty.

'It's too simple,' Marteinn said as she explained her theory to him over the phone as she drove back towards the motel.

'Maybe,' María said. 'But maybe not. Sometimes things really are exactly what they appear to be. Maybe this shortage of aluminium is just that: a shortage of aluminium.'

'Too simple,' Marteinn said. 'And *maybe* I could think there's some other reason why you're prepared to swallow such a simple explanation, María.'

'Hey, come on!' María was taken unpleasantly by surprise to discover that Marteinn's determination to see conspiracies everywhere had brought him to this point. He clearly hadn't managed to get his medication tuned. 'No bullshit, Marteinn. I'm looking for support here, and if you're not prepared to help then just let me know and I'll find someone else.'

She was sure that, at the other end of the phone, his eyes were narrowing as his suspicion evaporated, and he was hunching over and hanging his head.

'What do you need?' he asked in a low voice.

'It seems that as much goes into the warehouse as goes out,' María said. 'So I was wondering if you could go through directories online and find one or two people who do business with Meteorite Metals and store aluminium there, so I could try and talk to them – ask them about it.'

They ended the call and soon she was outside the door to her motel room. She parked and got out of the car with an uncomfortable feeling: Marteinn's medication was still out of balance, and she wasn't in Iceland to keep an eye on him. Going by the directions he was going in, she ought to call his column 'The Voice of Suspicion' instead of 'The Voice of Truth'.

The air in her room was stale and she went into the bathroom and pushed the window wide open to let some fresh air in. The mosquito net was rusted to the window frame, so she couldn't pull it fully across before turning on the shower, but she decided that a few more bites would hardly make much difference.

34

In the background there was some TV show about a couple renovating an old house. As soon as Agla registered what she was watching, she switched channels. She had been staring numbly at the screen without taking in what was in front of her. Instead, she'd been focused on the confused images passing through her mind – of Elísa buying herself ice cream, eating a hot dog at Bæjarins Besta or sitting in a darkened cinema. It was like a guided tour of Elísa's life, seen through her bank statements. But this nonsense dissolved when she saw a young couple on the TV, painting the walls of their future home. She felt a stab of pain in her belly. She had looked forward so much to moving into the new house with Sonja. She had relished the idea of turning that white concrete lump into a home, having coffee in the mornings with Sonja, looking forward to being with her in bed, bathed in sweat and groaning with pleasure.

Elísa was having a bad effect on her. Since she had arrived, Agla had been confused; it was disconcerting to be so unsure what to make of the young woman, never certain what she would do next to offend, anger or simply leave her speechless. All the same, she had to admit that life in this cage wasn't as dull as it had been.

These two feelings – heartache about Sonja and the boredom of prison life – seemed to sit at either end of a scale; seemed to pull her in opposing directions. But all of them – the psychiatrist, the prison chaplain, the prison officers – said there would always be emotional turmoil in the wake of a suicide attempt. So maybe this mental restlessness wasn't just because of Elísa.

Agla switched off the television and left the room. Guðrún was on duty so Agla took the opportunity to ask to go to the library. She was only supposed to work during the day, but she told Guðrún that she was bored. Having been with her at the hospital, Guðrún was inclined to let her have her way.

'An hour,' Guðrún said, shutting the door behind Agla, who pretended to examine the books. As soon as the lock clicked shut behind her, though, she sat at the computer. They often forgot to switch off the wifi in the evenings, and she was in luck – they had tonight too. In her experience the best remedy for heartache was work; it led the mind along other avenues – the right avenues.

She started by going to Companies House to look up William Tedd's activities in Britain, before moving on to the US and French registries. He sat on the board of so many companies it was difficult to count them all, but after scrolling halfway down the list, she found the confirmation she had been looking for. He was on the board of Meteorite Metals. Agla clicked the blue tab to call up all of the board members' names. She didn't know a single one of them. This had to be a sham. There was every chance that the real power behind the company was William and Ingimar. She was about to take a closer look at the board members, but all the links were dead. No internet connection. The wifi had been switched off.

She went instead to Meteorite's annual reports, which she had downloaded into her hidden folder. She had already been through a decade's worth of reports and she only had the last two left to read. She scanned the balance sheet, and then switched back to the annual report from three years before to make sense of the figures, but without success. William appeared to have had his bank in Paris buy the company three years before, when it had been in poor shape. Since then it had run at a heavy loss. The amounts of money it had lost over the last two years were astronomical. This was bizarre. She knew William had an impressive track record of buying poorly performing companies, refinancing them so they could get their acts together, before selling them for many times what he had paid for them. On top of that, he was a genius at sniffing out cheap debt all around the world. So it wasn't like him to buy a company that was doing badly, and then let it get worse. She contemplated a number of possibilities, while searching the reports for information that might confirm her theories, but none of them worked out. He did not appear to be using Meteorite as a dumping ground for losses incurred by other companies, as there was nothing to be seen in the figures to show that Meteorite had increased its borrowing or taken over any loans. The company did not appear to be buying the aluminium it was storing, as there were no stocks listed among its assets. She couldn't understand it, and that was frustrating. There was no way that the bank, the owner of the company, would tolerate such heavy losses for long. Although William was in a key position at his bank and she knew it was keen to retain him – they were happy to pay him all kinds of hefty bonuses every time someone else made him an offer – she was also well aware that the bank had little patience for loss-making ventures.

'Cut your losses – stop bleeding' was a phrase she had drummed into her own staff at her bank in the past.

All this could mean only one thing. If William was running some dubious scheme with this metal-storage company, the bank had to be a part of it.

35

The little diner next to the motel had both filet mignon and surf 'n' turf on the menu, but María decided that the burger was likely to be just as good. There were very few customers in the place and the aircon had been cranked up so high that goose pimples appeared on her arms, so she decided to have her food to go. She asked for extra mayo and some plastic cutlery, which the elderly waitress made a fuss of searching for. Once she was outside, though, María decided to drive to the aluminium warehouse and eat in the car then rather than in her motel room.

She parked behind the aluminium store, out of sight of the road, on a gravel track that had to be a service road for the water pipes and air-conditioning units that sat outside the warehouse's perimeter. The burger was a good one, and she squeezed ketchup into the mayo to mix herself a cocktail sauce that she dipped her chips in. There wasn't a single window on the high perimeter walls facing her; she was put in mind of a dark, impossibly steep cliff face. She finished her food and slurped up what was left of her Coke, the generous amount of ice the waitress had given her crunching in the bottom of the cup.

María got out of the car and took a deep breath. This was certainly an adventure, although maybe not as exciting as her sweating palms indicated. She only intended to get inside the building, into the section where the aluminium was supposed to be stored, and make sure that it really was empty.

At the front there were plenty of lights, but here at the back, there seemed to be very few. What was more, when she approached the exit through which the trucks emerged, she found that the chain holding the gate closed was slack, allowing her to slip easily through the gap. Inside the perimeter now, she listened out expectantly for the sound of an alarm. But there was nothing.

Next to the goods-out exit she spied a little door with a window in it. She found a large rock on the ground nearby, picked it up and hammered at the glass. She was surprised to find the glass didn't break. For a moment she stood still, listening, but she heard nothing but the cicadas and the hum of traffic on the distant highway. She wielded the rock again, harder this time, and the glass gave way. She used the stone to tap the remnants of glass away from the edges of the frame. Then she stretched a hand inside and was relieved to find a normal lock, rather than the padlock she had expected. She turned the handle and the door opened.

She stood for a while in the doorway before setting off cautiously, still concerned about setting off any alarms, but after a few paces she was certain that there was nothing. She reflected that it probably wasn't easy to steal aluminium – anyone trying to would need a fork-lift and a truck; and there needed to be some aluminium in the warehouse to steal – which she was sure wasn't the case.

María tiptoed along the passage. To her right were locked doors, probably leading to offices, while ahead there was another door. She tried the handle and was pleased to find it was unlocked; she was relieved not to have to do any more damage. Easing the door open she found herself in a vast storage area. There was a row of illuminated green EXIT signs overhead, clearly intended to show drivers the way out. They cast a dim light across the space, which was far from empty. In fact, the opposite was true. This cavernous building was stacked to the roof with tightly stacked aluminium bars, criss-crossing each other like a huge, three-dimensional puzzle. Running through the centre of the space, from the exit doors next to her, all the way to the entrance at the far end of the building, was a clear strip that reminded her of a swept mountain road after a heavy snowfall; it was just wide enough for a truck to pass through, beneath the towering stacks of metal.

María pulled out her phone and took a picture of the area. But it was too dark, so she switched the flash on to take another, and emailed it to Agla:

The warehouse is packed! There are thousands of tonnes here!

She had just tapped the send button when she became aware of rapid footsteps behind her. Someone took hold of her shoulder, at the same time gripping her arm and propelling her forwards so that she cried out in pain, then landed on her knees on the concrete floor.

36

Anton sat helplessly while Júlia wept. They had been playing Yahtzee, sitting side by side on his bed, and Radio Edda played from his computer's speakers. The station's phone-in was in progress, and one listener after another had called in to describe the overwhelming threat from Islam.

'*Those bastards want Sharia law, hate Jews, they want to Islamicise the West and they support Hamas, which is hell-bent on destroying Israel. Those Muslims love Hitler because he killed Jews,*' one furious caller railed. '*And we're supposed to accept this scum that wants to murder the Jews? Are we going to watch history repeat itself?*'

'*They should all be sent home! What are they doing here in Iceland if they don't want to be Icelandic? In Iceland we eat pork and we wear normal hats, not these rags that their women wear,*' rasped an elderly woman Anton had often heard before during phone-ins.

'*Now they're demanding that we stop making pork available in schools. Next they'll start blowing us up if we don't do what they want!*' yelled the latest caller, who was quite obviously drunk. Anton's mother would yell in just the same way when she been drinking, even if everyone around her agreed with what she said. In just the same way, the Radio Edda presenter sympathised with the opinions of the drunk caller, but they still felt the need to shout.

'*They want to circumcise women,*' said an older woman in a measured tone. '*How are we, who have fought for women's rights, supposed to accept that? Get rid of the lot of them, I say.*'

'What on earth is the future going to look like?' Júlía sniffed.

Anton stroked her back in a helpless attempt to reassure her.

'I don't know,' he whispered. And it was true – he had no idea. The way things were shaping up was alarming. For a moment he wondered whether or not to tell Júlía about the bomb, to give her some hope. The struggle would provide hope. Maybe it would reassure her to know that he was planning to take matters into his own hands. Surely she would be pleased that he had no intention of doing nothing as society fell apart around them. But maybe she would be even more afraid. She was such a sensitive soul.

'Don't cry,' he whispered, placing his arm around her shoulders and squeezing. Her hair smelled so sweet – not exactly of shampoo but more of blossoming flowers. For a moment his thoughts wandered and he imagined burying his face in her hair.

As if she sensed what was in his mind, she stood up.

'I'm so frightened,' she said and sniffed. 'I don't know how it's going to end if things continue like this.'

She was right. Things couldn't go on as they were. He would have to find a solution to the detonator problem. He just had to, and sooner rather than later, as her birthday was approaching.

'Is everything all right?' his father asked from the door.

'Yes,' Anton replied.

'Why are you crying, my dear?' he asked, clearly worried. 'Isn't Anton behaving himself?'

Júlía wiped her eyes and smiled at his father.

'It's all right. Anton is always good. There's just something else that I'm sad about.'

'Let me know when you need a lift home,' his father said.

Júlía smiled at Anton.

'Shouldn't we finish the game?' she asked. 'I'm winning.'

It was just as well that his father had interrupted them. It had stopped him telling Júlía about the bomb. Now wasn't the right time. He had to wait until her birthday, when it would be set off.

37

Agla dried the dishes listlessly. Neither of them had said a word since Elísa had announced after dinner that she and Agla would clear up. The bookkeeper, whose turn it was to wash up, had stood up and left the room in obvious relief, and Elísa appeared to pay no attention to the looks of surprise on the faces of the other women. Agla thought that Elísa had made the suggestion to ensure the two of them were alone in the kitchen, and that there must be something she wanted to talk about. But she hadn't yet said a word.

Elísa rinsed the last plate but one and handed it to Agla, who toyed with the thought of mentioning the dishwasher. This was a constant subject of discussion; or, rather, the lack of a dishwasher was the source of endless speculation. The prison authorities seemed to have been provided with funding to build a new prison, but not to furnish it, so this large, white building was a coldly empty place. It had occurred to Agla simply to buy the required furniture and give it to the prison, but that would lead to a media storm. Bankers sitting out sentences were carefully observed, and whatever they did was interpreted negatively and plastered over the newspapers.

Elísa handed Agla the last plate, and she wiped it dry while Elísa scrubbed the sink clean. This seemed to be unnecessary, so maybe Elísa was dawdling, waiting for Agla to say something.

'Who's Katrín?'

She had said it unintentionally, without giving herself time to think.

'How do you know about Katrín?' Elísa asked, the sink forgotten.

'I don't know anything about her,' Agla said. 'I just saw her name on your bank statement the other day when I was helping you. I wondered why you pay her most of the money you get.'

This was true, although Agla did not mention that she had continued to examine Elísa's bank statements ever since, checking her every transaction.

'Katrín's just ... sort of, a girlfriend ... kind of. We saw each other for a bit, and it didn't work out. I think she was sleeping with the Boss as well, and then I was arrested in Holland, and all that. It was all a fuck-up.'

Elísa smiled and shrugged as she spoke, as if this were all some trivial matter. But Agla could hear a tremor in her voice; it gave away the hurt beneath – the kind of pain she knew all too well.

'Oh,' she said, folding the dishcloth. She wanted to say something encouraging, but nothing suitable occurred to her.

'Yeah. A massive fuck-up.'

Elísa sniffed hard and turned off the tap.

Agla knew words would do little to assuage the pain of lost love, but this little confidence they had exchanged was too valuable; she couldn't now walk away as if nothing had happened. She hadn't experienced intimacy – in any form and with anyone – since the prison doors had closed behind her. In fact, she'd experienced nothing of that nature since her last real conversation with Sonja. As much as she tried to be sincere when she spoke to the prison psychologist, their sessions always seemed to be driven by what she knew she ought to say. But now, she felt all her caution and suspicion drop away, and she wanted to tell Elísa what she had told no one else.

'There was a woman who was important to me as well,' she said. 'I bought her a house and tried to get her to move in with me. But she freaked out and disappeared.'

Elísa turned to face her with a look of sympathy on her face.

'Shit,' she said, and Agla nodded.

Their eyes met for a moment and Agla could feel her face begin to colour – she had said something that might have been better kept to herself.

But then Elísa smiled. 'The ungrateful bitch,' she said.

'What?'

'This woman. What an ungrateful bitch, not wanting the house. And you.'

A few minutes later Agla shut the door of her cell, her heart still hammering, as it had since Elísa had added the words 'and you' to her sentence. She had said it with vehemence, as if Agla were someone who deserved to be desired; as if Elísa felt that she was desirable. This had taken her by surprise. And there was no teasing behind it: it was clear she wasn't trying to aggravate Agla or wind her up. She meant it. But Agla wasn't going to let herself be rattled by this girl. She had no intention of being caught up in any emotional nonsense again.

Agla had hardly finished muttering this, trying to convince herself it was true, when the cell door opened and Elísa stood there, dressed in a singlet. Somehow Agla's hand stretched out to Elísa's arm, touching the tattoo, which seemed to come alive beneath her fingers, moving in the flow of warmth. Then Elísa's lips were on hers, and as quickly as she had appeared, she was gone, leaving Agla with her heart fluttering and a sob in her throat. Damned, damned nonsense.

38

The handcuffs bit deep into her wrists; María quickly realised that they would soon draw blood if she didn't keep still. In any case, wriggling wouldn't help. She wouldn't get these things off by herself. The warehouse's night watchman clearly had no sympathy for her when she complained that he had put them on too tight.

'Ma'am, you were trespassing,' was his retort.

He stood looking at her thoughtfully for a while, before turning and walking away with his phone in his hand, leaving María alone, sitting on the floor, handcuffed to one of the stacks of aluminium. As he opened the door that led to the little office she had come through, she heard him talking on the phone, but the door closed behind him and she could no longer make out what he was saying. He had to be calling the police. Then the lights went out and for a while everything was black.

As her eyes adjusted to the darkness, in the green glow cast by the EXIT signs María was able to make out the stacks of aluminium that towered over her. Every sinew in her body was tense and it was a battle to stay still as her insect bites itched, but the pain in her wrists meant she had no choice. Her bottom was numb from sitting on the concrete floor, and she almost hoped that the police would come quickly to release her from the discomfort. It would be a relief to sit in a patrol car's soft seats for a while. She bent her knees and tensed her bottom, one side at a time, to keep her circulation going. But although she tried not to move the upper half of her body, her wrists still rubbed against the handcuffs and the pain was such that she was sure they were bleeding. She wished he hadn't cuffed her with her hands behind her back.

A long time passed, but Maggi finally appeared in her thoughts, and before she could stop them, a few tears ran down her cheeks. If she had genuinely been able to hold her own, maintained her self-discipline and kept the promise she had made to her younger self – to think everything through twice before acting – then she would be asleep at Maggi's side right now, in their house in Iceland. She would have a few more hours to rest in the warmth from his body, before getting up to make porridge and then go to work at the prosecutor's office, or even at the Competition Authority. That would be on the dot of eight o'clock. That was the way it would have been if she had not encountered Agla. But because Agla had become part of her life in the aftermath of the financial crisis and upset the delicate balance she had worked so hard to build, now she was sitting handcuffed on a hard concrete floor in a shithole town in Indiana, in the power of men who were obviously working for a big corporation that would stop at nothing to protect its interests.

The tears continued to run down her cheeks in a strange blend of regret at losing Maggi and anger at Agla, and at the stupidity of Iceland, a state that couldn't see the wood for the trees, allowing its resources to be sold at a knock-down price to a corporate giant that was behind sinister goings-on in metal storage units around the world, and which handcuffed innocent journalists. She whimpered to herself through the tears, until the lights came on in the warehouse. Then she quickly sniffed hard, wishing she had a hand free to wipe her face.

The door at the far end of the room opened and the night watchman walked towards her, accompanied by the man María recognised as the one who had spoken so rudely to her earlier in the day. Donald. He had a phone to his ear and was clearly holding a conversation with someone.

'Yes. It's the woman who was here today, asking questions. The Icelandic journalist.'

He listened for a moment and took another phone from his pocket. María immediately saw the Squirrel sticker she had stuck on it, in the hope that it would be returned if she were to lose it.

'Wait a second,' she heard him say into the phone at his ear before he crouched down in front of her. 'We need the code for your phone,' he said politely.

María laughed coldly.

'Who are you speaking to?' she demanded. 'Who's on the other end?' she said, louder, so that her voice would be heard by whoever he was in touch with. 'Go on, call the police!' she yelled finally.

She was prepared to let the police take a look at her phone, but not these aluminium goons. They had no right to demand to examine it.

Donald nodded to the night watchman, who immediately responded by drawing his pistol and placing the muzzle against María's cheek.

'The code for your phone?' Donald repeated, still managing to sound courteous – his tone at odds with the cold steel against her cheek.

María felt as if she had been plunged into freezing water, and all the blood in her body rushed to her belly as danger threatened. She could hardly speak or move. She was like a frozen waterfall – her whole life came to a halt and the only sign of life inside was the forlorn hope that one day spring would come.

'The code,' Donald repeated. Any courtesy had disappeared – his voice had become a hiss. At the same time, the night watchman pressed the gun hard into her cheek so that the sharp pain brought her out of her daze.

'Twenty-eight-zero-eight,' she whispered, and saying the number out loud brought the tears back. It was Maggi's date of birth.

39

It was almost three in the morning when Ingimar's phone woke him. He felt that he had only just fallen asleep. As so often, in his dreams he had been at sea with a group of other young men, working as a team to shoot a seine net into the water in filthy weather. As he came to, for a moment he missed the camaraderie of the crew. A joint effort could make the hardest of circumstances pleasant.

'Hello?' he said into the phone.

He fumbled in the darkness for his reading glasses. Once he had started to wear them, it was as if he could no longer use the phone without putting them on. Somehow, he felt that he could hear better with the glasses on his nose.

'There's a problem at the warehouse. The journalist broke in,' William said.

Ingimar sat up and switched on the bedside lamp.

'OK, I'll deal with them direct,' he said. 'Wait a second while I find a pencil to write down the number.'

'Do you want me to text it to you?' William asked.

'No, absolutely not,' Ingimar said quickly. 'No phone trails to follow, thanks very much.'

He felt in his computer case and found a pen, writing on his arm the number William read out for him.

He got out of bed and made his way quietly down the stairs, not that he needed to as both his wife and his son appeared to be able to sleep through practically anything. He went into his office and closed the door behind him. He sat at the desk, switched on the lamp and hunted through the desk drawer for the small mobile phone he used for just this kind of call. Its battery was flat, so as usual he had to hunt for a charger cable; at least he had sockets fitted to the desk. Otherwise he would have had to crawl along the floor to find somewhere to plug in the wretched thing.

He punched in the number on his arm, and the call was answered on the first ring.

'I understand you've had a visit from my friend,' he said, and the man on the other end answered with an all-American 'Yes, sir'.

'Did she get any documents?'

'No, sir.'

'Did she take any pictures?' he asked.

The man hesitated.

'We don't know. Her phone is locked.'

Ingimar sighed silently.

'Make her give you the access code,' he said. 'You might need to be ... persuasive,' he added gently.

The man hesitated again, then agreed. In the background Ingimar could hear a door opening and closing again, and a moment later a woman's voice, raised to a screech.

'Who are you speaking to? Who's on the other end?' he heard her yell, and he smiled to himself. The fact that she was shouting in English indicated that she had no idea there was someone from Iceland on the line. The shouts came to a sudden end and the man spoke again.

'We have her phone open,' he said. 'She seems to have taken two pictures. I'll delete them right now.'

'Good,' Ingimar said. 'Check and see if she sent them to anyone.'

There was a pause, and the man confirmed that she did not appear to have sent pictures as text messages or emails, and they were nowhere to be seen in her social media pages.

'That's fine,' Ingimar said. 'You can let her go. She's small potatoes. Just a pawn.'

Ringing off, he switched on his computer, went to The Squirrel's web page and scrolled down to find a picture of María alongside one of her articles. He opened Tinder on his phone and searched until he found a woman who resembled her. He stared at the woman's picture for a moment, imagining fucking her hard as a punishment for María's interference. But then realised that he had no appetite for it. Tinder was too easy. There was no victory to be had there, no challenge.

40

Agla hadn't slept much, and when the door was unlocked in the morning for once she was anxious to get out of her cell. All the same, she felt a certain trepidation at the thought of meeting Elísa at breakfast. This was going to be colossally awkward. She had spent the night trying to escape thoughts she could not control as they flitted from Elísa and the hot skin of her arm, to the fleeting kiss, which in hindsight could mean anything, then on to that crushingly terrible time when Agla had sat in a rental car outside the place where Sonja was staying in London, watching her but not daring to speak to her. It had been plain that Sonja had wanted to get away from Agla, their commitment too much for her. She'd clearly been overwhelmed by the vision of the future stretching out ahead of her.

A couple of times during the night she had managed to focus her thoughts on the various aspects of the bizarre aluminium conundrum. she had got out of bed and snatched up the raw materials market reports she had printed out, and then tried to work her way through the figures, attempting to get a handle on how the aluminium flowed on the market. What was clear was that the world market had changed and those changes had begun to occur just as William's bank had begun the col...

She felt as if her body was unable to remain still. She could hardly breathe for the lump in her throat that appeared when her thoughts went to Sonja. When they then turned to Elísa, her heart beat faster and the palm that had stroked the tattooed arm felt as if it were on fire.

Agla decided to take a morning shower instead of an evening one, hoping that Elísa would have left the kitchen by the time she got there, and she would be able to get herself coffee without having to face her. What would she say to her? What on earth had happened last night in the cell doorway? Was it something other than usual light-hearted clowning for Elísa? If it was, what would that mean for Agla? These thoughts were maddening, and for the first time since that first week in her frustration at the shower.

Getting out of the shower, she growled at the mirror, which suppos-edly showed her the neglected mop of hair that resisted any attempts to tame it — other than those made by the skilled fingers of her regular hairdresser, who normally thinned it for her and touched up the roots, which were now looking distressingly grey. It was a long time since she had last considered her own appearance, but now she wondered whether Elísa thought she looked worn out. She would definitely need a complete overhaul once this was all over: a haircut and dye, a facial with all the works, manicure and pedicure, and on top of that she would need some new clothes. The ones she had brought with her to prison were now hanging off her like sacks, she had lost so much weight. Her stomach lurched at the thought that soon she would be let out of this cage, but this time there was none of the old despair at the thought. Now there was work to be done ... she had to get to the bottom of whatever ... business William had his fingers in. She needed to find out how she could make herself part of this intrigue.

She met Elísa in the kitchen ...

... the wing was silent ... the pot?' she asked ... ... breakfast. She ... without looking at Elísa. She didn't wait for an answer: the jug was ... full, so she poured herself a cup. Then turned to find Elísa gone. Hell ... She could have said something else: 'good morning,' or anything other than asking if there was any coffee left.

41

'Good to see you on your feet!' Sonja said as Thorgeir made his way down the wide curving staircase. His heels ... ... had taken a bath floor as he made his ... ... in a decent bed, the foyer and ... now dressed in a suit. He looked human again instead of resembling a wild animal.

'How are you feeling?'

'As well as can be expected,' he replied, his voice still hoarse after the tears and his movements stiff from his long incarceration in the cage.

'There's coffee,' Sonja said, pushing the flask across the table to him and gesturing for Thorgeir to take a seat, which he did with a deep groan.

His appearance had changed little with the passing years, despite his lifestyle. It seemed to be a quirk of people who looked older while still young, that they hardly changed at all after middle age. His hair had always had the same streaks of grey, and his face had never been anything other than lined, while his frame was as skinny as a teenager's. He poured himself coffee, and Sonja could see that his hand shook slightly, although she couldn't be sure if this was the withdrawal symptoms at work, or simply fear. She relished being amiable to him, as it seemed that every time she passed up an opportunity to punish him it simply magnified his terror of the final reckoning. But Sonja had no desire for a dramatic showdown. This drawn-out, painful amiability was her revenge on him.

'You have to understand, my dear Thorgeir, that we can't have our people partying so hard they forget what they should be doing.'

He didn't reply, but looked downcast and stared at his hands.

'And you have to understand that we can't have people being sent back home to Iceland for treatment and going to AA meetings where they open their hearts.'

He looked up quickly.

'You know I'd never tell—' he began.

Sonja raised a finger indicating that he should keep quiet.

'The condition you were in when Sponge brought you here from Iceland didn't inspire a lot of confidence, so the only option for you was the cage. You understand, don't you?'

Thorgeir sighed and said nothing, so Sonja stood up and went over to him.

'Now, after a few days in the cage, you're a new man,' she said, placing a hand on his shoulder and feeling him flinch at her touch. 'So we did the right thing, didn't we?'

She squeezed his shoulder and he nodded.

'Yes,' he said. 'Right. Quite right.'

'And you understand that this wasn't a punishment, but a necessary strategy to get you back in line?'

'I understand perfectly,' he said, nodding again.

'Good,' Sonja said, letting go of his shoulder and sitting back down. 'You're booked on the evening flight back to Iceland from Heathrow, and you can catch the tube to the airport. And you keep yourself straight, or next time there won't be anything to soften the withdrawal symptoms in the cage. Understand? It'll be cold turkey and I don't give a shit if the cramps kill you.'

Hesitatingly, Thorgeir got to his feet, as if he hardly dared believe there was no more to come; that there was no further punishment to be meted out.

Sonja gave him a friendly smile.

'Have a good trip home, Thorgeir,' she said. 'Let me know when you're back on your feet, won't you?'

He sidled out of the room, crabwise, as if he wanted to hurry as fast as he could but dared not turn his back on her. Alex followed him out through the foyer and Sonja could hear him murmur a goodbye as he opened the heavy mahogany door and let him out. Then Sonja heard his rapid footfalls down the steps outside. At one time there hadn't been a single person in the entire world she had hated as much as she had loathed Thorgeir. Back then she could only look on as he had sent her travelling from one country to another, first with cash and then with cocaine; trips that marked the beginning of all her misfortunes. But her viewpoint had changed. She saw that Thorgeir was a junkie, so had never been entirely in control of his actions. And she had also admitted to herself, that she was completely responsible for her own misfortunes.

42

The sun was rising as Donald and the night watchman escorted María to the gate, making it plain that if she were to show her face again, the gun would be waiting for her. María nodded vehemently and was left in no doubt that they would shoot if she were to return. She wasn't inclined to find out. There were ways other than breaking in to find out what these men were up to.

'Did you find any of Meteorite's customers?' she asked as soon as Marteinn answered the phone.

'Yes,' Marteinn said. 'I emailed you the list.'

'Thanks,' she said. 'How did you get hold of that?'

He said nothing.

'Marteinn, where did you find a list of Meteorite's customers?'

'Why do you want to know?' he shot back at her.

'Just curious,' she replied. 'Marteinn, are you all right?' she added.

'That's a fucking sneaky question,' he snapped. 'You're on the other side of the world, so why stick your nose into stuff that doesn't concern you?'

María stopped and leaned on the fence that encircled Meteorite Metals. She had the sudden feeling that she was about to faint.

'My dearest Marteinn,' she said. 'Have you been to the clinic? You know you need help to get your treatment in balance, and if you're starting to be suspicious about me then there's something wrong.'

'Don't you try and use that against me,' he whispered, his voice laden with hatred. 'You pretend to be my friend, but I can see all the clues that tell me what you're up to. And the dangerous thing about all this is that I'm the only one who can see through you!'

He hung up and María drew a deep breath. By the time she arrived back home he would be seriously disturbed. His mother was dead, and his sister, who lived on the other side of the country, in Egilsstaðir, wanted nothing to do with him. So there was nobody to call other than the police or the mental-health clinic, and she knew from painful experience that it wasn't easy to have him admitted. On top of that he was still struggling to forgive her for having had him sectioned once already. It wasn't something she wanted to go through again.

She got into the car, started the engine and turned the heater up. The car had no aircon, but at least there was heating, which she needed as she was shivering with cold. Her teeth chattered and her hands were numb from the cuffs, which had prevented the blood circulating. She rubbed her wrists cautiously. Each one was marked with a deep groove, like a bright-red bracelet. There was no sign that there had been any bleeding, despite what her instincts had told her as she had sat on the cold warehouse floor. But instinct could lead you astray, as Marteinn demonstrated so clearly. The painful emotions that he experienced had no basis, but still caused him unending misery. In three days she would be home and then she would see what could be done for him. Now she desperately needed to get some warmth inside her, and make use of her time in America.

It wasn't until she was under the shower at the motel that she burst into tears. The flow of hot water seemed to melt the cold ice casing that had formed around her sensitive core as she sat on the cold warehouse floor, and now her body ached with pain. She could not fully straighten her back, her buttocks were sore, and there was so much pain in her hands it was as if they had been burned.

She could still feel where the muzzle of the pistol had been jabbed into her cheek.

The chlorine taste of the water made her gag, but she gulped down three painkillers, and forced herself to drink more water to make them work faster, before throwing herself onto the bed, hair still wet. She set her alarm, giving herself two hours, and was instantly asleep.

43

Anton stared at the dynamite and was worried. The undersides of the sticks all seemed to be damp and the paper wrappers were wearing through. He had felt all over the boiler room floor and there was no damp to be found anywhere. Maybe it hadn't been a smart move to keep the dynamite lying on a plastic bag. He picked up one stick and carefully unwound the paper. It was wet to the touch; in some weird way, it seemed to be sweating. The damp seemed to come from inside. It was like when his father took fish from the freezer to let it defrost in the kitchen, and the carton would become wetter and softer through the day. But the dynamite hadn't been frozen, and if anything, it was now uncomfortably warm in the boiler room.

He hoped that the dynamite hadn't become useless. If it wasn't usable, then he had no idea what he would do. His plans would be back at square one. He sat on the camping chair and took out his phone. He would have to sort this out. School would just have to wait; this was much more important.

Searching in Icelandic yielded no results, though, but a search for 'sweating dynamite' in English did. He read through a couple of cha-troom posts and a wiki article that matched what he was looking for. Apparently, the nitroglycerine was leaching out of the dynamite; to stop it happening he needed to turn the sticks regularly. He didn't waste time reading all the words of warning about how sensitive nitro-glycerine could be; he knew perfectly well that explosives needed to be handled with care. He gently turned every stick over so that the damp side was facing upwards. That way he hoped the liquid would leak back into the sticks. The worrying thing was that, according to the wiki article, dynamite ought to be kept somewhere cool. The tem-perature in the boiler room could vary. Sometimes the hot water pipes running along the wall from the inlet valve would hiss and then it would become warm, and at other times it was quite cool down here. But there was no point worrying about it. He had no other place to keep the explosives, and he preferred to have it somewhere close by, where he could keep an eye on it.

There was, however, a bigger headache – and that was how to solve the detonator problem. All this explosive was of no use if there was no way of setting it off remotely. He shut the boiler-room door behind him and so that he wouldn't be heard walked lightly up the grass verge rather than the steps. Not that he needed to bother; his father had already left and his mother was asleep, and would sleep well into the day.

Outside, on Tjarnarbakki, he saw a man looking at the sky, his phone in his hand. Anton watched his strange behaviour, until he heard a buzz and saw the drone whizz across the lake.

'It's a no-fly zone,' he said to the man in English, assuming he had to be a tourist, as this was common knowledge. 'This is the approach path for passenger aircraft landing at the city airport. You could cause an accident.'

The man quickly landed the drone.

'Sorry, I didn't know,' he said.

'But the drone should know. It should be programmed so it won't work in a no-fly zone.'

The man smiled apologetically.

'You can get round anything,' he said. 'A computer is just a computer.' He packed the drone away into its case. 'You live in one of these houses?' he asked, gazing along the street with admiration.

Anton pointed to their house and the man nodded as he admired it.

'Lucky you,' he said.

But Anton's thoughts were elsewhere as he walked away. A solution to the detonator problem was taking shape in his mind.

44

Agla looked at the blurred picture María had attached to her email. Despite the heavy grain and the green cast, it seemed to support what her short message said. The warehouse at Meteorite Metals was full to the rafters. Agla had learned that sometimes things were just what they appeared to be, and this seemed to be one of those instances. Apparently, the Icelandic smelter was producing aluminium that was registered on LME, but instead of being sold, it was put into Meteorite's warehouse, where it was stacking up. But despite all its activity, Meteorite Metals looked to be in poor financial shape, and things were deteriorating. The outgoings on its balance sheet had not been itemised, though, so it was impossible to see where the money was going.

It was obvious that William and his bank were running a scam of some kind, undoubtedly with Ingimar's involvement, that revolved around stockpiling aluminium. But the reason why they were doing this remained a mystery. At some point there had to be a use for it all. Maybe it was an attempt to lift the world price, but as this was governed by demand rather than production capacity, such a venture was doomed to failure. International regulations would have to be changed before stockpiling would have any effect on the world market price; these rules had been put in place explicitly to prevent stockpiling. Yet it was clear that neither the smelter in Iceland nor Meteorite Metals was selling the aluminium. It was all very strange. Agla sent a message to María, asking her to follow one of the trucks. It wouldn't do any harm to know where they were taking aluminium.

She suddenly felt a shudder of discomfort pass through her, of the kind she had not felt since her first few days in prison. She had to stand up, move her legs and use every ounce of willpower not to scream in frustration. She had to get out of this place; she needed to go where she wanted, to breathe fresh air, to be herself. She jumped a few times, forcing herself to draw breaths that went all the way down to her belly. She lay on the library floor, closed her eyes and concentrated on a mental image of the ceiling of her bedroom at home. In her mind she lay in her own bed, free to stand up, walk out and go wherever she pleased.

Agla was startled when the door opened and one of the warders let Elísa in.

'Hey, do you want to come to my room at eight tonight?' Elísa whispered, glancing at the security camera as if she was sure that it recorded sound as well as images. 'They're all going to an AA meeting – everyone except the bookkeeper – and I'm going to pretend to have a headache. We can have an hour to ourselves with nobody to disturb us.'

45

Her phone's alarm chimed for a long time before María finally woke up. She stretched for it, hit the snooze button and closed her eyes again. Despite the painkillers, her whole body hurt. She lay still. That was best. As she drifted between sleep and consciousness, Maggi seemed close to her, performing the gentle caresses he always woke her with on Sunday mornings, a clear day ahead of them with fresh bread from the bakery and the weekend papers to be read in bed.

The alarm called out to her a second time. As she was about to tap the snooze button again, she was startled to see a message from Agla on the screen. It was painful and difficult to sit up. She lifted her hands above her head to stretch her spine. But the pain in her back shot all the way down her right leg to her toes as she got to her feet. It would be a while before she would be ready for anything.

She limped back and forth, picking up her things and throwing them anyhow into her case. The old María had had a linen bag for underwear that she packed before arranging everything else in orderly rows; but in this grubby motel, bruised and stiff from the beating she had endured while carrying out Agla Margeirsdóttir's assignment, she admitted to herself that she hadn't just changed in the last few years, she had become a different person. Maggi had been quite right when he had said that she was no longer the woman he had married.

Agla's message was short: *Follow a truck and find out where they take the aluminium.*

María sighed. She had meant to start working on the list of business contacts that Marteinn had sent, but this sounded like a better plan. The trucks appeared to arrive full and drive straight out again. There was no space to load or unload them, so this had to be for show. It was therefore key to work out where they went after leaving the warehouse. Did they go round in circle after circle, or stop off somewhere? If they did, where might that be? She sent a reply that was as brief as Agla's message had been.

OK. There's something fishy about all this, and they threatened me with a gun.

She had finished packing her case and just dropped the room keys off in the box at reception when her phone rang. The caller was identified on her screen as the Hólmsheiði Prison.

'Will you accept a call from Agla Margeirsdóttir?' asked a voice with a strong Eastern European accent. She had hardly said yes before Agla was on the line.

'Are you all right, María?' she asked, and she felt a pang inside at this unexpected concern.

'I'm not entirely sure,' she said. 'I'm not used to having a gun in my face.'

'What happened, exactly?' Agla whispered as if to stop anyone listening, although they both knew that prisoners' calls were often monitored.

'I broke into the warehouse last night, and they caught me. I was thrown out. It was all very heavy-handed.'

As she thought of the pistol barrel being rammed into her cheek, the feeling again came over her that she was about to faint. She sat down on the kerb outside the motel.

'I had no idea I was sending you into anything dangerous,' Agla said. 'Maybe it's best if you just come home. We'll leave things as they are.'

'No chance.' María felt the obstinacy well up inside her. She wasn't going to give up right away. She wasn't going to let these scumbags scare her off. 'If they had nothing to hide in that warehouse, then they would have called the police and had me arrested. But instead they called someone who told them to erase the pictures from my phone and to check the messages.'

'Do you think they saw the message you sent me?' Agla asked.

'No,' María replied. 'I fixed the settings so that outgoing messages are deleted – just like you showed me.'

Agla laughed and María couldn't help smiling as well. This had been the focus of endless questions when she had been at the special prosecutor's office and Agla had been a person of interest under interrogation. María had asked again and again if Agla had replied to this or that message, while across the table Agla had sat silent and impassive. There had been nothing for it but to take all kinds of roundabout routes to get to her emails.

'Take care, María,' Agla said at last.

María said 'yes', and 'thanks', and ended the call with the bizarre feeling that Agla was her thoughtful friend instead of her sworn enemy.

She threw her case into the back of the car and limped over to the diner, where she ordered two American pancakes and bacon. When the food arrived, she squeezed a generous helping of maple syrup over everything and tore into it. She asked for coffee in a take-out paper cup. This was one shithole she couldn't wait to leave behind her.

46

Anton would really have preferred orange, but he thought it would look immature to wait for a boy two years older than he was and already in college with a glass of fizzy orange in front of him. So instead he ordered a latte and stirred two spoonfuls of sugar into it. That made him a grown-up man meeting another guy in a coffee house to discuss serious business. He had to play the part properly. That was why he hadn't brought Gunnar along. He would have screwed things up with some crap about Molotov cocktails and fireworks. Anton sipped his coffee, which wasn't too bad once there was sugar in it. He would have much preferred hot chocolate.

As soon as Oddur walked in he stood up and waved, and asked him what he wanted to drink. Oddur asked for a cappuccino, and Anton made a mental note to ask for just that next time. There was something cool about the way Oddur said it – 'cappuccinothanks', all one word, as if this was something he had ordered a thousand times before but somehow still looked forward to; as if there was something special about that kind of coffee.

'We were at school together,' Anton said with a smile.

'Yeah, that's what you said in your message,' Oddur said. 'Sorry, man. I don't remember you at all.'

'That's all right,' Anton said. 'You normally only remember the older kids. That's why I remember you but you don't remember me.'

In fact, he was relieved that Oddur hadn't remembered him, as two years ago he had been a stick-thin spotty weakling; not exactly the slick business type he wanted Oddur to see now.

'Excuse me a moment,' Oddur said, looking at his phone. He seemed to be reading messages and answering them; he held the phone in both hands and tapped with his thumbs at incredible speed.

'I saw in the paper that you won an honorary award in the university robotics competition,' Anton said as Oddur put his phone down.

'The engineering students' competition,' Oddur said. 'I would have won if I had been old enough to take part. But I'm still at high school, so they gave me an honorary award instead. My robot, Wrangler, was the best of the lot.'

'That's fantastic!' Anton said, raised his cup in appreciation and sipped, as if he was toasting Oddur's success.

Oddur lifted his cup at the same time and when he put it down again, it was clear that the moment had come when he wanted to know what Anton's request to meet him was about.

'You're interested in robotics?' he asked.

Anton shook his head.

'No,' he said. 'That's why I need your help.' He moved his chair closer to the table, leaned forwards and dropped his voice. 'Let's say, for example, that I needed a remote-control system that could light a fuse leading to some dynamite to blow up an old shed. Is that the kind of thing you could produce?'

Oddur stared at him in surprise.

'Why on earth would I do that, even if I could?'

'Because I'd pay you. As much as you want.'

Oddur shifted in his chair and sat very upright, as if his body had stiffened.

'What are you going to blow up?'

Anton was slightly taken aback by how abrupt Oddur's manner had suddenly become.

'It's just an idea,' he said to calm Oddur down. 'Just an idea, you know. Let's just say that I want to do something a bit special as a surprise for my girlfriend's birthday, and I'm taking her and some friends for a picnic. The best part might be when we blow up a rotten old shed that's in a place I know.'

'And you think your girlfriend's going to enjoy seeing some shed blown up?'

'Yep. She loves a bang, y'know.'

Now Oddur smiled awkwardly.

'That's the weirdest thing I've ever heard,' he said and shook his head in disbelief.

'She just loves explosions,' Anton continued excitedly. 'New Year's Eve is her favourite. She'll just love it.'

He could hear the lies in his own voice and hoped that Oddur wouldn't see through him.

'Then why not just have a firework display for her?'

'That's the plan,' Anton said. 'But blowing up the shed is the high point of the firework display.'

He was taken by surprise by just how quickly the lies had spun themselves. It was as if all this make-believe emerged effortlessly.

'And where are you going to get the money to pay me?'

'I have money,' Anton said. 'I'm a silver-spoon kid.'

Oddur smiled again.

'I need to think it over,' he said. 'I can easily make what you're looking for, but I'm not sure that I'd want to. It depends whether I want to take the risk that someone could get hurt and it would be my fault.'

Anton nodded gravely to show that he appreciated Oddur's concerns.

'That's why I wanted to ask if you could come up with something smart. My friend offered to make some kind of a detonator using a petrol bomb. That sounds far too dangerous.'

It had the required effect. 'Christ...' Oddur breathed.

'I reckon there's far less risk of someone getting hurt if you could make a high-tech remote control,' Anton went on. 'I want everyone to be well clear when the dynamite goes off.'

'You're completely off your head,' Oddur said, getting to his feet. 'Thanks for the coffee. I'll think it over and let you know.'

Oddur had left the coffee house when Anton remembered something important: he should have mentioned that this had to remain strictly between the two of them. He hurried after Oddur, who turned as he heard Anton call his name.

'Hey,' Anton said. 'Don't forget this is just a *potential* scenario, and we keep it between you and me.'

Oddur waved a hand and nodded, but his eyes flashed nervously from side to side, so that Anton wondered if a boy two years older than he was, a coffee-drinking robotics genius, was actually frightened of him.

47

María didn't have to wait for long for a truck to turn up at the warehouse. She had been parked in the shade of a threadbare tree for only a few minutes when two trucks drove up at the same time. She sat up straight and finished the weak coffee in her paper cup. She knew the trucks spent around a quarter of an hour inside the building before emerging at the far end. Considering how packed the place was, there was unlikely to be any loading or unloading going on, so she guessed that the fifteen minutes were simply a coffee break for the drivers.

She pulled out from under the tree, and with the engine running waited in the side road from where she could see the exit. As the second truck crossed the speed bumps by the gate she swung the car out onto the road.

She kept a safe distance behind the trucks as she followed them through the town, but closed up the gap as they approached the freeway, for fear of losing them in the traffic. With less than a mile to go before the turn-off, the trucks dropped into separate lanes. For a moment María wondered whether they were aware of her and were splitting up as a way of confusing her. But that was a ridiculous idea, and to avoid switching lanes and drawing attention to herself, María decided to stay where she was, following the second of the two trucks. It took the bend towards the north and Fort Wayne, while the other went under the bridge, taking the Indianapolis road.

Following the truck was no problem. It stayed in the right-hand lane and its speed remained steady. Once again María kept a distance behind it, sometimes allowing another car to drop in between them, but never letting the truck out of her sight. After half an hour she began to feel herself getting sleepy. She hoped that the truck would stop at a diner where she could get something stronger than the dishwater she had been given that morning, which hadn't seemed to contain even a minimal amount of caffeine.

She didn't need to think too long about coffee, as her phone rang and the sight of Marteinn's name on the screen brought her back to full alertness.

'*Hæ*, Marteinn, my darling,' she said and immediately sensed that her warm tone had taken him unawares.

'*Hæ*, María,' he said humbly. 'I think I was a bit over the top earlier.'

'Maybe a little, my dear Marteinn,' she said. 'You know, if you think of all the time we've worked together, you'll know I sincerely want whatever's best for you.'

Marteinn broke into tears.

'I know,' he snivelled. 'But it's so hard to not be angry when there's so much going on in the world. And now that you're getting mixed up in this metal stockpiling business I have to be careful in case you're part of the big conspiracy.'

'I'm not getting caught up in any metal stockpiling, Marteinn. I'm digging into it.'

'And who got you to do it, eh? Who was it who put you onto this?'

María swallowed. She hadn't told him that she was working on this for Agla. But it was difficult to keep anything from him. She had had a suspicion that he was reading her emails. Now she was sure he was.

'Agla Margeirsdóttir asked me to do it, Marteinn, but that doesn't change anything. She gets the information she's looking for, and I get a hell of a scoop.'

'I'd never have believed that you would be on Agla's side.'

María sighed. Not all that long ago she wouldn't have believed it herself. There was no way to explain it or excuse herself other than with the plain truth.

'To be completely open with you, Marteinn, she's paying me a pile of money for this and I couldn't see any way of turning her down because it's what's keeping The Squirrel and me from bankruptcy.'

'So you're for sale like everyone else?' Marteinn yelped, hardly holding back his sobs of frustration.

'I'm truly sorry to disappoint you,' María said, and meant it.

'My disappointment doesn't mean a lot when you're working for the corporate giants fighting for ownership of metals. And metal is the only thing that will be recognised as currency once the magnetic storm hits.'

As often happened during conversations with Marteinn, María was failing to keep track.

'Magnetic ... what?'

'Look back at all economic systems and you can see the pattern. First banknotes replaced metal as currency, and from banknotes we went to plastic cards, from electronic to digital and when the magnetic storm hits us and all digital records are destroyed, nobody will be able to prove they own anything. There's a new world order coming and they will control it with magnetic pulses and blame it on solar activity.'

The words tumbled out of Marteinn's mouth as he went into an even more convoluted explanation of his latest conspiracy theory. He spoke so quickly, María struggled to follow what he was saying. The only thing she understood was that those who would end up with the world in their hands were the same people who now had warehouses stacked high with metal.

'Marteinn, I have to go now,' she said as gently as she could.

The truck was indicating that it was about to turn right.

48

The counsellor stared at Agla with concern.

'Are you sure this is a good idea?' she asked, her brow furrowed and two deep grooves appearing between her eyebrows.

'I don't know,' Agla said. 'We'll find out. I've owned this house for almost six years and have never used it.'

'But you're aware she's an addict?'

'Yes. I know that.' Agla was fighting to maintain her composure in the face of this complete stranger's interfering attitude. She had never met this counsellor before and couldn't see that it was any of her business who she was letting live in her own house. 'It wouldn't worry me if she wrecks the place. I've no attachment to it.'

That wasn't strictly true; there were plenty of emotions tied to this house, but they were all negative ones. She could see herself, childishly cheerful as she painted the living room, Sonja having changed her mind about the colour after the painters had finished. They had lain in bed after making love, ordering furniture online. And then she saw herself sitting in despair on a box as she read Sonja's farewell message again and again.

It would be perfect to bring some fresh spirit into that house. Although she hadn't set foot in it for years, she had never had the heart to put it on the market.

'Well, if you're happy about it,' the counsellor said, as if she wasn't satisfied with the idea herself.

'Of course I'm happy with it,' Agla said as firmly as she could without being downright rude. 'I've made her the offer, and I'm delighted to be able to. It's completely ridiculous that Elísa won't be allowed out on probation if she doesn't have anywhere to live.'

This was one of the system's strangely inflexible rules that she couldn't fathom. Each prisoner was required to demonstrate that they had a place to live before they could be released, even though everyone was sent to the Vernd probation hostel for a while once their sentence at Hólmsheiði was over. Wherever she lived, Agla couldn't see how Elísa would be able to pay her way. The wages for the job she had been able to arrange, behind the supermarket tills at Bónus, wouldn't go far.

The counsellor set her lips in a firm line, as if she wanted to stop herself from responding. She inspected Agla with an expression that could have been one of exhaustion or disgust. For a second it occurred to Agla that the counsellor knew what she and Elísa had got up to the previous evening, but that was impossible. They had been in a corner of Elísa's cell, where they couldn't be seen through the peephole in the door, and they'd been as quiet as possible, so nobody passing by could have heard their nervous giggles and stifled gasps. All the same, Agla could feel her heart pumping blood into her skin, and she blushed to the roots of her hair.

'As the landlord, you need to sign this,' the counsellor said, sliding a form across the table. It detailed her consent for ankle-tag monitoring equipment to be installed in the house. Agla signed it and slid it back.

'Well,' the counsellor said. 'We need to discuss your own move to Vernd and your release on probation. It says in your file that you are financially well off and live comfortably. But the staff here say that you show considerable apprehension about being released.'

'No,' Agla said. 'Not any longer.'

'No nerves at the thought of walking out of here and getting to grips with life outside?'

The counsellor leaned forwards and gave her a friendly smile.

'Not at all,' Agla said, standing up. 'I can't get out of this cage soon enough.'

49

It was as if his mother could sense that this time he really wanted her to go to bed early, because she did just the opposite. She sat in front of the television, drinking slowly, making weird comments about the presenters on the news, mostly reflecting on their clothes or their family connections. On a normal evening he would have enjoyed it and laughed with her, sending a few examples of her odd turns of phrase to Júlía, but now he needed some time with the middle floor of the house to himself for a while – before his father came home.

'That hairdo doesn't suit her, and that can't be a woollen dress. Wool would be much too hot in a TV studio,' his mother muttered, slurping her white wine.

'Hmm.'

Anton had no opinions on what material the presenters' clothes were made from. They didn't choose what they wore – they had stylists for all that; and their clothes weren't even their own, so didn't say anything about their personalities. It was pointless thinking about it.

'I reckon he's better-looking now that his hair's gone grey,' his mother said, pointing at the screen.

'Who?' Anton asked, looking up from his phone.

'Him, there,' she said, pointing again. 'The son of that bloke ... the minister.'

She was forgetting names now, so it wouldn't be long before she would go upstairs to bed. Anton stretched to reach the wine bottle and refilled his mother's glass. She took a long swig, and then he filled it to the brim.

'Thanks, darling,' she said, knocking back half a glass as if white wine was a soft drink. Normally she drank vodka, so for her white wine must be tame stuff. Anton was never going to drink, and he was never going to take any kind of pills; and he would never marry a woman who drank or took pills.

He looked through everything that Júlía had added to Stories on Snapchat, then went to Ask and sent a few questions her way, which he knew she would realise came from him. When she answered, he always got a warm feeling inside, like he was the coolest, best and smartest kid she knew. When he looked up, his mother was asleep, her head thrown back on the back of the chair, snoring quietly with her mouth wide open and the empty wine glass in her hand.

She would undoubtedly sleep there well into the night. He got quietly to his feet and tiptoed cautiously to his father's study, where he carefully shut the door behind him.

The safe was behind a painting that was fixed to the wall on a set of hinges. When he had been a kid it had been fun to swing the painting aside and show his friends the hidden safe. He had often seen inside the safe when his father was using it, and knew that as well as the documents, it held stacks of banknotes. Under normal circumstances he would never steal money from his father – he had never needed to. He had always been given money for everything he had asked for. But this time it wouldn't be easy to explain why he needed such a large amount.

Oddur had sent him a message, saying he would make a remote-control detonator, but it would cost half a million krónur. He seemed to be surprised when Anton replied and accepted the offer. More than likely Oddur had thought that this would be so much that Anton would not be able to raise the funds, and the matter would be forgotten. But it actually wasn't so much that it would make a dent in his father's cash reserves. He probably wouldn't even notice that anything was missing. It wasn't as if he sat there and counted the cash every week. And if he were to notice, then Anton would reply with what his father was always telling him: money in itself had no value; money was a tool.

Anton spun the combination lock a couple of times. He didn't need to be a genius to crack this lock. His father used Anton's date of birth as the key to practically everything.

50

María picked up her phone and took a picture. She could hardly believe her eyes. In another small town in another state was a warehouse identical to the first; the only visible difference was that this one was branded OR Metals Inc. Even the fence around the perimeter was exactly the same as the one surrounding Meteorite Metals.

María sent a picture to Marteinn with a short message:

Another metal storage unit in Ohio, the name is OR Metals. Can you check it out for me?

If anyone could find something out, then that person would be Marteinn. The question was whether he was so disappointed with her, he wouldn't bother to reply.

She waited for the truck to emerge on the other side. She didn't need to check that there was an exit, like there was at the other place, so she parked by the side of the road near the entrance so the driver wouldn't see her when he drove out. She wondered if this warehouse was also stuffed full of aluminium, but didn't have the courage to go inside and check it out. Meteorite had a night watchman, and this place was exactly the same. The prospect of another cold pistol muzzle in her face wasn't an attractive one. She rubbed her wrists and decided that she would continue to follow the truck to see if it made a call at yet another warehouse.

Twenty minutes later the truck appeared, driving back past the perimeter fence. María waited a moment before starting the engine and following it through the town the way it had come. It was getting dark now, and after a monotonous hour on Highway 90, heading east, she was struggling to stay awake. She opened a pack of potato chips and a bottle of water, and reflected that if the truck didn't make a stop soon at a diner, then this would have to pass for dinner. She wound down the window to let in more air and set the radio to search, hoping for a station that offered something other than country and western and advertisements.

She was fighting to keep her eyes open and was scanning the side of the road for motels when the truck finally indicated and turned off into a rest area.

There had been diners and shops at some of the rest areas she had passed, but this one had nothing more than a shack containing toilets and coin-operated showers, and a large, empty parking zone. María was hoping that the driver had stopped for nothing more than a quick call of nature and would then drive on a little further to somewhere there would be a place to eat. But he took care to park the truck in one of the large diagonal parking bays in the middle of the rest area; it looked like he was stopping for the night.

She got out and went over to the toilet block where the smell smacked her in the face. She tried to breathe through her mouth as she peed, relieved that she had pocketed a serviette, as there was no paper. She washed her hands and eased the door open with her elbow so she could get out without having to touch the handle. Walking back to the car, she saw the driver with a bag in his hand, making his way over to a wooden table under some trees. She sat in the car and watched as he lit a lamp and sat at the table. He was better prepared than she was. She checked her phone to see if Marteinn had replied, and he had:

They own two warehouses.

She sighed with relief. It was good to have Marteinn on her side. She would try to explain things for him in more detail when she was home and he was feeling more like himself.

So Meteorite Metals had a warehouse and OR Metals had two, which meant there was every chance there would be more companies and more warehouses, and the amount of stockpiled aluminium might be considerable. But she still failed to understand the reason for the truck movements. She got out of the car and set off across the rest area. She had learned during her time at the special prosecutor's office that sometimes there was no need to work your way around the edges, trying to discover everything for yourself. Often a straight question was the best way to get answers.

'Hi, I'm María. I'm a journalist from Iceland,' she said, holding up her press card.

The driver stood up, still with his mouth full and a beer bottle in his hand. He leaned forwards to peer at her card.

'Journalist, yeah?'

'I've been tailing you today, and I can see you're driving a loaded truck from one warehouse to another. Can I ask why?'

'What paper do you work for?'

It was a question María was ready for. It was what everyone asked. But it was less embarrassing to explain to a foreigner: he wouldn't know that The Squirrel was just a tiny online venture.

She accepted the beer he opened for her, perched herself on the edge of the table and gave him a quick lecture about The Squirrel's importance to Icelandic investigative journalism.

'I'm interested to know what you drivers are doing. The warehouse in Indiana is stacked to the roof, so why are the trucks driving in and out all day long? Can you help me? I can keep your name out of it, of course,' she added. 'I'll just say I have an anonymous source.'

'What's in it for me?' the driver asked.

'We should be able to pay you something in return for information,' María said quickly. She had no doubt that Agla would cover the cost.

'I don't mean cash,' he said. 'It gets lonely on the road, y'know.'

He took two steps towards her, standing close and trapping her between his heavy frame and the wooden table, which was bolted to the ground.

'Excuse me,' María said, taking an instinctive step to one side, but his hand closed around her arm, and she realised just what a dangerous position she was in. She was alone in a vast, deserted parking lot, and even if she managed to squeeze out a scream, it would be drowned out by the roar of traffic from the nearby freeway, and there was nobody anywhere near to hear it.

Time suddenly began to take on a strange elasticity as she was faced by the imminent danger. The clear thought formed in her mind, that if she did not react right away, within a few seconds, she would be petrified with fear, just as she had been when she had felt the pistol's muzzle pressed into her cheek.

She leaned forwards and sank her teeth deep into the man's arm. As he yelped and relaxed his grip, she sprinted for her car, not daring to look back to see if he was following her. As she dropped herself into the driver's seat, she heard him yell 'Stupid bitch!' She started the engine and fumbled for the door lock at the same time, and a moment later the tyres screeched as she hurtled down the slip road to the freeway.

As she bullied the car up to eighty, she could feel there was no strength in her legs. A deep wave of nausea suddenly swept over her. She slowed down, pulled over, put her head out of the window and vomited onto the verge. A powerful smell assailed her senses, and her limbs were now so weak, she felt paralysed. It all merged together in her thoughts: the man's sweat-damp face in the darkness and the stench of piss from the toilet.

51

'I'm sure you'll do a good job,' Ingimar said into his phone as he weighed a perfect green avocado in his hand, applying gentle pressure to gauge its ripeness. It seemed fully ripe – a rarity in Iceland, where the distance that products had to be transported meant imported fruit and vegetables were generally sold unripe and needed a few days on the kitchen windowsill before they were edible.

Today everything was going his way: a friend on the south-west regional police force had promised that on her return to Iceland, María would get the treatment she deserved for her interference; the avocado in his hand was just right; and in front of him was a woman who ignited something inside him, so waiting in the queue for the checkout was no hardship. She wore a leather jacket and a pair of skin-tight leggings that hid nothing. He held his phone in front of him so it was not too obvious that he was checking her out. Occasionally he would allow himself to ogle women, but it was rare for him to start a conversation or make a move to pick them up. Maybe he was getting old. Any thoughts of sex were tinged with sorrow, and sometimes he felt that a moment's delight was hardly worth the effort. As she filled her bags at the checkout, the pretty woman's jacket flapped open to reveal a low-cut top offering him a glimpse of her cleavage.

The woman looked up and caught him staring at her, but instead of taking offence she smiled briefly, and he smiled back, apologetically, placing his basket on the counter and emptying its contents onto the conveyor. Once the woman had paid and had finished packing her purchases into her shopping bag, she sent him another smile, as if in farewell. Ingimar felt warm inside. The smile told him that if he had made the effort, he could have got somewhere with this woman.

'There's an offer on avocados,' the lad behind the till said. 'Buy one, get one free.'

Ingimar grinned.

'Great,' he said, and jogged back into the shop to pick up a second avocado from the fruit stand. He didn't need a second one, but he took it as a symbol of how life was treating him today. He was certain that this evening, when he had blitzed it in the blender with tomatoes and spices, and put it on the table with a bowl of nachos, it would taste wonderful.

Ingimar dropped the bag on the back seat of his 4×4 and got in. It was unfortunate that he wouldn't be able to see the expression on María's face tomorrow, when she found the police waiting for her. That was something he would have enjoyed. Maybe he would be able to get his friend to take a picture of her meeting the reception committee. He would undoubtedly do that for him. Ingimar counted himself fortunate that he had many good friends and generally didn't find it hard to get people to do him a favour.

He started the car and glanced in the rear-view mirror, but it had been moved slightly, so instead of seeing the view behind the car, he found himself looking into his own face. The second he looked into his own eyes without intending to, the warm feeling of luck and happiness vanished, and he could no longer face the thought of going home. Rebekka would be waiting for him, either drunk or asleep, doped up with pills, along with an unhappy and hungry Anton, who could not be pleased, it seemed. A snarling revulsion at the thought of home welled up inside him.

Across the car park, the pretty woman was taking her time arranging stuff in the boot of her car. Hell, it couldn't take that long for her to sort out her shopping, could it? She had to be waiting to see if Ingimar stopped to speak to her. If he did, he'd have hooked her within a few minutes, and in an hour he would be getting out of her bed, and looking for ways both to escape and to rid her of any expectations about seeing him again. He couldn't be bothered with it. Fate constantly sent him tempting offers, just like a buy-one-get-one-free avocado, but that didn't mean he had to accept them all.

He took out his phone and called *her*.

Experience told him that whenever he felt there were too many signals from various directions flagging up how fantastic and smart and fortunate he was, it was time for some abuse.

'Get yourself over here,' she ordered. 'I'll be furious if you're not here in thirty minutes flat.'

Once he had been flogged, he would be relaxed and satisfied with his lot, which in reality was no better or worse than anyone else's. Then he would go home humbly and make the most of the evening with Anton, just like any normal man. Because he was just a normal man. *Just a mortal man.*

52

Agla found herself sliding into a deep depression as she watched Elísa finish packing her belongings. Agla fussed and repeated yet again all the things she had been through with her twice already.

'Call as soon as you get to Vernd, and my lawyer will bring you the phone and the car. It needs to be charged up every four hundred kilometres, but to be safe it's worth doing it when it's down to twenty per cent. If you can't plug it in somewhere, then just go to a fast-charging point. It doesn't cost anything.'

'I know,' Elísa said and gave her a beautiful smile.

Agla wondered what it had been that had initially repelled her, as now she felt herself melting when Elísa smiled at her.

'Work hard and make sure you're back at Vernd for dinner at ten to six – be sure you're not late. And aim to be sure you're home at ten to eleven so there's no chance of accidentally breaking the rules.'

'I know it's strict,' Elísa said.

Agla realised that Elísa knew all this, but somehow felt that she wasn't taking it seriously enough. There was something about the look on her face that indicated a disregard for the probation regulations. Breaking the rules even once would mean being fast-tracked back to Hólmsheiði.

'I'll be at Vernd in a week, and then we can help each other out,' Agla said.

Elísa reached for her hand and pulled her to the corner, out of sight of the window. Agla felt herself flush with excitement as Elísa pressed herself against her, but was too flustered with concern to risk a hurried fumble. The prison officer would arrive any moment to drive Elísa to Vernd.

She held Elísa's face in both her hands and looked into her eyes.

'Be good, my darling. Seriously. Be good.'

'I promise,' Elísa whispered and smiled awkwardly. 'I promise not to fuck things up.'

She pulled away and picked up her case, two plastic bags and a couple of extra garments she hadn't been able to fit anywhere.

'I'll come and get you when you're released,' she said from the doorway, and grinned with a mixture of shyness and teasing impertinence.

Agla smiled back. In a week Elísa would drive up to the prison in the Tesla, and Agla would walk out of the turnstile gate, ready to breathe in the aroma of Elísa's tousled hair and the Tesla's leather upholstery. For the first time she was not only free of the fear of being released from the cage, but was actively looking forward to it.

53

The source lived in Morgantown in West Virginia, so it was convenient for María to drop by on her way to Washington for the next morning's flight home. She had arranged to meet him at a coffee house, as after the incident at the rest area, she had no desire to meet a trucker anywhere other than in a public place.

She had arrived early and had been to a bank to fetch the thousand dollars that was his price for the information, according to Marteinn, who had found the source and set up the meeting.

Marteinn hadn't wanted to explain in too much detail what he had done, but it seemed that he had managed to hack into Meteorite's staff lists, identified some of the drivers then been through their social media pages until he found one who had let negative comments about his work slip out. Using this as a starting point, Marteinn judged that this man would be likely to spill the beans on his employer. He turned out to be right. The man was prepared to tell María everything she wanted to know about the trucking operation, in return for anonymity and a thousand dollars. María had to admit that it was smart of Marteinn to find a source this way. Her own approach would have been to call every driver on the list, which would not have led to such a quick, accurate result.

This driver turned out to be nothing like the one who had threatened her at the rest area the night before. This man was young and small, neat and well dressed, with a strong smell of aftershave about him that reminded María of something – she just couldn't think what. He shook María's hand courteously as he introduced himself, and she took a seat opposite him and slid the envelope across the table.

'I appreciate this,' he said, folding the envelope away into his jacket pocket. 'What do you want to know about Meteorite?'

María had made notes on her phone of the questions she wanted to ask, but had no need to look at them. She knew precisely what to ask.

'Why do you drive the trucks into the warehouses and out again without loading or unloading?'

It was the key question, and the one most in need of an answer.

'Because all the stores are full,' the driver said. 'Although the Massachusetts store is normally empty. That's where the aluminium arrives before it's shipped out to storage somewhere else. There are new stores being built and they're filled up as soon as they are ready.'

María nodded and made a note of Massachusetts. So there were more warehouses than the three she already knew about.

'Why all the driving in and out all day long?'

'That's because there are international rules that say there has to be a flow of aluminium. So the load I bring in is booked into the store and then booked out again. The stores are all run under different names, so the metal is booked as going from one company to another so it doesn't look like aluminium is piling up. But in reality, Meteorite owns all the stores.'

'Do you have any idea how many stores there are altogether?' María asked hopefully.

'I don't,' he said, pausing for a moment's thought as he counted on his fingers. 'I've been to at least fifteen, and I've heard other drivers mention at least a couple more.'

María swallowed the saliva that had formed in her mouth as if she had been starving and could smell a delicious meal cooking somewhere close by. This was big news. This was the scoop she had waiting on for so long. She shifted in her seat, but tried to appear calm so as not to startle the driver.

'And who owns all this aluminium? Do you have any idea who's behind it?'

'Different people. There are funds that trade in metals, some companies, sometimes the smelters themselves. You can see it all on the transport documentation that goes with each delivery.'

María could feel her heart jolt in disappointment. She had been sure that she had solved the mystery for Agla at the same time as coming up with a major news story of her own. She had been certain that there had to be a single entity stockpiling all this aluminium.

'You're sure?' María asked, staring hard at the driver's face as he nodded emphatically.

'Absolutely sure,' he said.

'But why would all these different companies suddenly decide to start stockpiling the aluminium they produce, or buying it up so there's a world shortage? It's a weird coincidence.'

'No. It's not a coincidence,' the driver said. 'Meteorite pays them to store it.'

54

Agla had to tell María to speak slowly and clearly, as her internet connection seemed to be poor and the Bleep app didn't seem to be able to keep the sound quality clear. The image broke up into blocks and pixels, but Agla could just make out that María was on the move, holding the phone in front of her with one hand while she steered with the other. Now was exactly the time when a proper phone would have been handy, one on which they could have held a normal conversation, but that wasn't an option at Hólmsheiði. Instead she sat hunched in the library with the screen turned away from the all-seeing eye on the ceiling, so that no one would realise she was using the computer to make a call. Fortunately, by now the warders trusted her completely and only checked on her every couple of hours.

'The owners store the aluminium in the warehouses, get a payment for taking delivery of it, and immediately apply to have it released, which can take a long time. Sometimes that can take close to two years. And then they simply put it straight back into storage to get another payment, instead of selling it. It takes a week to get aluminium into storage, and never less than a year to get it out again. So the overall storage time for all the metal gets longer and longer. And Meteorite buys more and more warehouses as they fill up. Strictly speaking, they're not stockpiling it, but they're still restricting the flow onto the market, and that's how the price of the aluminium available on the open market rises.'

Now Agla was starting to see a clearer picture.

'I'd bet...' she called into the screen in the hope that María could hear her. 'I'd be ready to bet that the payments from Meteorite for storing aluminium from the Icelandic smelter go direct to the smelter's parent company abroad. That way the parent company doesn't care if the smelter sells its production very slowly – they still get an income from the storage payments. Undoubtedly other smelters do the same thing. It's better for the parent company to get paid for storing production, and then they can always sell it later for the same or more than they would get for it today. It's absolutely brilliant!'

Bleep lost the connection and some interference came out of the speaker.

'What did you say?' Agla asked.

'Everyone except the taxpayer comes out a winner,' María repeated. She always had to make some kind of point like that, Agla reflected. 'Just as long as there's no tax paid on production in Iceland.'

'The taxpayer just wastes it on some crack-brained nonsense,' Agla said in irritation.

'Like building prisons...?' María said and the connection was lost.

That was typical of both María and Bleep. It was as if both of them had conspired to break the connection before Agla could come back with a suitable riposte. This Bleep software wasn't as good as Skype or FaceTime, but had the advantage of being encrypted so that any trace of a conversation was erased as soon as it ended. As far as Agla was concerned, the prison authorities had no need to be concerned over things they knew nothing about.

Agla checked the clock. It was finally time to call Elísa. She rang the bell and when Ewa appeared, she let her know that she needed to make a call. She waited by the phone in the hallway for a little while, until Ewa had gone over to chat to Vigdís, so neither of them would be listening in.

'Hæ. How are you?' she whispered when Elísa answered.

'Agla, you're awesome! Your lawyer brought an iPhone 7 for me! You're something else; any old phone would have been enough for me. And the car! Jesus! I hardly dared get in. This isn't real! You should have seen their faces at Vernd when the guy came and handed me the keys.'

'How are you feeling?' Agla broke in.

'Well, just great. It's half past five and I'm fine, just waiting for dinner. I'm on the rota to wash up tonight, and then I'll go for a drive around town with my friend. We'll go and get ourselves ice cream somewhere, but I promise I won't let her eat it in the car, so don't worry.'

'I'm not worried,' Agla said, although that wasn't completely true. The car wasn't a concern, but the thought of Elísa going for a drive with a friend troubled her. She hoped it wasn't Katrín, the former squeeze; and she hoped it wasn't one of Elísa's druggie friends, who might be a bad influence on her.

'Tomorrow I'll start looking properly for a place to live. It'll be easier now I can meet people face to face, because everyone who advertised a room for rent online was a bit strange when I said I was calling from Hólmsheiði...'

'But you have the house,' Agla said. 'You can stay there for as long as you want.'

'Oh.' Elísa fell silent for a moment. 'You were serious about me moving in there?'

'Of course,' Agla said, surprised at how Elísa had misunderstood her.

'I thought you were just doing that so I could be registered somewhere, so I'd be allowed out on probation.'

'No, my sweet. You can have the house. I have an apartment somewhere else, so the place is empty. And it's crazy for you to be holed up in a room when there's a house going begging.'

Elísa said nothing and Agla waited with growing trepidation. That wretched house was probably too much for any woman, and like a fool, she was trying to pass it on to Elísa. She would probably be no keener on the house than Sonja had.

'But of course you don't need to move in there, if you'd prefer to find yourself a room somewhere else. I was just trying to help you out; a way of solving your problem,' Agla said quickly.

'Shhh, Agla,' Elísa whispered, and sniffed. 'Of course I want it. Don't be daft. I'm just having a bit of a cry.'

Agla wondered what she could say. She had no idea what she had done that would make Elísa cry. That had certainly not been her intention. But before she could figure out some way to reply, Elísa coughed and spoke.

'Hey!'

'What?'

'It's going to be fucking brilliant fun when you're out and we'll be together at Vernd and free. Or, y'know, freer.'

'What sort of fun?' Agla whispered, and she felt a surge of relief like the kick from a drink. 'Tell me what kind of thing you're thinking about.'

'Just, y'know. All sorts...'

Now Elísa was whispering, and Agla closed her eyes, imagining her face with its shy smile and the teasing flash in her eyes.

'Tell me how,' Agla said again.

Elísa giggled into the phone.

'Stop it! Just ... you know.'

'I know,' Agla said and laughed with her. 'I'm just teasing you.'

Long after Elísa had put the phone down Agla felt she could hear her breath, the low giggle and her bubbling cheerfulness echo inside her.

'Finished?' Ewa the warder asked, startling her.

Agla had been standing there by the phone for a good while, grinning into space like an idiot.

55

Sonja stood in the storeroom doorway and stared at the cage. Alex had disinfected it before leaving, so now it was clean and ready for the next candidate in need of a little discipline or a spell of cold turkey. Sometimes she felt as if her whole life revolved around that cage. It had become symbolic of her whole existence, ever since she had walked into Thorgeir's trap eight years ago and found herself coming to this house to collect a shipment to take to Iceland.

Sometimes when she looked at the cage it felt as if she herself was its occupant, her existence fenced in by immovable iron bars, but still able to look out through them and see the life she could have had. A life in which Tómas would have lived with her instead of spending much of each year at a boarding school. A life in which Agla would have woken up every morning beside her and cooked a meal every evening.

Sonja banged the storeroom door shut and locked it. These days it was rare for her thoughts to turn to Agla, which was a relief as she always felt sad when they did. There had been such a powerful attraction between them that it had been painful to end their relationship. She had suffered nightmares for weeks after she had abandoned Agla, and often thought she had caught a glimpse of her on London's streets, in the shops and even in a car in the street outside as she sat by the window in the evening darkness.

She went upstairs and walked through the large rooms that surrounded the imposing hallway. The cleaners had gone and the place smelled of soap and vanilla-scented candles. She glanced at the clock; Alex would be about to land in Amsterdam to catch his connecting flight. Once Tómas was in the car with him, she would call and let him know of the change of itinerary. This time she was going to have them fly direct from Zürich to London, and then weave a puzzle with trains and cars on the way from the airport. Giving them an extra two- or three-hour flight would try her patience too much; she was bursting with anticipation at the prospect of seeing Tómas again.

She started as the doorbell chimed, and then remembered that this had to be the delivery she was expecting from the shop. On the intercom screen she could see a new delivery man standing on the steps with a box in his arms.

She pressed the intercom button.

'Leave the box by the door,' she said.

The delivery man looked around in surprise, and then he saw the camera over the door. For a moment it was as if they looked at each other through the lens, and for a second Sonja was taken by his surprised brown eyes. But as they so often did, her senses were deceiving her. It was all too easy to convince yourself that you could know someone from their eyes. She had learned from bitter experience that there could be a single-minded determination to kill hidden behind innocent brown eyes.

'There's a tip for you under the flower pot. Thank you.'

She waited for a while after the delivery man had gone before she cautiously opened the door, brought the box inside and then shut and locked the door again. As she brought the box into the kitchen, her phone rang and she saw it was Alex calling.

'Any changes to the itinerary?' he asked.

'Not yet,' Sonja replied.

'It's a lot better for me if I know in advance what the route is, so I can be prepared,' he said. 'You could try trusting me.'

She could hear in his tone that he realised it was a hopeless suggestion.

'There's nobody I trust,' Sonja said and put the phone down.

It was true. There was nobody she could trust completely, although Alex would certainly be at the top of the list if she were forced to put her life in someone else's hands; he had been ever since he had put himself between her and her rival's hitman, taking a bullet in his side in the process. But she knew exactly how the Mexicans worked, and also knew there was nobody who couldn't be bribed or tortured. So she would never be able to trust anyone again.

She put the shopping away and went into the long, high-ceilinged living room that had once been Mr José's dining room, where he had received guests and where the tiger had also lived in its cage.

Everything was ready for Tómas's arrival, even down to their favourite Shakira CD in the player, although they no longer danced on the sofa when they were together. The joy that had always been a feature of their reunions had gradually faded over the years, replaced by a certain mutual guardedness, which they both hid well, but which prevented them from being completely open with each other. All the same, it didn't do any harm to have Shakira ready, just in case Tómas came home in a particularly good mood. All she would need to do was to press the play button and they would both abandon themselves to the delight of being together.

June 2017

56

The flash from the doorway was so bright, it was painful; María felt as if the light cut deep into her head. She rubbed her eyes and waited for them to acclimatise to the darkness again. This was the tenth or eleventh time this had happened – that the door to the dim corridor opened, the silent figure of a man appeared in the doorway and then there was a blinding flash as he took a photograph. After that she heard the sound of him pushing a tray of food across the floor with his foot.

Each time the man opened the door, she tried her hardest to read the sign on the wall in the passage behind him, but it disappeared when she was dazzled by the flash. It seemed to say *Evacuation Route*, and then there was some smaller lettering that she hadn't been able to make out, although she was sure it was in English too. The sticker on the door was also in English, and when the bag had been removed from her head and she was thrown in here, she had seen something to the effect that these doors must always be kept locked.

She knew she had to be in Iceland. She had taken a flight home and it had landed at Keflavík airport, where two policemen were waiting to arrest her. They had spoken in Icelandic and apologised for the hand-cuffs when they saw the bruises on her wrists. Looking out of the car window, she had seen that they were driving out of the airport area, and were heading for Reykjanesbraut – the long, straight road leading into town, when the officer in the passenger seat had leaned back and pulled a cloth bag over her head.

Once she had finished yelling, she tried to get her bearings and keep track of what was going on around her as best she could. It had felt like they had driven around in circles for a long time before she was transferred to another car. She had been treated gently. Someone took her arm and a hand guided her head so she didn't crack it against the roof of the car as she was pushed into the seat. In this car she could hear two men talking, but was unable to make anything out over the loud music they were playing. Then there was a long drive, some of it clearly on an unmade road, as the car shook and juddered. But now, after a long time in this dark cell, she was beginning to doubt the evidence of her own senses; her mind seemed to present different versions of her travels. Maybe that second car hadn't been a car at all, but an aircraft, and the gravel road not an unmade track but turbulence in the air. It wasn't just the signs in English that indicated they were in America rather than Iceland, but the shape of the door handle, the little dark window with its bars, the carpet on the floor and the smell of disinfectant that flowed into the travel toilet in the corner when she pressed the button on it. There was nothing she could put her finger on, but there was something American about the strange blend of menthol and flowers.

It took some time before her eyes became accustomed again to the gloom. Once she could again make out shades of grey in the darkness, she crawled over to the tray and sat down by it. The food was the only thing that had changed during the three or four days she had been here. She groped cautiously for the tray to see what was on offer today. The first couple of times she had ignored food in protest against this bizarre captivity, but by the third time she had been so ravenous that she had swooped on the food so eagerly that she had upset the glass of orange juice, and now there was a patch by the door that was so sticky, she stuck to it if she sat there.

This time the food seemed to be some kind of meat fried in breadcrumbs; two thin slices that sat on the plate along with three lukewarm potatoes. There was something cold in a tub next to the plate and María tasted to be sure that it was coleslaw. It seemed to be hospital food, or a dinner tray from an old people's home. She used a little of the water in the flask to rinse her hands and wiped them on her trousers. She put one of the potatoes in her mouth and then took a bite of one of the slices of meat. She had given up using the plastic cutlery that came with the tray, and ate with her fingers instead, except for the dessert, and then she used the plastic spoon. Dessert! This looked to be either lunch or dinner, so there had to be a dessert. There was always a dessert with a cooked meal. She felt around with her hands, but there was no dessert to be found. She passed her hands over the tray and was certain there was nothing more than the plate of food, the tub of coleslaw and the flask of water. The tears flowed and she burst into sobs. She couldn't understand why she was in tears over a missing piece of pie or cake, but in some odd way she saw the missing dessert as a deep betrayal. She had looked forward to eating the entire meal at a slow, leisurely pace, while she thought of something other than the fact that she was locked away in a dark cell, practically a dungeon that could be anywhere. Somehow the dessert was the most important part, a kind of sticking plaster for her own miserable circumstances, a final pleasure that she could string out as long as she could.

María sniffed hard and wiped her nose on her sleeve. She must be suffering from Stockholm syndrome, or some kind of condition that makes captives so crazy that they're grateful for the slightest display of kindness from their captors; such as a tub of dessert. She ate a second potato and bit into the second piece of meat, and felt over the tray for the fork to eat the coleslaw. It had been cut too fine and was too moist for fingers. Her fingers came to a halt on something plastic, and she felt it to be sure if it was the knife or the fork. It turned out to be a spoon. The tears flowed again, falling down her cheeks. How vindictive it was to put a spoon on the tray but no dessert?

She carefully put the salad tub down and crawled on all fours towards the mattress in the corner. She would finish eating later. Now she was going to curl up on the grubby bed and cry. Her hand touched something and it rolled away. She stopped instantly and patted in front of her with her palm, moving forwards and feeling the floor with both hands. Her right hand touched a round plastic tub and she stopped. She picked the tub up and could feel that it had an aluminium cover. This was the dessert! It must have fallen over and rolled off the tray when the man had pushed it into the cell with his foot.

María's heart beat faster as she rolled the tub in her fingers. This meant far more than just the all-important final piece of a meal. The plastic tub itself gave her a clue as to where she was. With her limited sense of time and space she had become completely lost, unsure now whether she was in Iceland or in America.

57

Oddur still looked as if he couldn't believe his own eyes. His forehead was furrowed right up into his hairline, so that in the morning light he looked like an old man weighed down with worry. He ran his thumb back and forth along the edge of the wad of notes, as if it were a pack of cards he was about to shuffle.

Anton fidgeted on the bench. The old cemetery was still mostly grey-brown, but some newly sprouted grass around the graves was starting to give the dead leaves on the ground some competition and the lichens seemed about to change colour. He was cold and wanted to get this business out of the way before anyone came along to disturb them.

'So we're all square?' he said, getting to his feet.

Oddur remained on the bench, fondling the notes in his hands.

'What did you say it was that you're going to blow up?' he asked.

Anton felt his patience ebb away.

'Nothing you need to worry about,' he said, his voice sharp. 'Just an old shed. Something a bit special for the girlfriend. Something she'll never forget.'

Oddur nodded and stood up, drawing out the moment, and Anton wanted to snatch the bag of equipment from him.

'All square?'

'Yep.' Oddur stuffed the notes into his inside pocket and opened the bag. 'Here's the battery. The plate is just to keep it all secure. This is the detonator itself,' he said, pointing to a little box with a printed circuit board. 'You just stick the fuse from the dynamite into this hole, clip it together to keep the fuse in place and flip this switch. When this little light goes red, you're ready to go. When everyone's a safe distance away, you use this remote control, and *bang*. It has a range of around a hundred metres.'

'Brilliant. Thanks.'

Anton made to take the bag, but Oddur seemed reluctant to let it go.

'And you remember what I said about a safe distance,' he said. 'The delay is only about forty seconds, unless you use a longer fuse.'

'OK.'

Anton stood with his hand holding the bag, but Oddur continued to hold it tight. Anton didn't want to wrench it from his grasp.

'Anything you want to ask?' said Oddur.

'No.'

Anton made as if to leave, pulling on the bag a little, telling Oddur that it was time to let go. But he still seemed reluctant to let it out of his hands.

'You want me to go over all that again?'

Anton grinned and patted Oddur's shoulder.

'Take it easy, man! It's not that hard. I got it all the first time. Now we're all square, right?'

Oddur finally let go and Anton folded the bag under one arm.

'See ya!' he said, turning and walking away, but Oddur came jogging up behind him.

'Hey ... I was just wondering.'

Oddur shivered, his hands thrust deep into his pockets.

'What?'

'You're not going to use this to kill anyone, are you?'

58

It was early in the day when Agla stood outside the prison building, taking deep breaths of cool air. Freedom was as refreshing as a cold drink on a hot day; in fact it was a surprise how much fresher the air seemed outside than it did in the little exercise yard at the heart of the prison complex. She went to the turnstile gate, pushed her way through with her suitcase in her arms, put it down and went back through the gate to fetch the box and her computer case. It was unbelievable how much junk she had accumulated over a few months, even though she had brought only essentials into prison with her. She put the case on top of the box and stood outside the inner gate. She glanced each way along the road, but there was no sign of Elísa.

She wondered whether she ought to make the two trips through the outer gate and up to the road, wait with her belongings there, but it would be a nuisance to have to keep ringing the buzzer to be allowed in and out; it would only attract attention that she could do without. After a while she checked her watch. Elísa should have been here to meet her twenty minutes ago. The suspicion crawled into her mind that maybe Elísa wasn't coming. She decided to give it another ten minutes; half an hour would account for a traffic jam or having to recharge the Tesla. She had no desire to go back inside the prison building. She should have had the lawyer collect her, she told herself. He would have brought her phone and some decent clothes. Instead she was standing here like an idiot in tracksuit bottoms, not even able to call herself a taxi.

Finally, with heavy steps, she walked back into the building. She could feel every fibre of her body rebelling, sending stomach acid rushing to her throat and giving her an instant flash of heartburn as she opened the door and stepped back inside the prison.

'Could you call a taxi for me?' she asked.

Sigurgeir, the officer at the desk, nodded, the look on his face saying that he could have told her Elísa wouldn't be here to pick her up. It was just as well that he was on duty and therefore wasn't able to repeat his offer to drive her down to the probation hostel at Vernd, as that would have been one humiliation too much.

When the taxi driver arrived, he got out of his car by the outer gate, ready to help with her luggage, but sat back inside as soon as he recognised her. No doubt it had already been all over the media that she was about to be released on probation, and there was also no doubt that the entire nation agreed that it was far too early. The boot opened with a click, and she lifted her box and case into it before sitting in the back seat and bidding him a good morning. The driver didn't return her greeting, but asked abruptly where she wanted to go. Banksters didn't deserve courtesy, she reflected.

Outside her apartment building she took some notes from her wallet and weighed up whether or not to ask for a receipt, just to annoy him by forcing him to put it through his books. But instead she added an extra three thousand krónur on top of the fare and told him to keep the change. The boot clicked open, and she barely had time to take her luggage before the car swept away, its boot still open. She took out her keys, went to the shelter at the side of the building and dropped both box and case into the bin. Then she went upstairs with only the computer case on her shoulder.

This wasn't the release day she had been expecting. She had indigestion and a headache, but she certainly wasn't going to sit down and weep bitter tears because some fool of a junkie had let her down. What the hell had she been expecting? That the girl was genuinely fond of her? That a fumble and stolen kisses in the corner of a cell were the basis for something special? Bullshit!

She cleared her throat hard, stripped off, threw the clothes into the bin and opened the fridge. She had to use all her willpower to resist the sudden longing that gripped her when she saw the bottle of beer on the top shelf, reaching instead for a can of Coke, which she took with her to the bathroom, drinking it as the bath filled. There was no chance that she was going to risk her probation with a beer, or by being a second late for the evening meal or lights-out at eleven. She had no intention of breaking even a single one of the rules and regulations that were all part of being allowed out. She could pee into a bottle whenever they wanted and they wouldn't find a trace of anything stronger than Coca-Cola.

She crushed the aluminium can and weighed it in her hand. She would have to focus her mind on aluminium over these coming days. She would systematically concentrate on this pale, lightweight metal that so many people seemed to want to own. The best remedy for mental turmoil, she reminded herself, was a complex problem to solve.

59

The yoghurt was wonderfully sweet; much sweeter than any she'd had before, and the obviously synthetic fruit taste was a clue that this was an American product. There were many brands of yoghurt in America that María had never tasted, but she had tried practically every one available in Iceland, and this one wasn't familiar. She stretched her tongue as deep as she could into the tub and used her fingers to clean it out. She was going to keep hold of this and try to read the lettering on it the next time the door opened and some light was let in.

If this meal had been lunch or dinner, then there would be a snack next – one for either the afternoon or evening, so now she just had to wait. She lay down on the mattress, the yoghurt tub still in her hand, and spread the blanket over her, more to give herself a feeling of security than because of the cold. The cell was neither hot nor cold; instead there was a steady warmth that told her that this place wasn't dealing with the Icelandic climate's fluctuating temperatures.

She lay still and tried to control her train of thought. She needed to trace things back to their origins – to what had put her in this position. Her interest in aluminium producers and how some of them worked went back a long way, all the way to her time with the special prosecutor's office, when she had done her best to get to grips with the extent of the whole aluminium issue. While she understood that every company wanted to maximise its profits, there was something about the way these international corporate giants treated tiny, stupid Iceland that made her furious. One smelter produced as much pollution as all the cars in the country put together; the Icelandic energy companies had made huge investments so they could provide the smelters with enough power, which the energy companies sold to the smelters at knockdown rates. All of this had been done under the pretence that the smelters would generate jobs and revenue for Iceland; but the fact of the matter was that some smelters brought in labour from overseas and a significant chunk of any profits they made remained abroad. The foreign parent companies invoiced their Icelandic subsidiaries for hefty sums, which meant these subsidiaries' books showed minimal profits, and the parent companies avoided paying almost any tax in Iceland.

'Cooking the Books Still in Fashion' could be a good headline for an article in The Squirrel. She could detail how little had changed since Halldór Laxness first spoke about this phenomenon back in the forties; and demonstrate that Iceland had then been in much the same position as other former colonial nations that found themselves newly independent – easy meat for international finance and greedy traitors.

Now one such company was engaged in an even worse kind of swindle, that wouldn't withstand much scrutiny. And that's why she was here, locked away to keep her quiet. She hardly dared imagine how long her incarceration would last.

She woke up sensing Maggi's presence, instinctively put out a hand to feel for him, and had a few happy seconds before she realised where she was. She breathed in deeply through her nose in the hope that the dream had left some trace of his smell; the scent she always woke to in bed in the mornings; the aroma of security and love. But the only smell was from the lousy floral disinfectant in the travel toilet, blended with her own sweat, which filled her with revulsion. It wasn't the heat that was making her sweat, but the stress. Initially she had hammered on the door in the illogical hope that she might be let out; then later she'd been haunted by the recurring nightmare that she could find herself locked away for a very long time.

She couldn't be sure how long she had dozed. There was no way to estimate the passing of time. She crawled towards the door – she found it safer to be on all fours. Her sense of balance had worsened, and every time she stood up she felt faint and struggled to concentrate. She sat by the door, on the side that opened, so that she would be able to hold the yoghurt tub in the triangle of light that would shine in first, and read the lettering on it. That would remove all doubt as to which country she was in.

She kept the tub clamped between her legs so as not to lose it and reached out to count the trays that she had piled up by the wall next to the stacks of plates and cups. To begin with she had been too upset to clear up after meals, but after she had stepped on a fork and hurt her foot, she took to piling everything by the wall. Her fingers passed over the stack of trays as she counted under her breath.

'Meal, snack, meal, snack, meal, snack.'

If this were to be an accurate way to gauge the passage of time, then she would have to know how many meals were served each day, which was impossible as she no longer had a sense of time. She also couldn't know if there was a regular interval between meals; or if there was a longer interval that indicated a night. But if she were to guess three snacks and two meals a day, then this had to be her third day. It was unnerving to think that despite her discomfort and the fear that plagued her, she was in fact precisely where she had always dreamed of being: at the centre of events.

All her work up to this point, first at the special prosecutor's office and later as a journalist, had centred around examining events from outside – an observer desperately looking for explanations, searching for experiences that would provide her with understanding. Now that was exactly what she had been given. She was part of the course of action, a genuine participant in a series of events that one day would be examined by journalists and prosecutors.

It could have been that only a moment had passed; but at the same, it could have been a whole lifetime before the door opened. Sitting in the darkness, she was startled when she heard the key turn in the lock, and she immediately raised the yoghurt tub, taking care to concentrate on it and not be dazzled by turning her face to the light.

The surprise was the wording on the tub: *School Yoghurt*, in Icelandic. But what was even more of a surprise was that instead of the usual blinding flash and a tray pushed through the door, the man stepped into the cell.

'Well, then,' he said in plain Icelandic.

60

Agla felt like she was putting on her old self as she pulled up her tights and tied a scarf under the neckline of her white silk blouse. The black Versace suit with its pearl-strung pockets maybe wasn't the least eye-catching outfit, but these were the only trousers that weren't baggy around her rear end; they had been too tight before she had gone to prison. She would have to replace her wardrobe and eat well. That would be easier now that she could have lunch wherever she saw fit. Dinner would have to be at Vernd, though.

Make-up done, she packed some cosmetics into a case and put it in with the clean underwear and toothbrush. That was all she was going to take with her to Vernd. She put a grey overcoat on over the suit, even though it was a mild day. It was so long since she had worn a coat that there was a special feeling to it. Although the day had started badly, she was going to make sure to enjoy what she could of it.

It was a shorter walk than she remembered to the hotel that housed her hair salon, and she was tempted to take another circuit around the block and take more lungfuls of fresh air. But the hairdresser was waiting and she couldn't be seen walking around town with her hair like this.

'Hello, my darling!' Thorbjörg exclaimed. Agla was taken aback by her sincerity, as she hugged her close and drew a hand through her hair. 'We're going to have to do something about this,' she said.

For the next ninety minutes she sat in the chair and listened to one report after another about Thorbjörg's children, grandchildren, daughters and sons-in-law and friends, without having to answer any questions other than whether or not the food in prison had been acceptable. This was what she had hoped the day would bring – that someone would be pleased to see her. Of course, she had hoped that person would be Elísa, but she decided that it was as well to take what was on offer.

She inspected herself in the mirror while Thorbjörg put the cash away, and was satisfied with what she saw. Her hair was now an attractive sandy blonde and reached halfway down her neck, no longer lapping at her collar. She was ready to take on the world, dressed as her preferred persona and wearing the armour that hid the weak inner self she had discovered in prison – the opposite of the person she had believed herself to be.

Maybe it was symbolic of that inner weakness that before she knew it, she was walking over to Bónus with a hazy idea that she would go up to Elísa, smile and ask for the Tesla's keys. She would act as if nothing had happened, without showing the least sign of disappointment and without reminding her that she had been supposed to collect her that morning.

Her intentions came to nothing, as Elísa wasn't at work. The manager looked from Agla to the front page on the newsstand, and back. 'Agla Margeirsdóttir on Probation at Vernd', the headline read, below which was an old photo of her slapped on top of a photo of the Vernd building.

'Elísa didn't turn up for work this morning, and she hasn't called in sick, so I don't know what's happened to her,' he said.

'Oh, I remember now,' Agla said. 'She texted me to say she wasn't well. Flu, or something.'

'OK, I'll put her down as sick. But if you see her, could you tell her that she needs to call in before ten in the morning to let us know?'

Agla nodded, as the man's eyes flickered once again, as if by accident, to the front page of the newspaper. She couldn't understand why she was lying on Elísa's behalf. She wasn't even sure what on earth she was doing looking for her in Bónus.

⊞

Elvar the lawyer got to his feet and came over to her the moment she walked into his office.

'Where the hell have you been?' he asked, in the concerned tone of voice she had learned to appreciate over the years. 'The prison said you'd left in a taxi. I could have come to get you.'

Agla sighed. It would have been so much better if she had asked Elvar to collect her.

'I went home and then had my hair done,' she said. 'And now I'd like to get my phone and to hear what's new.'

Elvar opened a drawer and took out her phone.

'I've charged it up,' he said. 'And, forgive me, but I thought the girl who was to take your car was a little ... what shall I say? Dubious? So I put a tracker in the car.'

'What's that?'

'A small positioning transponder that connects to an app on your phone. Open the tracker app and you get a map that shows you where the car is. Here's the spare key.'

Agla took the key and swallowed down the shame that had tightened her throat. Elvar had seen through Elísa right away, while she had duped herself with rose-tinted dreams of something that didn't exist in reality.

To his surprise, she planted a kiss on Elvar's cheek, and he squeezed her shoulder amiably. This handsome young guy always put her in mind of a tired old man, and she suspected that she and her affairs were sucking all the energy out of him.

'I need you to do some organising for me,' she said from the doorway. 'As I'm not able to leave the country, I have to invite a French banker to a meeting here in Iceland. Can you send him an invitation if I send you all the details, and fix up a jaunt in a helicopter or a day's salmon fishing for the old fellow?'

Now it was all about aluminium.

61

María fought tooth and claw, but the man held her tight in his arms and didn't seem to be breaking a sweat. She was sure she could hear him sniggering to himself, as if she were a naughty child who didn't want to go home from play group and had to be carried by Dad out to the car. A naughty child with her head in a bag; a petrified child with her head in a bag and her limbs shivering after being cooped up for days in the dark, in solitary confinement.

She kicked with her heels, hoping to land a blow to his balls so that he'd drop her and she could pull the bag off her head. But the man held her high so that her kicks connected with nothing but thin air. Steadily losing power, she gave up after a while and lay in his arms like a sack. She heard the creak of a door and the click as it shut behind them. She instantly felt the cold air envelop her. They were outside, and she renewed her efforts to fight back – outside there might be an opportunity to escape, to run and maybe get away from this man and whatever he meant to do to her.

'Here's the tape,' she heard the man say, and at the same moment she felt someone grab her feet, tying them tightly together. So either there were two of them or the man had four hands. More than likely they were the same two men who had picked her up at the airport. They had been dressed like police officers and were driving a squad car – but she hadn't been aware that the police put bags over people's heads or tied them up with tape. This was all terrifying and impossible to understand; she had the urge to give way to tears and to wail into the bag, but she judged that she should hold herself back. She could hardly draw breath inside the bag, so tears and a blocked nose wouldn't be much help. She felt the second man wrap tape around her midriff, so now her arms were tight to her sides and she was unable to move at all. She was lifted, felt herself laid on something soft, and then hands were placed on her ankles and her legs folded into place, followed by the familiar click of a car door closing.

The car's engine started then it moved off, its movement rocking her around. She was sure she was lying on the back seat. She could hear the indistinct mutter of the men's voices, but as before, music played. She was certain that it was the same music as before – when it was played far too loud in the car that had taken her from the airport.

At first the road they took felt smooth, and then the car shook and rattled for a good way, until they were on a proper road again. Finally they made a few tight turns, as if they were taking one roundabout after another.

She was becoming sleepy now, and was wondering if she was gradually being suffocated in the bag, when the car stopped. She held her breath, her heart hammering in her chest, as she listened for every tiny sound that might indicate what was to befall her. The car doors opened, her legs were straightened out, and she felt herself being pulled, ankles first, then by her legs. Finally she was placed upright. She felt something hard run down her back and heard one of the men speak.

'Cut here.'

Her legs were freed so that she could move them apart and get her balance. Then she heard footsteps and the sound of two car doors closing, one after the other. Last of all the sound of a car driving away.

She wriggled and felt her arms coming free. Instinct made her immediately rip the bag from her head, and she gasped down a lungful of cold outdoor air, the sudden daylight dazzling her. At the same time a loud howl of a car sounded from somewhere and she crouched down. It seemed to be driving straight at her at great speed, but then it flashed past her. It was followed by another howl and another, and she realised that she had to be beside a main road. She rubbed her eyes and gradually her sight became clearer, although it hurt to do anything but squint. She ripped the tape from her feet and from around her middle, seeing that the thick wrapping had been sliced through.

There on the road was her handbag, lying in a puddle as if it had been flung from the car. Her wallet, keys and other small items were scattered around it. She picked up her things and looked about. There were no people around, but there was loud traffic noise somewhere nearby and above her was a concrete bridge or road. She walked from under the bridge, holding a hand to her forehead to shield her eyes.

Once she was clear of the bridge, her eyes had begun to adjust enough for her to take in her surroundings. She was standing by a little roundabout with slip roads leading to and from it up to the road the traffic noise was coming from. In the other direction there was nothing to be seen but jagged, moss-covered lava that stretched away as far as the eye could see.

She realised that she had been dumped underneath Reykjanesbraut, the road leading from Keflavík airport to the city.

62

Anton had turned the detonator over and over, examining it carefully from every angle, and had come to the conclusion that it was convincing. He sat wearing his head torch in the boiler room, which was gloomy despite the daylight outside, waiting for Gunnar, who was supposed to be going to a builder's merchant after maths class to buy fuse wire.

He stretched for the little radio and switched it on, but there was only a fuzz of interference so he had to turn the dial to get Radio Edda. Their broadcasts often seemed to be poor quality, which was why he generally listened to the station online. There was nothing much to listen to now, just a discussion between the presenters about old-fashioned Icelandic cuisine. He had no interest in pickled rams' testicles or blood sausage. That was the kind of food his father occasionally ate from a plastic tray as his mother scoffed. On this subject he was completely in agreement with her: this so-called 'traditional' food was disgusting.

He heard a gentle knocking at the door and clicked off the radio.

'*Hæ*,' Gunnar said, removing his helmet as he came in. 'How are things?'

'Fine,' Anton said and pointed at the old toolbox he had taken from the storeroom.

'Hey, where did you get that from?' Gunnar asked.

'Nicked it from the cellar,' Anton said. 'The old man will never notice it's gone. I didn't want to use a new box for the bomb, because the fragments could be traced once the police start investigating.'

'Yeah, OK.'

Gunnar sat down on a garden chair. Anton could see that he wasn't at ease.

'What?' he demanded. 'What's up?'

'Well, just ... I was wondering if the police will be able to trace the fuse as well. I just bought it; I must be on every security camera in the fucking place, a big grin on my face.'

Anton laughed.

'The fuse burns up, you idiot. But the metal from the box will break up and there'll be splinters everywhere.'

At any rate, that was what he expected to happen. He had read somewhere that a stronger box would magnify the power of the explosion, which meant a metal box would be better than a cardboard one. He didn't know what his grandfather's tool box was made from – probably some rubbish metal like aluminium – but it had to be better than cardboard or plastic.

'Yeah, all right. Of course.' Gunnar giggled awkwardly. 'I hadn't thought of that.'

That was one of Gunnar's good points. He took it well when his errors were pointed out to him and wasn't fussed about having things explained.

'You brought the scales?' Anton asked, and Gunnar patted his backpack.

Anton's mother had thrown their bathroom scales out in a fit of fury and neither he nor his father had seen any reason to replace them. He had no worries about his weight and, anyway, it was mostly girls who thought about that kind of thing. So he hadn't needed scales until now ... when he wanted to weigh the bomb.

63

María could smell the stink coming off her body as she opened the door into her hallway. Her clothes reeked of stale sweat. She was so ashamed of the smell, she had had to apologise to the lady who had picked her up on Reykjanesbraut. The woman had asked repeatedly if there was anyone she could call for her or if she should take her to A&E, but María had just shaken her head and said that she needed to get home for a bath.

Going by the stench that erupted from her as she took off her sweater, there was no doubt she needed one.

She unzipped her trousers and kicked them off in the hall, along with her socks. She really wanted to throw these clothes away, but they had been her favourite jeans; they had cost more than she would usually spend on clothes. She decided to see if she could live with them once they had been washed.

She hadn't even got as far as the bathroom door when she was startled by a cough – the sound of a throat being cleared to let her know that she wasn't alone in the flat. She instinctively folded her arms over her breasts and slowly turned to see Ingimar Magnússon sitting on her old Ikea sofa with a smile on his face.

'You look like shit,' he said with what was obviously false concern. 'It looks like you didn't get much of a welcome when you came home from your little research trip.'

'Get out of my house,' María hissed, aware of how powerless she was, standing in her underwear, with a barely suppressed sob in her throat. Things were coming together in her mind, but she had been taken too much by surprise to work it out properly.

'I can understand that someone in your position would call this a home,' he said, glancing around. 'But we could do something about that,' he added.

María forgot that she was wearing nothing but underwear, her rage overpowering any sense of caution.

'It's disgusting how people like you and Agla try to arrange everything the way you want it by throwing money at people. It's as if you think the whole world is for sale.'

'Show me someone who isn't,' said Ingimar.

María felt an overwhelming shame. This little research trip, as Ingimar had described it, had been at Agla's bidding, so it wasn't as if she could offer herself as an example.

'Get the fuck out,' she yelled.

Ingimar got to his feet and strolled towards the door.

'Interesting that you mention Agla,' he said.

María felt her stomach lurch. She was losing track of reality, was desperately tired and her thoughts were whirling through her mind. She knew that she certainly should not have mentioned Agla's name to Ingimar, but that would hardly matter. Ingimar took her phone from his pocket and placed it on the kitchen table.

'Apologies,' he said. 'I wiped it clean. Not too many personal memories, I hope.'

María kept herself in control until the door had shut behind Ingimar. Then she leaped at it, hooking the chain across it in a vain attempt to keep the world and everything that went with it at bay, including this vile man with his polished shoes.

She just managed to drop to the floor by the toilet before she vomited, and once she had finished retching, she hung onto the seat and wept into the bowl. Not only had the bastard had her abducted and held against her will for days on end, then broken into her flat and offered to bribe her, he had also wiped from her phone all the pictures she had left of Maggi.

64

The tracker showed her precisely where the car was: it was parked outside a shabby detached house in Fossvogur. This was one of the white, neo-modern houses built at the tail end of the twentieth century that had at one time meant money. But now the paint was flaking off and the garden had turned into a wasteland.

She could hear music blaring from the house as she stepped out of the taxi. She stood still on the street for a moment, wondering whether to just take the car or to knock on the door and ask for Elísa. Maybe she should let her know she was taking the car; and she could also ask why she hadn't come to fetch her that morning.

'Are you looking for your daughter as well?' asked a middle-aged woman, walking away from the house, leading a dead drunk teenage girl by the arm.

'Yes and no. Not my daughter. But I'm looking for a girl called Elísa,' Agla said.

'There are more girls in there,' the woman said. 'She'll be with the rest of his harem, no doubt.'

The girl seemed ready to pass out so Agla took her other arm and helped the woman walk her over to a red jeep parked on the pavement.

'His "harem"?'

'That bastard in there: the filthy lawyer who preys on junkie girls. It's like the arsehole hangs around for them as they come out of treatment to get them back on the drugs again. Do you want me to come in with you to find your daughter?'

'Thanks, but no. I'll find her,' Agla said, not inclined to explain again that Elísa was not her daughter. She wasn't even sure that she would go into the house to search for her. There was no guarantee that Elísa was in there, but if she was and was back on the dope, then she would hardly have much to say to Agla. It wasn't as if she was her mother. She had no right to barge in and fetch her.

'If she's not there, then she'll be up at Iðufell. At that bastard debt collector's place, fourth floor at the end, next to the shop.'

Agla nodded. She had little intention of running around town, searching for Elísa.

The woman fastened the seat belt around her daughter and shut the car door.

'This is the second time one of my daughters has got caught up in this,' she said, and looked at Agla. She didn't seem to see her clearly, though, as there was a mist in her eyes. 'The drugs took the first one.

I hope you don't have to experience finding your child dead from an overdose at one of those lousy men's parties.'

Agla swallowed hard. She wanted to say something to the woman but had no words, so she reached out and gently squeezed the woman's arm. The woman nodded a silent thanks for her helpless sympathy, and turned away. She didn't look back as she sat in the car and drove off.

Agla strode straight into the house and pushed her way through a gaggle of people, who were coming or going as if it was the evening, even though it was the middle of the day. They all seemed ready for some kind of nightlife. But after all, she thought, the June daylight did ensure there was hardly a border between day and night.

It made no difference anymore that she wasn't Elísa's mother; and she didn't care about the giant of a man facing her who demanded what she wanted. She simply slipped past him and glanced around the living room, where a few figures lounged in a cloud of smoke on the sofa. Then she headed up the stairs.

She found Elísa in the room at the far end, asleep on a sofa bed. Her mascara was smeared over her cheeks and her hair was one big tangle. She was wearing a grubby singlet and the Adidas tracksuit trousers she had worn most of the time at Hólmsheiði. Agla lifted her feet and placed them on the floor, then supporting her back sat her up. She shook her gently and after a while Elísa opened her eyes.

'Agla. Shit, what time is it? I was just about to come and get you.'

65

Ingimar's thoughts were dark as he left The Squirrel's office. It never ceased to amaze him how sensitive people could be. In fact he was surprised that the weirdo had managed to survive this long without topping himself. It was as if the poor bastard had been waiting for a reason to end his life, and when that appeared in the form of Ingimar Magnússon, it seemed to be a relief. He had been unbuckling his belt as Ingimar left.

Ingimar had intended to appeal to the man's greed, as he usually did in these situations, knowing that it generally worked. Greed and the hunger for life went hand-in-hand. He hadn't spent long talking to Marteinn, however, before he realised that fear was a more potent weapon in this instance. The man had no urge to live; only fear.

'Are you one of them?' Marteinn had asked, his tone of voice indicating that this was the moment he had waited for and feared, the one he had hoped would never come but had long ago accepted. So instead of asking who 'they' might be, Ingimar merely said yes and took a seat on the lop-sided office chair.

'I knew it,' Marteinn muttered again and again. 'I knew you would come. It was always just a matter of time.'

'You knew we would come sooner or later,' Ingimar echoed, watching him root through the piles of paper on the little desk in the corner that had to be his workplace. Next to it stood tottering stacks of paper and books that leaned against the desk as if they were supporting it. The chaos provided an insight into its owner's inner turmoil.

'Are you going to torture me?' Marteinn asked, turning to Ingimar, and his mouth trembled.

Ingimar shook his head.

'No,' he said.

'You have to understand that this is unbearable. Totally unbearable. I can't describe how hard it is to have an insight that nobody else has. It's not a burden I would wish on anyone.'

'In that case it's best that it goes no further,' Ingimar said, without any idea of what they were talking about. Not that it seemed to matter; whatever he said appeared to confirm some idea that had clearly taken root in Marteinn's mind long ago.

'So this ends with me?' Marteinn said.

Ingimar couldn't be sure if this was a question or a statement, so he agreed.

'This ends with you, here and now,' he said calmly.

'Here and now?' Marteinn asked in surprise. 'Here in the office?'

'Isn't that the best way?' Ingimar asked as Marteinn fell to his knees and burst into tears.

'I had never expected any mercy from you, but I'm grateful. Deeply grateful.'

Ingimar got to his feet, feeling in his heart a need to touch the man's head, to lay a hand on it, like a blessing, as if he were a confessor or a saviour, and not the bringer of death. This feeling was the reason why he sometimes got involved himself. He could easily have sent someone to speak to María and Marteinn. But then he would have missed out on seeing the fear in María's eyes and the delicate tremors that rippled her skin; and he would have missed seeing Marteinn's brimming eyes as he looked up at him.

'Are you going to do this, or may I deal with it myself?'

With one finger Ingimar wiped a tear away from the man's cheek.

'I trust you to do this yourself,' he said. 'Not everyone would be given such an opportunity, but you're special, and that's why I trust you.'

'It ends here and now,' Marteinn said, unbuckling his belt. 'You win. The world is yours.'

Ingimar left, letting The Squirrel's door lock behind him.

He reflected that the efforts of doctors, nurses, counsellors, friends and family over many years had undoubtedly gone into keeping this wretch of a man from taking his own life, but it had taken just one conversation to end his pain. Ingimar would have felt worse about it if it hadn't been so blindingly obvious that the man wanted to die. And it was as well for it to happen now. He was collateral damage.

Considering Agla was behind The Squirrel people's inquisitiveness, it was imperative to put a stop to their investigations right away, before Marteinn could come up with any more crackpot articles about Ingimar's connections to Meteorite. He acknowledged that if people heard something often enough, then it would start to sound plausible, and then other media would also start to poke around. That was something he wasn't going to allow.

66

Agla set the coffee machine to make a strong brew while Elísa dozed in the bathtub. She found a frozen loaf in the freezer, and the fridge revealed an unopened carton of long-life milk and a tub of butter. She took a couple of the least dried-out slices from the middle of the loaf, slotted them into the toaster and scraped the yellow rind from the butter to reveal the perfectly fine whiteness underneath. There was an unopened jar of marmalade in one of the cupboards that she couldn't recall having bought, and all put together, this was enough to provide an afternoon snack for Elísa. That was if she could be got out of the bath.

Elísa wept as she dried her hair.

'I'm so sorry I didn't come and get you,' she mumbled again and again, until Agla shushed her, her heart unaccountably full of warmth. Elísa hadn't given her the cold shoulder or forgotten about her. She had been doped up, not knowing if she was in this world or another. Her obvious misery at her failure to turn up made Agla forget the morning's disappointment.

'I was just going to have coffee with my friend and she wanted to stop off at a little party,' Elísa said. 'Those fucking pills are no good for me. They just knock me right out and I feel like I'm suffocating. I'm a lot happier with speed.'

She struggled to eat, saying she was feeling nauseous, but Agla encouraged her, heaping praise on her for every mouthful she swallowed and every sip of coffee she drunk. It was almost four o'clock, and they had to be at Vernd before six. There was no way that Elísa could turn up clearly drugged and in filthy clothes. Agla left her swathed in a towel on the sofa and rooted through her wardrobes. Most of her clothes were too big now, and would be far too big for Elísa, who was ten centimetres shorter than her and as thin as a rake. She picked up a shapewear top and a pair of leggings, went back to the living room and handed them to Elísa.

'Put these on,' she said. 'We'll stop off at a shop on the way and get you some clothes.'

It was a quarter to six when Agla swung into Laugateigur after calling at a clothes shop where she had hurriedly bought jeans, a shirt and a leather jacket, and explained to the stunned staff that Elísa, still half asleep and dazed, would wear them out of the shop.

A couple of cars marked with various media logos were parked outside the probation hostel. Agla took a deep breath.

'You remember what we're going to do?' she asked, and when Elísa didn't answer, she jabbed her with one elbow. 'We're here, Elísa, at Vernd. Here's the bag. You remember what to do?'

'Yeah, I remember,' Elísa said. 'Hold the bag in front of me, say I've been throwing up all day, ask if I have to be there for dinner or if I can go upstairs and lie down.'

She opened the car door and walked up to the house. Agla was relieved to see she was no longer slouching. The photographers snapped a couple of pictures of her, as if for show, and turned to Agla as she got out of the car. The reporters crowded around her, and Agla wrapped herself tightly in the ash-grey overcoat, as if it could protect her from the flood of questions and the clatter of clicking cameras.

67

'If you want to take tricks and win the game, then it's best if you call trumps,' Sonja advised Tómas as he hesitated, concentrating on the cards in his hand. 'Even if you don't have great cards, stay high so you keep the lead. If you wait and see, then you're playing against someone else's call, and that way you'll always lose.'

Alex nodded, as if in agreement with this lesson in whist tactics, while Lucia repeatedly rearranged her cards, the same look of confusion always on her face. Sonja wasn't sure that she actually understood the rules as occasionally she would play a different suit, but she always welcomed an invitation to join the game. It made a change from the kitchen.

'And what if I have a few good cards in one suit and only bad ones in another?' Tómas asked. Sonja delighted in hearing how deep and musical his voice had become. He had gone through puberty late and it had taken a long time for his voice to change. But that was all behind him and he now sounded like an adult. He was as tall as a grown man, and still growing.

'Then go for your weaker suit,' she said.

She was about to give him more advice when the doorbell rang. Alex was on his feet in an instant and left the room, and she followed to peer over his shoulder at the intercom screen. Húni Thór and another man stood on the steps outside, both of them holding their hands open to demonstrate that they were unarmed. This was strange. It was unusual for him to call without warning.

'Only let Húni Thór in,' she muttered to Alex. 'And search him to make sure. I don't trust him further than I could throw him.'

'I'm not sure you could throw him at all,' Alex replied.

'Precisely,' Sonja said and went back to the living room. Tómas and Lucia were sitting with their cards still in their hands, holding a conversation in a weird blend of English and Spanish.

'There's a man come to see me who I need to talk a little business with, so it would be great if you could help Lucia get supper ready in the kitchen.'

Tómas stood up, throwing his cards on the table in irritation. Lucia looked questioningly at Sonja, who winked. Lucia nodded once. She struggled to understand the card game's rules, but she was from Mexico and understood what real life was all about. She would lock the kitchen door and smile as she melted cheese onto the tacos, but she would still be ready with the pistol she kept under her apron if anyone tried to break in.

Húni Thór extended a hand to shake as he walked into the living room. He was always relaxed and courteous, so while Sonja had no fear of the man himself, it was his plotting that concerned her. He had plotted to place her where she was now. The two most momentous moments of her life had been arranged by Húni Thór. It had to be something big that brought him to her now.

'I need to get to the store,' he said.

Sonja stared at him in astonishment.

'The store?'

'Yes. I'll take the whole lot off your hands now, one big shipment.'

Sonja went to the bar and poured cognac into two glasses. She didn't want a drink; quite the opposite, as she needed to keep her wits about her, but she also needed to buy herself a moment. The store was her business; her insurance – it ensured her position in the chain.

'I don't need anything taken off my hands,' she said. 'I maintain a steady flow and I can increase it quickly if that's what you need. You always get your cut of everything, so if you need money then there are ways to make that happen.'

Húni Thór smiled and took the glass from her hand.

'Iceland is bouncing back,' he said. 'Coke is selling like it did before the crash, and all the other shit – the steroids and speed – is booming as well. There's a million tourists, and Icelanders are rich again.'

'How much are we talking about?'

'I'll take the whole store now,' he said. 'It'll be restocked bit by bit and you continue as usual.'

Sonja felt the sweat breaking out down her back. He was cutting her out, and there was nothing more terrifying in this business than being surplus to requirements.

'And what does Sebastian say—?' she began before Húni Thór interrupted.

'Sebastian knows about this and is in full agreement. It's vital to have a secure supply to the market.'

Sonja forced herself to smile. If there was anything worse than Húni Thór's plotting, it was he and Sebastian making plans together. It was precisely such a plan that had changed her life permanently, torn away every vestige of innocence and given her endless nightmares, which seemed to get worse with the passing years. They were the ones who had decided between them that she would murder someone.

She stood up, went to the statue of Thor on the mantelpiece and plucked the key from the niche in its back.

'This is one of the keys,' she said, handing it to him. 'Miguel has the other.' She sat at the coffee table, picked up a pen, tore a page from the crossword book and wrote a number on it. 'This is Miguel's number. He'll tell you where to go and will go with you to the store. I'll tell him to expect you.'

Húni Thór took the scrap of paper and stuffed it into his trouser pocket along with the key. There was no point protesting or delaying. The only thing that would work with Húni Thór was to plot a strategy of her own – something realistic. First she had to figure out what transport route he had found. It would have to be something special to empty the store, which was now several dozen kilos. She stood up and went with him to the door.

Once Alex had closed it behind him, she clapped a hand on his shoulder.

'Pack your toothbrush, Alex. We're going to Iceland.'

The lesser of two evils was always to be in the driving seat, even on a road leading straight to hell; it was better than drifting without knowing where you would end up. Life was like a game. Even with a handful of bad cards, it's better to be the one calling trumps.

68

'What do you mean, this ID number doesn't exist? It's my ID number. Do you think I don't know my own ID?'

María gaped at the bank cashier, who shook her head apologetically. 'I'm sorry,' she said.

'You're sorry?' María felt the rage swirl inside her. 'What you're saying is that something seems to have gone wrong with the bank's computer system so that my ID number has dropped off the registry, which means I – a customer – can't withdraw anything from an ATM or over the counter, in spite of waiting for a quarter of an hour and just getting a cup of piss-weak coffee! And you're *sorry*?'

'I'll fetch my supervisor,' the cashier said, standing up and disappearing into a room behind the tills.

María waited, drumming her fingers with impatience on the counter. A man at the next till and the cashier serving him looked sideways at her, and she knew she had raised her voice unnecessarily. A glitch in the system obviously wasn't the unfortunate cashier's fault, but María's whole body was as tense as a spring, after two mugs of coffee and the Modafinil she had taken to stop herself wailing over Ingimar Magnússon, and of course she was still feeling the after-effects of her time in that dark dungeon, the trucker in the States who had frightened the life out of her, and everything else she had been through in the last few days. She stiffened as the cashier returned, accompanied by an older woman, who looked questioningly at María.

'What does the problem appear to be?' she asked in a neutral voice.

María could feel the anger rushing to her head as she filled her lungs and exhaled slowly, forcing a smile as she did so.

'The problem is,' she said, placing emphasis on the *is*. 'The problem is that my ID appears to have disappeared from your computer system.'

She held the smile and forced herself to remain calm while the woman took a pair of reading glasses that hung on a chain around her neck, put them on and peered at the screen.

'What's your number?' she asked, and María repeated it yet again. The woman shook her head. 'You're sure that's the right number?' María nodded and maintained her plastic smile so as not to find herself dropping an inappropriate word. 'Let's look in the National Registry,' the woman said and asked María for her full name.

'María Gunnhildur Jónudóttir,' María said, and the woman's head tilted back as she looked down to type the name into the National Registry. It was clear that her reading glasses weren't up to the job.

'Jónsdóttir?' she asked.

'No. Jónudóttir,' María replied. 'My mother's name is Jóna.'

'I can't find it in the registry,' the woman said, tilting her head forwards this time to look at María over the top of her glasses.

'That's impossible,' María said. 'Of course I'm in the National Registry, like every other Icelandic citizen.'

The woman tapped at the keyboard again and shook her head. The cashier, who was standing quietly at her side, looking at the screen over her shoulder, shook her head in sympathy.

'Is this some kind of joke?' María demanded, aware that her voice was becoming shrill.

'The only explanation that comes to mind,' the woman said, taking off her glasses, 'is that you've recently adopted your mother's name, while the registry still has you under your patronymic.'

'No,' María replied. 'It's years since I changed my name. You must be using a version of the National Registry that's years out of date, which I can't believe.'

'Well, no. We get an amended version every day. You'll have to talk to the National Registry. There's nothing we can do about it here. I'm sorry.'

'You're not the only one who's sorry,' María said. 'And I'll certainly be taking my business elsewhere in future.'

She reflected that there might be some value in her threat, as, while the bank staff didn't have her ID, they wouldn't be able to see that her accounts were generally either empty or overdrawn.

She spun around and marched away, and as she reached the automatic doors, she noticed out of the corner of her eye that the cashier who'd served her grinned at the one at the next desk and tapped her head.

'I saw that,' María yelled, but as the doors hissed shut behind her, she was gripped by a feeling closer to despair than fear.

69

His fingertips were sore, but Anton was satisfied with his day's work. The bomb looked convincing, and as long as the detonator did its work, then all that would be needed was a little common sense to make sure the dynamite went off at once. In fact, the tool box looked harmless. Closed, there was nothing to indicate this was anything other than a well-used box that had once been shiny and new, but which was now endearingly worn, with a few paint splashes and stains, sustained over a couple of decades of use by his grandfather, after which it was left in their basement.

Opening the box, however, revealed the sticks of dynamite, a fuse leading from each one and fastened with garden wire to a longer fuse. On top sat the detonator, which he hadn't yet dared switch on. He really didn't want to have Gunnar anywhere close by when he tried it out. He was so clumsy and prone to fiddling that he would undoubtedly mess with the remote control and unintentionally blow them both up.

Gunnar had only just left, and Anton was mustering the courage he needed to put the end of the fuse wire into the little hole in the computer board, as Oddur had shown him, when his phone rang. His heart sank as he saw it was his father calling, as if he had been caught red-handed in the boiler room.

'Where are you, son?' his father asked, and Anton breathed a sigh of relief. Of course he had no idea what was going on in the basement. The stress was starting to get to him.

'I'm with the boys,' Anton said. That was an answer that always worked on his father, as if this was a catch-all explanation for any absence. *With the boys.*

'That's fine. I didn't mean to disturb you. I just wanted to say that I've booked you and Júlía a table at a fantastic place, and it's on me. OK?'

'Sure, yeah. Thanks, Dad. You're the best.'

'You're welcome, my boy. See you this evening.'

His father ended the call and Anton wondered if he was somewhere in town or working at home. Sometimes he would come home during the day and lie down for an hour in the living room, so it was possible that he was in fact lying directly above the boiler room.

The fuse wire had a ragged end, so Anton snipped it off clean and pushed it cautiously into the hole in the detonator, then snapped shut the red plastic cover to hold it secure. He took the remote and put it aside on the other garden chair. That way there was no risk that he could nudge it by accident as he tried it out. The remote looked like a doorbell; maybe Oddur had used a doorbell to make it. He was so clever in using all kinds of basic electronic stuff to make his robots. But that meant there was no security cover on the remote, of the kind Anton had seen in movies, so it was bound to be sensitive.

He took a deep breath and examined the bomb one more time. It looked good, convincingly bulky, and, going by the amount of dynamite and the information he had gleaned from the internet, it should be powerful enough to do its job.

Oddur had said that clicking the switch would make the bomb active, and a red light would come on. Anton's heart beat hard enough to burst and his finger trembled as he placed it on the switch.

70

There had to be a limit to how long Meteorite could continue to accrue losses, and as things stood, the company's owner, the bank in Paris, had to be getting nervous. It was this nervousness that Agla intended to home in on when she met the bank's director. Tomorrow she would speak to Elvar about what he had found to entertain the director during his visit to Iceland. It would be important to make a serious effort to pamper him before they talked; she needed to put him in a positive frame of mind. All the same, she was not nervous about taking her proposals to him; this was something she could do better than most people.

She opened the online banking page to check on her Icelandic hedge funds. She made a point of having a stake in as many of them as possible, as spreading your assets around could work out well. It had also been to her advantage during her case, as she had been able to challenge the impartiality of one of the judges as he had investments in the same fund. It was the minor details that made the difference, something that so many investors overlooked. It wasn't enough just to watch the big figures.

Invalid ID, the computer flashed up as she tried to log into her bank account.

She tried again.

Invalid ID.

There had to be a glitch in the bank's system. She tried once again, closed the computer and stood up. She would try again once she had checked on Elísa, and then she'd go to bed herself.

Agla walked down the corridor, slipped past the big potted plants and the grandma-style side tables, which were intended to give the house a homely feel but really just resulted in clutter, and pushed open Elísa's door. She was lying in bed, and at first Agla thought she was asleep, until she heard her sniff.

She sat down on the edge of the bed.

'Everything all right?' she asked, and Elísa shook her tousled head against the pillow. 'What?' Agla asked.

'Sorry I didn't come and get you. I fucked up.'

Agla placed a hand on her head and stroked her hair. It felt thin and dry to the touch.

'Shh, Elísa. It's all right. Don't think about it now.'

'You're so good, helping me out, and I do nothing for you. I even screw up picking you up from prison,' Elísa said, struggling to form the words through her sobs. 'And I ought to know what it's like having nobody to meet you when you come out of jail.'

'Don't cry. Shake it off,' Agla said. 'It's a new day tomorrow, and a new day brings new opportunities. I'll wake you up tomorrow, and you'll go to work and apologise to the manager at the shop for forgetting to call in sick. Then I'll collect you after work and we'll go for ice cream.'

Ice cream was the only thing that came to mind that might cheer Elísa up. She had seen how fond she was of it when she'd looked through her bank statements. It seemed to work – Elísa's tears dried up.

'Thanks,' she whispered into her pillow.

Agla leaned over, kissed the top of her head and tiptoed out, quietly closing the door, as, judging by the sound of Elísa's breathing, she was asleep already.

It was almost eleven, and for the first time in months Agla realised she felt tired. She again sat on the bed and looked around the small room. It had obviously been furnished with the help of IKEA, with a pinewood bed and a white plastic-laminated dresser, but the framed prints on the walls were something even her mother would have deemed out of fashion.

With the laptop on her knees she made another attempt to log in to her online account. Again, access was refused, so she tried logging into her accounts in the other Icelandic banks. She had the same result.

She decided to try her Swiss account, and was able to log in as usual, so it had to be a problem with the Icelandic central banking data centre. It was giving her the same result everywhere she tried.

Invalid ID.

71

The lock was stuck and it was dark inside The Squirrel's office so it was clear that Marteinn wasn't there. María wiggled the key impatiently, pushing at the glass door at the same time, until the key turned and the door opened.

From the moment she had opened her eyes that morning, everything had worked against her. First the glass jug of her coffee machine had broken, so there had been no choice but to resort to instant coffee; and then the National Registry had been monumentally unhelpful, expecting her to fill in a whole stack of forms. Now the office light switch wouldn't work, so she had to feel her way in the dark to the switch on the far wall, between her desk and Marteinn's. She reached out a hand to turn on the light, her shoulder brushing against something as she did so. She was startled, unable to stop herself from calling out. She didn't dare put out her hands to touch whatever it was in the dark, so she quickly switched the light on.

She didn't recognise him as Marteinn. The blackened face was nothing like him. But as she stared at the man hanging from the ceiling, it gradually dawned on her that the mustard-yellow corduroys were Marteinn's trousers and the worn leather shoes on the lifeless feet were Marteinn's shoes. The corpse slowly turned through half a circle and then back, making the leather belt sitting tightly around the dark-blue neck creak; Marteinn's cowboy belt.

Before she realised what was happening, Radio Edda's manager was at her side, trying to get her to her feet. She didn't realise why he was there all of a sudden, until she realised that she was screaming with all the power in her body.

'Come on out of here,' the radio station's manager said, pulling her towards the door.

But she didn't want to leave Marteinn like that. She wanted to cut him down to see if he would start breathing again. The manager told her repeatedly that he was cold and that it was too late. She couldn't understand how he could know that. Then she found that she could hardly stay upright, and the man half-carried her out into the corridor. She sat shivering against the wall while the man fetched his phone, standing over her as he called the emergency services.

It seemed as if she could hear the sirens wailing the moment the manager put his phone down. As the sound approached, it filled her with some hope that Marteinn might still be alive, and that was why the ambulance had its siren on. With that thought in mind, she stood up, rushed back into the office and up onto the desk, where she hauled at the belt that held Marteinn's corpse as it swung gently.

A moment later she was back in the corridor and a police officer was asking her all kinds of questions. She answered everything calmly, and the policeman left, and then the radio station's manager brought her coffee in a Radio Edda mug and she drank it in one gulp, hoping that it would bring her round from this nightmare.

72

Agla withdrew as much cash as each of her Swiss cards would allow then stuffed the notes into her wallet. The ATM had declined each of her Icelandic bank cards, debit and credit cards alike. Now, however, having received a confused call from María, she was beginning to join the dots in connection with this mysterious glitch in the banking system. She had struggled to understand what María was saying through her tears; she had skipped from her ID number to being imprisoned illegally and then to something about a dead man. She seemed petrified and said she was completely penniless, so Agla stopped off at an ATM on the way to pick her up outside the supermarket beside The Squirrel office.

'I think somebody might be watching me,' María said as she got into the Tesla. 'Drive, drive.'

Agla drove away slowly and watched María out of the corner of her eye as she twisted round in the seat to check the street around them.

'What was that about your ID number?' Agla asked as she turned onto Sæbraut.

María finally sat back in the seat with a deep sigh.

'It's gone!' María said. 'It's simply disappeared from the system. The National Registry said they'd check it out, so I filled in some forms, and the staff there put my name and number into the registry, but neither were there. They looked at me as if I was crazy.'

Agla couldn't stop herself from cracking a smile. This confirmed what she had suspected. There weren't many people who would be able to arrange something like this.

'You wouldn't happen to have encountered a certain Ingimar Magnússon since you started looking into this aluminium case for me?'

María sighed again.

'Yes,' she said, taking a tissue from her pocket and dabbing at her eyes. 'Ingimar was sitting in my flat when I finally got home after days of being held illegally in some empty jail or hospital up there on the old US military base. He tried to threaten me, to stop me from investigating the aluminium storage units. And now he's had Marteinn murdered – my assistant.'

'Murdered?'

'Yes. Marteinn is dead. I found him hanging from the ceiling when I got to the office this morning.'

Now the tears were running freely down María's cheeks. Agla pulled off the road into the coach park next to the *Sun Voyager* art installation on the sea front overlooking the bay and stopped the car.

'I know Ingimar well,' she said. 'He's a wolf and he'll stop at nothing when it comes to business. He plays dirty tricks on anyone who gets in his way; it seems to boost his ego. But he wouldn't go as far as killing someone. I can't believe that, María.'

María buried her face in her hands.

'I don't know what to believe anymore,' she said. 'The police said they'd look at every angle and wouldn't just assume that it's suicide,' María said, sniffing. 'Or maybe they do that with every fatality they investigate, I don't know. I'm absolutely not my usual self right now. And now the police will come and pick me up when they find out that the ID number I gave them doesn't exist. And I can't be locked up again, because I'm sure I'll freak out completely if I'm put in a cell. I mean really go crazy.'

Agla couldn't help feeling a twitch of satisfaction deep inside that María had had to experience incarceration for herself; after all, she had said often enough that she hoped Agla would spend as long as possible behind bars. But Agla kept quiet, took out a stack of notes and handed them to María.

'Do you have a place to go where you can keep out of sight for a few days? A friend out of town, or a summer house; anything like that?'

'Can't you just talk to the police and explain everything?' María asked.

'That's going to be a headache and a half,' Agla replied. 'I'm guessing that you mentioned my name to Ingimar, as my ID number has disappeared as well.'

María groaned, but took the bundle of notes as she got out of the car.

'I'll walk home from here,' she snapped. 'Call me when you've found out how I can get myself back again.'

She slammed the car door, and Agla drove away. It wasn't until she was passing the Harpa conference centre that she realised she had forgotten to give María a few encouraging words. It wouldn't have done any harm to show a little empathy – show that she had some understanding of what María had been through. Agla growled with irritation at her own shortcomings. There were good reasons why María and pretty much everyone else didn't like her.

She found Elvar's number in her phone then linked it to the Tesla's hands-free system. She would have to bring forward the French bank director's visit to Iceland. Sorting this whole affair out was becoming urgent. She signalled left and turned onto Hverfisgata. She would be at Bónus in time to collect Elísa as her shift ended.

73

Anton felt that he had never been more alert than at that moment. He was physically tired and his back was sore after bending over the bomb for so long the day before, but his senses were sharp and ready to react, and it felt as if his eyes saw everything more clearly and his ears picked up even the tiniest sounds. He lay in bed, admiring the pattern of roses that surrounded the light in the ceiling and listening to the hot water gurgle in the radiators.

Straight after school he had gone down to the boiler room to arm the bomb again, and then deactivate it, just for the kick that came with it.

It felt like the adrenaline his body had injected into his bloodstream had wiped clean his mind and senses so that he had gained a clearer awareness of the world. It seemed to have made him even more convinced that he was doing the right thing; that the bomb would change the state of things in Iceland. That could only be a good thing.

The first time he had clicked the switch on the bomb yesterday, he had done it with his eyes tight shut, his body tensing unconsciously; but when he opened his eyes and saw the red light on the detonator and the remote control on the garden chair, just a metre away, he felt a burst of pleasure. It wasn't unlike when he and a friend had tried vaping. The nicotine mist with its menthol taste had enveloped him, he had felt his legs go weak under him and was filled with delight – that was until the nausea took over. But this time there was no nausea, just a clarity of thought that he had never before experienced. The little white doorbell button on the remote, which sat just an arm's length away, marked the dividing line between life and death. Anton felt himself swell, as if this power nourished him and the skinny, spotty boy he had so recently been vanished for ever.

He was startled from his reflections by the doorbell ringing. He jumped to his feet. It had to be someone looking for him, as his parents never had visitors.

'I'll get it,' he yelled down the corridor. But he was too late, as he heard his father opening the front door.

He went quickly to the bathroom, ran a comb through his hair and splashed on a little aftershave, in case it happened to be Júlia dropping by. With his mind so clear, he was sure he would be able to dazzle her with all kinds of ideas. He loved it when she looked at him with adoration as he told her about something he had discovered on the internet, such as the work of Ocean Cleanup founder, Boyan Slat, or Deepika Kurup's water-cleaning bottle, which had made it possible for people in developing countries to have clean water to drink. They both liked hearing about initiatives by young people that made the world a better place, and they agreed that it would be so much better when their generation took over running things. Their parents' generation had done nothing but screw the world up.

He took two strides down the steps but then came to a halt in the middle of the stairs. It wasn't Júlia, but a man with a shiny bald head who followed his father inside.

'We can go to my office,' he heard his father say as he pointed to the door to his room.

The blood froze in Anton's veins, and in a flash the clarity he had experienced since activating the bomb turned to fog and confusion. His body felt heavy; the same feeling he got when he received a low mark in an exam or lost at cards with the boys, but magnified a thousand times. The thought that he might be found out before the bomb went off had never entered his head, but now that possibility was staring him in the face. Accompanying the bald guy into his father's office was a police officer with a tool belt and a hissing radio.

74

The sobs had come to an end but the tears hadn't; they poured down María's cheeks all the way to Thingvellir. She had stopped at the filling station on Ártúnsbrekka, filled the car's tank, thrown a few snacks into a bag and paid with notes from the wad Agla had given her. Even in the shop the tears had continued to flow freely from her eyes, as if her body had finally given up all resistance, allowing the sorrow and fear free rein.

She took the Nesjavellir road up to Thingvellir lake, even though she had never wanted to go that way when she and Maggi had been together – she had found it easier to take the straighter Mosfellsheiði route. Now she drove cautiously through the Hengill area, terrified of coming off the road, as her tears occasionally obscured her vision.

She felt a lump in her throat as she turned down the track at Grafningur and headed towards the summer house. She had always loved coming here, and it was among the few material things she had missed after the divorce. But as Maggi had inherited the place from his parents, naturally, he still owned it.

She parked the car behind the boathouse so it couldn't be seen from the road, deciding there was no point in attracting too much attention.

There was a scent of budding birch in the air. The water lapped at the shore as if it didn't have a care in the world, and the lively birdsong around the summer house sparked a glow of joy in her heart that ended the flow of tears but immediately made her feel guilty. Somehow it seemed wrong to let herself feel any happiness on the day Marteinn had died.

Maggi had never been one to change old habits; the key was in its usual place, under the flower pot by the door. María went inside. A respectable stack of firewood by the stove indicated that it hadn't been long since Maggi had been here, and she knew she needn't worry about him taking her by surprise. He never went to the summer house except at weekends, Christmas, and for the summer holiday he always took in July.

When she had unpacked her snacks – a two-litre bottle of Coke, two prawn sandwiches and a bag of chocolate raisins – and put them in the kitchen, she sat down and felt the quiet surround her. There was nothing to be heard but birdsong, and there was nothing to disturb her. After everything she had been through she finally had peace to think.

75

The smell the cleaners had left behind was so strong that Agla started by going into each room and opening the windows. Elvar had done well, preparing the house as she had asked. Most of the furniture was new, and Agla was relieved that there was now little in the house that would remind her of Sonja. Everything they had chosen together had gone to a charity, and Elvar had also rearranged the furniture so that it felt to her like a different house. She opened the sliding door in the living room and looked out over the garden, which wore its light-green spring colours. She would have to get a gardener in; the hedges were starting to run wild and there was moss on the patio.

'You're not serious?' Elísa said, wandering through the house in a daze and repeatedly asking if this was some kind of joke. 'It's a well cool house. Are you really going to let me live here?'

'Yes,' Agla said. 'I bought it for ... well, a woman. And I've no desire to use the place myself.'

'Bad memories?' Elísa asked, in clear concern.

Agla felt her throat constrict, so she nodded and turned away. Coming in here had affected her more than she wanted to admit, even to herself.

'Surely you just need to make some newer and better memories to go with the house?' said Elísa.

Agla's heart leaped as she wrapped her arms around her from behind and squeezed.

'What are you doing?' She tried to shake Elísa off; she wasn't ready for this. A strong combination of emotions welled up inside her – the image of Sonja and some kind of feeling of responsibility towards Elísa. 'That's not what I had in mind for the house,' she whispered. 'You don't owe me anything and don't have to do anything for me in return.'

'You think I'm doing this for you?' Elísa tugged at the front of Agla's jacket, pulling her close and kissing her hard on the mouth. 'Come on, Agla. It's three hours until we have to be back at Vernd, and we're alone here. All alone, at last, with a bed and a whole house to ourselves. Come on!'

Elísa's eagerness, her smile and the hands that snaked inside Agla's clothes broke through the barriers Agla had swiftly erected as she stood alone by the road outside the Hólmsheiði prison. She felt the blood burning through her veins in a wonderful mixture of tenderness and passion, and she let Elísa lead her to the bedroom.

She had thought that Sonja had been her only opportunity in life to experience such emotions; an opportunity she had lost. But now she was here with this young woman she hardly knew at all, the blood rushing through her, her body alight with desire. She let go of the fear that this desire would turn against her, the fear of opening her heart only for it to be broken again; the fear that this time she wouldn't survive the heartbreak.

Elísa pulled her down onto the bed.

'Kiss me,' she said. 'Kiss me.'

Agla unbuttoned Elísa's shirt and unclipped her bra.

'I'll kiss you,' she whispered. 'I'll kiss every part of you.'

76

The man had introduced himself as a detective, but Ingimar had immediately forgotten his name and couldn't surreptitiously check the man's card, as he had just placed it in the desk drawer.

'Is it right that you went to the office of The Squirrel website yesterday?' the detective asked as Ingimar gestured for him and his uniformed colleague to take a seat.

'Yes,' he replied. There was no point denying it. It was true, and, anyway, they would hardly be asking if they didn't know the answer already. He took a seat himself, drew it up to the desk and rested his elbows on it, hands clasped together as if he were a receptionist waiting for a customer to announce their reason for calling. This was one thing he had learned from the shipping company owner he had worked for in the old days; the old man had always done this when someone wanted to discuss their pay. It was a fixed position, hands locked together with no chance of fidgeting or fiddling, and leaning forwards over the desk in a firm stance; nothing defensive. The last thing he needed now was to appear to be fighting a rearguard action.

'And could you tell me what took you there?' said the detective.

'Yes. It may sound silly, but the way they have been writing about me has been upsetting,' Ingimar said. 'So I decided to go there and talk to someone.'

'Someone? You mean Marteinn Árnason?'

'Yes. Marteinn, or María, who owns the thing.' Under circumstances such as these, Ingimar knew he had to take care to tread a fine line: telling the truth as far as was possible, and if he couldn't stick to facts, talking around the subject rather than lying outright. It was always surprising how many people sensed instinctively when they were being told a lie. 'I was hoping to persuade them to tone down the rubbish they've been publishing. It's not comfortable to be the subject of this kind of coverage. Not that many people pay attention to that kind of journalism,' he said, drawing invisible quote marks in the air around the word 'journalism'.

'But you had already spoken to María before you went to The Squirrel yesterday. Isn't that right?'

Ingimar felt something harden deep in his gut, but he nodded as if nothing was wrong.

'Yes. I went to her home first to try to speak to her and ask her to stop the witch-hunt that The Squirrel has been running, but I didn't have any success. I know it doesn't sound pleasant, but these people are completely nuts. I don't know which of them is worse, María or Marteinn. Anyway, can I ask what this is all about?'

The question wasn't because he didn't already know, but to reaffirm his innocence.

The detective studied his notebook.

'María claims that you broke in to her apartment yesterday morning. What do you have to say to that?'

'Broke in? That's rich,' he said, feigning astonishment. 'If that's what this is all about, then there's a simple enough explanation. When I got to her place, the door was wide open. I called out and took a couple of steps inside, and found she wasn't there. When she did show up she was pretty out of it, and looked rough, the poor thing. I have to say that calling this a break-in is – what shall I say? – exaggerating the couple of steps I took into her flat. I wouldn't have thought that would be a police matter.'

The policeman jotted something in his notebook with a bored expression on his face. His shoulders slumped and, judging by the dark rings under his eyes, Ingimar guessed that the man hadn't slept much recently.

'When you arrived at The Squirrel's office, was Marteinn alone?'

'Yes, he was there on his own. I tried to have a conversation with him, but I quickly saw that he was in no mental condition for anything like that.'

The detective looked up from his notebook and met Ingimar's gaze; his sleepy eyes were suddenly wide awake. 'What kind of mental condition would you say he was in, then?'

'He was agitated and seemed to believe that I had been sent by *them*. I don't know who *they* are supposed to be or what he was thinking. I didn't stay long as I could see it was pointless talking to him.'

'Did you feel that Marteinn's condition was such that he might have required medical attention?'

'Yes,' Ingimar replied.

'And did you call a doctor or other assistance?'

'No, I didn't.'

'Why not?'

'Well, with respect, I had the feeling that he was like that all the time. You only need to read the articles he writes. Judging by what he has been writing about me recently, his hold on reality is pretty tenuous. Has something happened to him?'

'It has,' the police officer replied. 'He was found dead this morning at The Squirrel's office. You appear to be the last person to have seen him alive.'

Ingimar dropped his head and stared down at his desk for a while.

'I should have called a doctor,' he said quietly, before looking up.

The policeman shrugged wearily and stood up.

'We'll be in touch if there's anything else.'

Ingimar went with them to the door, nodding to each of them as they went out onto the steps. He had almost pushed the door closed when the tired-looking detective pushed it open again.

'One more thing,' he said. 'Could you have touched Marteinn in any way when you met yesterday?'

'Touched him?' Ingimar thought for a moment and was about to say no, when he remembered his hand on Marteinn's head, the reassurance that his touch had given this troubled man, the finger that had wiped a tear from his cheek. 'I may have ... well, patted his head,' he said.

'You patted his head?'

'Yes, if I can put it like that. He was sitting down, and I may have given him a friendly pat on the head.'

Ingimar could hear how strange this must sound, in spite of it being largely the truth.

'Hmm,' the detective nodded, a curious expression on his face. Ingimar could see that the tired eyes were again wide awake.

77

Agla had never much enjoyed helicopter flights. While the boys at the bank had always found them hugely exciting, the aircraft's gentle movements normally left her nauseous. However, as the helicopter's altitude dropped over Thingvellir National Park, and they flew along the ravine in the summer brightness, Agla had to admit that it was a magnificent sight.

Pierre, the bank director, revelled in every second. 'It's so beautiful!' he called out.

Agla smiled. She didn't like to speak through the headset, aware of hearing her own voice, and reluctant to risk being misunderstood, so she smiled and gave the occasional thumbs-up to demonstrate how much she agreed with the banker. After a circuit around Thingvellir, the helicopter swept out over the lake, where the pilot took them lower and angled the machine over the islands so they could have a better view of them. Pierre was so absorbed by the sight that his exclamations were coming in French. Agla just raised her thumb again and smiled. The smile was a real one and she was genuinely happy; so happy that she could almost burst. She felt that a decade had fallen off her that day, and her heart was still tender. She and Elísa had sat over the evening meal at Vernd and grinned at each other foolishly. Agla had found it difficult to part from her afterwards, but she had to spend time with the banker before getting back to Vernd for eleven.

The helicopter came to land on a flat-topped peak, the name of which escaped Agla, but which provided a fantastic view over the Hengill region. The co-pilot left the helicopter first with a small table and a generous hamper. Once the rotor blades had come to a halt and the passengers had stepped out, he opened the hamper on the table so they could enjoy the delicacies Elvar had provided for them. Agla felt a pang as the pilot poured champagne into the glasses. This was a particularly good champagne that Agla had always made sure she had a stock of for special occasions. Now she clinked glasses with Pierre, lifted the glass to her lips and only pretended to drink. She didn't dare take even a sip. She had promised herself that she would follow the probation conditions to the letter and take no risks, especially now. It wasn't worth being locked up at Hólmsheiði again while Elísa was still free, just for a few mouthfuls of champagne – never mind how good it might be.

They strolled around the edge of the flat mountain top with their champagne flutes and looked down over the valley below, where little pockets of mist had collected in the cool evening air. Agla took the opportunity to pour a little from her glass occasionally onto the ground, while Pierre systematically emptied his own glass, and, with the bottle in her hand, Agla made sure he was kept refilled.

'Such hospitality!' he said contentedly.

'I'm delighted that you're satisfied,' Agla said, filling his glass one more time. 'Tomorrow you get a chance to bag a salmon. A gillie will collect you from the hotel and he'll cook for you at the lodge and keep you company.'

'And you? I don't get the pleasure of your company while we fish for salmon?'

Agla had no inclination to explain to the man what it meant to be out on probation. He could Google her and would find out that she had been in prison; but it seemed he hadn't done that, so she would simply rearrange facts into a more palatable form.

'I'm pretty tightly booked but I plan to drop by and cast a line with you during the day.'

That meant that she would leave at seven in the morning, the earliest she was allowed out of Vernd. She would walk the riverbanks above Borgarfjörður with him in rubber waders until the afternoon, and be back at Vernd before six for the evening meal. As with helicopter flights, she failed to see the fascination men had for fishing salmon. She enjoyed salmon for a meal, but preferred to buy it in a shop.

'You mentioned Meteorite,' Pierre said, turning to her with eyes that were remarkably clear considering how much champagne he had drunk. 'What is it you want to discuss?'

Agla coughed. It was time to get serious. She raised her glass and clinked it against his.

'I'm hoping that you're open to a proposal; it's a little business venture that could be good for both of us.'

78

Anton woke after a restless night with his determination renewed. He had passed through doubt, fear, hopelessness and then finally returned to optimism, coming to the conclusion that anything worthwhile in life involved taking a risk. That was how it had been with Júlía. He had taken a colossal risk by asking her to go out with him. She could have said no, which would have hurt; and she could also have said no, laughed and told everyone, which would have left him a social outcast. But she had said yes, and their time together had been completely worth the risk, although when he had stood in the school dining hall with his palms sweating, trying to summon the courage to approach her for the third day in a row, he couldn't have known that. It would be the same with the bomb. He was frightened now, and the visit from the police had magnified the risks, but once the bomb had gone off, it would all be worthwhile and the world would never be the same again.

He knew that his father was up and about, because he could hear the clack as the newspaper was pulled free of the letterbox, but instead of the morning shower and the usual routine, he could smell waffles. He leaped out of bed. These days were the best days, the ones when his father didn't go out, but instead pottered around the kitchen well into the morning. Anton pulled on his dressing gown and followed the waffle smell down the stairs.

'*Bon appetit!*' his father said, placing a stack of waffles on the table, along with butter and cheese. This was their personal foible. His mother liked her waffles with jam and cream, but he and his father buttered their waffles and put cheese on them.

'Did you look into all that stuff about me going to sea?' Anton asked.

'Isn't youth work enough for you this summer, my lad?'

'Yes, I'll do that. But there are only five weeks on offer and there's no money in it.'

'You know that money isn't a problem in this house,' his father said.

Anton had heard it all before. This wasn't the first time they had been through this. Before long the lecture would come about how dangerous fishing was, and that he was so precious. He would have to find a way to explain to his father, without going into detail, that this summer would see his life change direction. Soon everything would change, and he would take on adult responsibilities, be his own master.

'You went fishing when you were my age. You talk about it all the time.'

'You and I are different characters,' his father said. 'We have very different backgrounds.'

'But, Dad, you always said that fishing was what made a man of you.'

His father sighed. He looked at Anton for a while, shook his head, grinned, and nodded his head.

'All right,' he said. 'I give up.'

'Promise?' Anton wanted to hear him say it. His father had said several times that he'd look into it, that they'd see, and made all kinds of excuses. This was the first time that he had come clean.

'Yes. I give up.' He took out his phone, tapped at the screen and passed it to Anton. 'That's a twenty-five-metre trawler with a steel hull,' he said as Anton peered at the picture. 'I've bought it for us, you and me, so we can go fishing together this summer.'

'What do you mean? You own this boat?'

'That's right. I've had a hankering for a while to get back into the fishing business, and since I can't seem to rid you of this obsession with the sea, then I'll go as well and can keep an eye on you. We'll take on a skipper, I'll sail as mate and we'll be fishing for langoustine off the east from Hornafjörður.'

A whole series of questions spun through Anton's mind. This wasn't something he had expected.

'What about Mum?'

'We'll find a home help to look after her,' his father said quickly. It was obvious that he had thought things through.

'And me? What's my job on the boat?' he asked, suddenly fearful that he would be given some stupid, old-fashioned title such as 'ship's boy' or 'deckie learner', or something like that.

'You'll be the deckhand,' his father said.

Anton breathed a sigh of relief. Deckhand was fine. That was something serious, something grown up. He put out his hand to his father's, who took it and squeezed.

'Thanks, Dad,' he said. It wasn't quite as cool to be at sea on his own father's boat, but if those were the conditions on offer, then it was still better than messing about with youth work or some other rubbish all summer.

'You're welcome,' his father said. 'Soon it'll be time for you to take over waffle-making duties as well. My little boy's becoming a man.'

Anton was sure that his father was proud of the stubbornness he had shown, despite until now having been completely opposed to all of his dreams of going fishing.

'Cool boat,' Anton said, adding a generous layer of butter to a waffle and placing a couple of slices of cheese on top.

'Forward wheelhouse, three winches for twin-rig trawling. Built in 2000. It's coming here from Scotland.'

Anton bit into his waffle, and butter leaked out, down his chin; he wiped it off with the back of his hand. He looked at the picture of the boat and imagined himself coming ashore with a sea bag on his shoulder, Júlía waiting for him on the quay. She would kiss him and look at him as his father was doing right now, seeing him not as a boy but as a man. After the explosion, everything would be different.

79

Ingimar had overindulged in the waffles and felt uncomfortably full as he went upstairs to shower. All the same, it had been good to spend the morning with Anton. It wasn't often that the lad allowed him any insight into his thoughts. He was unnervingly cagey and often seemed troubled. Part of this was undoubtedly down to his mother. It wasn't good for a youngster to live under these conditions. Maybe his yearning for the sea was a need for some sort of escape, a desire to get away from home. And maybe that wasn't such a bad idea. This would be summer fishing so bad weather was unlikely and Ingimar would be there himself to keep an eye on the boy, to steer him clear of the most dangerous tasks. Maybe what he had said himself was right – some heavy work would toughen Anton up.

All this fatherly sensitivity, which always came over him when he was close to the boy, was washed away in the shower and while he shaved his mind turned to practical matters. He had already ensured that the María problem would now resolve itself. It didn't matter what accusations she threw at him, as far as the police would be concerned she would just appear increasingly unhinged. He was secure, as he always was. His understanding of how life in general functioned was clear. Sometimes this filled him with a sense of loneliness, as he seemed to be one of the few people who had this level of comprehension. He often felt that he was the director in a theatre where it had been decided in advance that the show would be a success. Sometimes all he needed to do was say a few words to nudge things in the right direction. The image of Marteinn came to mind – weeping and crouched before him – along with the emotion that he had experienced as he laid a hand on the man's head. Power. Dominance.

He found his phone and called *her*.

'Already?'

She seemed taken by surprise, and he was no less surprised to hear noise in the background.

'Yes. Circumstances are such now that I think I need it.'

He twisted his upper body so he could see his back in the mirror. There were still wheals there from the last time, but that wouldn't be a problem.

'I'm abroad, coming home tomorrow,' she said. 'How about late tomorrow evening?'

Her manner was unusually formal, so it was clear that she was in company. Normally she would have told him to get his arse over there right away and not forget what a shabby and insignificant worm he was. That was her script; it reminded him that he was mortal.

'Thank you, ma'am. I'll accept whatever you have to offer,' he whispered.

'That's just as well for you,' she retorted and hung up.

Ingimar felt a shiver of the anxiety; it was part of the anticipation – what he always felt when he was on the way to *her*.

80

In some inexplicable way María could sense Marteinn's presence as she sat at her desk in The Squirrel's office and hammered at the keyboard. It wasn't an uncomfortable sensation; quite the opposite: it was something of a comfort to be in the place where he had spent the last moments of his life.

As soon as she entered the office, she had looked in their secret place – behind a wall panel by the radiator – and saw that he had done as she had asked and put all the information relating to the case there. She felt a warm glow as she held the printouts and the flash drive containing the data in her hands, and made herself a solemn promise to do the best job she possibly could on this story, and to do it for both of them. It was the least she could do for Marteinn, after she had let him down so badly just when he was at his most vulnerable.

María had cried herself to sleep the night before, lying in the narrow bed in the summer house. She wanted to believe that her tears were for Marteinn, but in fact it was the bra hanging from a hook on the back of the door that had set her weeping again. It all mixed together in one deep well of sorrow inside her – Marteinn's miserable death and the new woman Maggi had clearly spent time with in the summer house.

Reading through what she had written the night before, when she had sat on the porch under the midnight sun, wrapped in a blanket with her laptop on her knees, she was surprised just how much anger there was in her words. She could see that it needed to be toned down and framed in neutral terms, so that the piece wouldn't read as a hysterical rant. A measured, impartial viewpoint was essential. While it was difficult not to be caught up in her fury at the financial bandits sucking the country dry, she needed to remain impassive. She needed to employ her journalist's detachment in order to keep clear of the maelstrom and look at things dispassionately. She would redraft it all in the third person, which would also increase the chances of one of the larger media wanting to buy her report. The Squirrel needed to establish itself in people's minds as a medium for genuine investigative journalism.

The course of events as she had described them read like a foreign thriller. She imagined people sitting, glued to their screens as they learned how The Squirrel's journalist, María Gunnhildur Jónudóttir, had investigated a case that pitted her against ruthless people with a great deal to lose; then the gun at her cheek, the incarceration in a dark cell, the smelter's spin doctor inviting himself into her home... Into this she would weave a detailed account of how the aluminium produced in Iceland didn't find its way onto the market, but instead was destined to be stockpiled in warehouses in America so that the parent company and a few greedy men in Iceland could push their profit margins through the roof.

She would leave Agla out of it, as she had been asked to, as she wasn't a directly involved party but had simply been brought in to investigate. The account would refer only to an unnamed source. There were plenty of other names she could drop in there; one smelter, one international bank, as well as Ingimar Magnússon, who was so closely connected to Iceland's business and politics. The big names would be the ones that would sell her report.

If everything went well, the piece might attract some attention. Maybe it would raise awareness of how these large multinationals behaved; how they used blackmail and every other dirty trick to channel all that wealth into the pockets of a few individuals, when by rights it belonged to Iceland.

81

Landing at Keflavík airport never failed to give Sonja a jolt of nerves, even though she had stopped carrying shipments herself long ago. Somehow she still felt there was the chance of being picked up – at the jetway, by the baggage carousel, or at the customs gate. To an extent she missed the elation that had followed every delivery she'd successfully brought through here in the past. But now she got her kicks from bigger business than a few hundred grams of cocaine.

The next piece of business was to figure out how Húni Thór was planning to bring the whole of her store's contents to Iceland in one go. There were two routes, air and sea, and she would have to be genuinely imaginative to work out exactly how he was planning to go about it. If he had discovered a new route, then she needed either to be able to make use of it herself, or wreck it for him so that she could make her own position secure. She could not accept Húni Thór and Sebastian cutting her out. She knew as well as anyone that once such a move had been made, it was customary to eliminate the person who was no longer needed.

The terminal was packed with people, and there was a queue for the duty-free store, so while Sonja waited by the carousel for their luggage, she watched Alex to make sure he didn't leave Tómas to himself, but followed a few steps behind him as he went into the shop, chose some sweets and checked out the electronics on offer. In a few minutes she would have to relax her grip on him and trust that his father would look after him properly. Adam was fully aware of her position and understood the importance of not taking his eyes off the boy, but he never wanted Alex to stay with them, and Sonja found that uncomfortable.

'I bought two boxes of chewing gum,' Tómas said as he appeared at her side. 'One for you and one for me. We check on each other every night and whoever finishes first wins, and gets massive jaw muscles.'

Sonja laughed. Some kind of competition between them every time they were apart had become customary. It gave them both a daily activity that kept them connected. Tómas was the only thing in her life that brought her real joy. Every other piece of business was just for the kick; excitement followed by elation, turn and turn about. This pattern had long dominated her life, like an addiction. Dope could be addictive in so many ways.

In the arrivals hall Adam stood on the left of the exit door and Rikki the Sponge waited on the right, near the shop. These two former colleagues and friends no longer spoke to each other, and each avoided even glancing in the other's direction. Sonja briefly hugged Tómas and made him promise to be careful, then she nodded to Alex to indicate that he should follow him all the way to the car with his father. She went over to Rikki the Sponge who took her case and greeted her shortly.

'Heard anything about this business of Húni Thór's?' she asked.

He shook his head.

'Nope,' he said. 'Not a whisper. Something weird's going on. But Thorgeir's been partying without a break since he came home. He's lined some girls up, so I hope he's not going to overdo it again.'

Sonja nodded and followed Rikki to the car. Thorgeir and his girls weren't a concern right now. It was the business with Húni Thór that she needed to resolve. Her eyes followed Tómas as he walked at his father's side to a big 4×4 on the far side of the car park, Alex following behind with Tómas's case.

Tómas always seemed happy to go to his father's, although she knew that father and son didn't get on particularly well. She supposed that it was a relief to escape her permanent vigilance, the locked doors and the bodyguard. She could understand his feelings; their life should never have come to this. Everything she had done had been with the aim of keeping him with her, but things hadn't turned out that way, to their shared distress. Now she was dreading having to tell him that he wouldn't be going back to the same school after the holiday – that he had to change yet again. Now that Sebastian and Húni Thór were plotting something ambitious, she couldn't risk someone finding him.

82

She wondered if she was being hysterical, but Agla felt uncomfortable as Elísa vanished right after dinner. She had said that she would get ready while Agla cleared up, and then they'd go for ice cream and a drive around the city. Agla had taken her teasing smile and the words 'go for a drive and check out houses' as meaning that they would go to her house and check out each other between the sheets.

'She answered a phone call and left as soon she had eaten,' said Kent when Agla asked if he had seen Elísa. 'She rushed off with the phone to her ear; from the expression on her face it looked as if someone had invited her to a pill-popping party.'

'Pill-popping?' Agla stared at him with her mouth open, and for a moment Kent stared back at her.

'You do know she's an addict?' he said, and Agla nodded. Of course she knew that Elísa was addicted, but it still took her by surprise that she could run off having made other plans. 'Someone came to get her. I didn't see the car, though, just heard it,' Kent continued without putting his book down.

He was the only prisoner who stayed at Vernd in the evenings. Apart from those who had some housework to do, all the others rushed off somewhere on the stroke of seven o'clock, while Kent sat in the lounge every evening with a book, reading or watching the TV. Agla turned and left the room, then stood in the lobby without knowing what to do. Should she go and look for Elísa, or just swallow her disappointment and use the evening for work?

'I'll come with you if you're going to fetch her,' Kent said, appearing in the lobby and shrugging a jacket over his shoulders.

That made up her mind. Agla snatched up her coat and followed him down the steps.

He sat in the front seat of her car and tapped at his phone. 'You know who her mates are?' he asked, and Agla shook her head. 'Give me the name of someone she knows so I can find her friends online; then I should be able to find out where she is.'

'How on earth can you do that?' Agla asked. It would be worth knowing what his method was, in case this happened again.

Kent shot her a tired look as if this was the most ridiculous question imaginable.

'This is my old life,' he said, tugging up the sleeve of his jacket to show the scars on his arm. 'It's not a big world and I know pretty much everyone. Any names?'

The sight of Kent's tortured skin made it difficult for Agla to think, so she closed her eyes and tried to remember if Elísa had mentioned any names while telling her far-fetched tales in prison.

'She used to be with a woman called Katrín,' she said, unable to remember any other names. 'And she's talked about some boss.'

Kent gave her a sharp look, as if she had mentioned the devil himself.

'The Boss? Boss with a capital B?'

Agla shrugged.

'Yes, there seems to have been someone who made her smuggle dope.'

'Shit.' Kent stared ahead with a concerned expression.

'What?' Agla asked. 'What's the matter?'

'Just. The Boss. That's what's the matter. Poor Elísa.'

Kent still had a distant look on his face as he slowly pulled his sleeve back down.

'So who is this Boss?'

'The Boss manages pretty much all of the drugs in Iceland. It doesn't matter if it's coke, or speed or E, or whatever. If you follow the trail far enough, you get to the Boss. And everyone seems to know, except the police. I don't know if they're stupid or if they're getting a cut. Considering how the Boss works, that wouldn't come as a surprise. It's all well organised.'

'Elísa said the other day that once she had finished her sentence she would be free of the Boss and the smuggling, so it's not certain she's still caught up in all that,' Agla said, but she'd hardly finished her sentence before Kent snorted dismissively.

'She can believe what she wants,' he said, shaking his head. 'But it's not that simple. Nobody ever is free of the Boss.'

83

It was a quarter to ten by the time Kent pointed to the right and she turned off Kringlumýrarbraut. He had made a few calls asking where a party might be found. This had led them to two places; Agla was still trying to digest what she had witnessed – she was made numb by the effort.

At the first place they had climbed the neat stairs of a three-storey building to an apartment that was so ankle-deep in garbage – they literally had to wade through it. The door hadn't been locked and Kent had just walked in. She had followed in the lee of his rawboned bulk, into the unknown. Everyone in the place was asleep. One of the two men asleep on the sofa in the living room raised his head and looked up as they entered. The atmosphere in the apartment was stifling, with a sour blend of sweaty bodies and garbage that was beginning to smell bad. Kent went straight towards the bedrooms. In one of them he approached a girl who was sleeping face down and rolled her over to see if it was Elísa. Then he turned her back to lie on her front.

'So she doesn't choke on her own puke,' he explained.

They then tried the other bedroom, where three people lay on a narrow double bed. Closest to them was a good-looking, dark-haired young man, bare-chested and with the needle still hanging from his red-mottled arm.

'Prescription dope,' Kent said as the door closed behind them on the way out. 'The junkies buy it from old or sick people who can't afford to eat. Then there are a few guys who'll sell prescription drugs for a fuck. Sometimes they sell access to girls who are knocked out. Great fun,' he said with quiet sarcasm, turning to her. 'Are you all right?'

Agla nodded, trying to hold back the nausea. The smell and the image of the slack face of the young man on the bed triggered an unexpected chain of thought: she imagined a woman holding a picture of a young man with a handsome smile, just graduated from college and looking to the future with optimism in his eyes. It was a ridiculous thought, but the weight of it remained until the nausea passed. Maybe somewhere, someone was looking for this young man.

The second place was the home of someone linked to the Boss, Kent had told Agla, and she saw immediately that it had a very different atmosphere. Lively music could be heard from outside the two-storey wooden house with its colourful corrugated iron cladding, which sat in the Thingholt district of the city. As soon as they stepped inside they were met by a young woman with a tray of drinks. Kent turned and looked at Alga as if he was waiting to see if she would take one, but she shook her head and he did the same. For a second Agla wondered if he would have taken a drink if she hadn't been with him. But he wouldn't have been there if it wasn't for her.

The house had been restored to its original style, and with surprise, Alga admired the artworks on the walls. Whoever lived here was no lightweight. In the living room the furniture had been pushed aside and a group of people danced on the wooden floor, which trembled beneath them. Kent threaded his way through the kitchen to the stairs, and had just placed a foot on the lowest step when a musclebound man in a tight T-shirt hurtled down the stairs and took a position on the third step, arms folded.

'What the fuck do you want?' he demanded, staring from beneath knitted brows at Kent, biting his teeth so hard together that the muscles in his broad jaw bulged.

'Elísa,' Kent said, not turning a hair at the man's attitude. It was a strange position. The big man was two steps higher and looked down at him, while Kent stepped onto the lowest step so that he was very close to the man, but no longer looking up at him.

'There's no Elísa here,' the man retorted, biting down hard again, and without looking away. Kent held his eyes for a moment, and then stepped back and down, backing slowly into the kitchen behind.

'Let's go,' he said, gently taking Agla's arm, and she meekly let herself be led.

'Kent Cook,' the man called out behind him. 'Kent the Cook is here to cook up something smooth for all of us!'

A gale of laughter followed them out, and Agla could feel the tension in Kent's body relax as he let go of her arm.

'How do you know that guy?' Agla asked when they were back in the car.

'I don't know him,' Kent replied drily.

'At any rate, he knows you and he knows you're a cook.'

'I'm not a cook,' Kent said.

'Oh? So Cook is a family name?'

'No. Hermannsson.'

'All right.'

Agla understood from his tone of voice that the name the muscle man had called out after him wasn't going to be explained, but that didn't matter. It now seemed unlikely that they would find Elísa before Vernd's eleven o'clock curfew.

'We'll check out one more place,' Kent said, pointing her towards the Kópavogur road, and Agla put her foot down.

84

'Sprint!' Anton called out as he overtook Júlía by the statue of Tómas Guðmundsson on the bench by the lake, and he heard her wince. This was their second circuit, alternating jogging and sprinting, and he was starting to tire. All the same he forced himself to continue, and hearing Júlía's footsteps behind him spurred him on. At Skothúsvegur he had to stop as there was a car in the road, so Júlía caught him up.

'Gotcha,' she said, slapping him on the back as she shot across the road and down towards the Hljómskáli gardens on the other side. He drew on his reserves of energy and was about to catch her up, when she realised he was close behind, shifted up a gear and left him standing.

'I give up!' he called out to her, and she slowed her pace, turned and jogged back towards him.

'Woo-hoo! I win!' she crowed, hands in the air as if she were completing a marathon.

'I let you win,' he laughed.

She pretended to be angry, jumping on his back and getting him into a headlock.

'I won! Admit it! Go on, admit it!'

He spun around a few times to try and shake her off, then tried to reach around to tickle her, but her headlock was too strong, so he stepped onto the grass and leaned down to try and dislodge her. He turned over to twist free, but she tightened her hold.

'I let you win,' he laughed. 'Because you're such a bad loser.'

Júlia shrieked and boxed his ears a couple of times until he pretended to submit.

'All right! All right, you won!'

In a second they were lying on the grass, their clothes damp with sweat, their breath coming hard, and all of a sudden Júlia, normally so physically hesitant, pressed herself against him, kissed his neck, slid a hand under his shirt and ran her fingers up his back. They kissed and kissed, until she pushed him away and jumped to her feet.

'Sprint home!' she said, setting off. He ran and caught her up, taking hold of her hand, but not with his little finger. That was too trivial now that they had broken all the rules by rolling on the grass together, so he took her whole hand in his and squeezed it tight.

'I love you,' he said.

She stared at him with a serious look on her face, smiled beautifully, but said nothing, letting go of his hand and setting off again. He jogged thoughtfully behind her. He could perfectly understand her unwillingness to say that she loved him; it was too binding, such words were too strong, and things with her dad were the way they were, after all. Once the bomb had gone off, everything would be different. Then she would see the world differently, and then she would certainly tell him what he wanted to hear.

85

'Take it easy, will you! I'm not the first one to take a turn on her tonight!'

'That's supposed to be some kind of excuse, is it?' Kent snarled, tightening his grip.

The youth stood on his toes, as if he was nailed to the wall, with one of Kent's hands at his throat and the other squeezing his balls. As far as Agla could make out, Kent was squeezing hard. They seemed to be functioning as one, as if Agla's fury at what they had found was manifesting itself through Kent's body; he had reacted precisely as she would have done if only she had the strength. She turned her back to Kent and the boy he was reading the riot act to, and kneeled by the bed. Elísa lay apparently completely unconscious, naked below the waist and with the turquoise Adidas top unzipped and her T-shirt hauled up above her breasts.

Agla could feel the pressure grow in her throat as rage swelled in her heart, and somehow what hurt the most was not what they had come across – the stupid boy who had decided to take advantage of Elísa's state, or her drugged stupor – it was Elísa's ribs, clearly visible below her little breasts. She was so thin – far too thin; her young body neglected for so long. And Agla suddenly realised that in all likelihood she would be unable to save her. This was an undertaking too big for her to handle. She pulled down the shirt and zipped up the top, but Elísa's trousers were nowhere to be seen in the gloomy room, so she pulled the sheet off the bed and wrapped it around her lower half.

'Can you carry her?' she asked Kent, who nodded.

'What are we going to do with her?' he asked, one hand still around the young man's throat, and Alga thought she could see his face darkening.

'I don't know,' Agla said, truthfully.

It was rare for her to concede defeat or to be unsure of what to do next, but at this moment she was unable to see any way forward. The best thing they could hope for was to get Elísa to Vernd before curfew.

Kent hissed a few well-chosen words into the boy's ear and let him go, allowing him to limp away, nodding his head ceaselessly.

Kent picked Elísa up, carried her out of the flat and laid her on the back seat of the car. Agla clipped the seat belt together before getting into the front. She needed to regain her composure, and Elísa's proximity brought back the painful pressure in her throat. Her head swam and she swore.

'Who the hell gains from all this?' she asked, half to herself, as Kent sat in the driver's seat and put out a hand for the keys.

'Gains?' he asked, starting the car and driving off.

'A situation in which everyone loses normally corrects itself, but for it to continue, there has to be someone, somewhere, who has something to gain from it.'

'You think of life in terms of profit and loss?' Kent said, winking at her.

Agla nodded.

'The fundamentals of existence,' she said.

There was silence in the car, until Kent brought it to a halt by the traffic lights on Miklabraut.

'Girls like Elísa are used as decoys,' he said.

'Decoys? What sort of decoys?'

'The Boss and all that crowd use girls like Elísa – junkies, kids they can control – and send them off as decoys.'

'And that means what, exactly?'

'The decoy goes abroad and is then sent back here on a flight, with a small amount of gear that's so badly packed that there's no chance of them not being picked up, while the real mule – who's often enough on the same flight, with a bigger amount, properly packed and hidden – just goes straight through because customs are busy with the decoy.'

'I can't see that Elísa is much use in the state she's in,' Agla said, 'either as a mule or a decoy.'

'No. They're working on her now. They're getting her ready, making sure she's broken and chaotic. After a few days of pill-popping and speed, she'll have breached her probation; she'll be hooked again and then she'll be offered a quick fix. They'll ask her to do one flight with some small amount, and in exchange they'll offer to fix her up in Copenhagen or somewhere with a stack of cash and all her debts paid. She'll be so fucked up that she'll believe it. I couldn't tell you how many times I've seen it happen.'

It was half past ten as they turned onto Laugateigur.

'We'll have to be quick,' Kent said. 'At quarter to eleven the night guy will be doing his rounds.'

86

Anton sat on the bench with one arm around Júlía and the other around the shoulders of his English friend, Tommy, while they watched his classmates playing the fool on the square. Somehow he felt that he had outgrown them. All the boys had stripped off their shirts and were in the middle of something that was halfway between a play fight and a wrestling match, the merciless spring sunshine giving their bodies pale-blue sheen. The girls sat on the benches and the flower tubs, chatting and giggling at the boys' antics. This had been a customary event for as long as the class had been together: to meet on the first sunny day after the end of term, go into town and treat themselves to hot dogs and ice cream. As Tommy was here as well, he had been brought along to join in the fun. It seemed to have been a good idea, as he laughed and laughed at the games the boys played, without taking part himself.

'These guys,' he spluttered, shaking his head as he laughed.

'They're a great bunch,' Anton said.

Tommy was like Anton – he seemed to be older than he was. He wore proper shirts instead of T-shirts and he read articles on the internet instead of watching TV. Anton surprised himself by having no desire to join in the fun. Instead he was satisfied to sit and watch, feeling Júlía's warmth against his side.

'When are you going to invite me to London to meet your friends?'

he asked, but wanted to bite his tongue the moment he saw the look on Tommy's face.

'Then you'll have to come to the school I go to in Switzerland,' Tommy said, and coughed, unscrewed the cap on a bottle of Coke and took a sip. 'I don't have any friends in London.'

'Yeah, I'd forgotten what a jet-setter you are,' Anton said, hoping to make up for his awkward question. He should have known better; Tommy had told him that he only rarely spent time in London with his mother, and there was something unpleasant about the whole arrangement. He should have taken care – he knew how uncomfortable questions about his own mother were. He turned to Júlía, to somehow put an end to an embarrassing situation.

'Not tomorrow, but the next day,' he whispered in her ear.

'What?'

'It's your birthday the day after tomorrow,' he said and smiled.

'You're more excited about my birthday than I am,' she said, elbowing him gently in the ribs.

'We're going somewhere really special for dinner,' he said. 'And there's a birthday present coming that is something you'd never guess in a million years.'

'You don't need to, well ... make a meal of it. There's no need to get excited about my birthday.'

'You're going to be sixteen,' he said, grinning. 'Sweet sixteen.'

Júlía laughed. 'You're the best there is,' she said, leaning in close beneath his arm.

'You're such a pair of sweeties!' called one of the girls, blowing them a kiss, and the others did the same. Júlía giggled, and Tommy gave Anton a slap on the back that told him he was the big guy. Anton smiled with pride. The two of them were somehow on a different level to the other youngsters. Maybe Júlía had always been on another level; she had always been different to the other girls, more serious. Now, in the square, under the spring sunshine, he understood why she had chosen him from among all the other boys in the class. He sat quietly on the bench with her, birthday celebrations on his mind, while the others strutted around and played the fool, with nothing on their minds beyond persuading as many girls as possible to suck them off.

'Not tomorrow, but the next day,' he whispered and kissed Júlía's cheek. 'Not tomorrow but the day after you'll get your birthday present.'

87

Sonja felt more depressed than she had for a long time, and the knot of anxiety in her belly grew with every hour that passed. Sebastian and Húni Thór had clearly emptied the store in an organised and efficient way, because she had spoken to everyone she imagined might have an idea about such a large shipment coming to Iceland, and they either knew nothing or were too frightened to say. The other option was so tough, Sonja couldn't allow herself to think it all the way to its conclusion. This was that everyone knew what was going on, but she had been taken out of the game.

She badly needed Bragi's help, so she had Rikki the Sponge drive her up to Lindargata, where she told him to collect her in two hours. Bragi wasn't someone she would open up to completely, but that wasn't what she was seeking. There was something about him that brought her down to earth – an authoritative, reliable energy about him that calmed her down. As they walked side by side to the lift in the sheltered accommodation apartment block where he now lived, she felt the tangle of nerves inside her soften. Bragi walked with a frame, painfully slowly, and although she longed to stride along the corridor, this leisurely amble was what she needed, enabling her to breathe deeply and tell him the news from London.

'Cutlets today,' Bragi said, smiling, as they went into the canteen. 'You chose the right day.'

They sat at a table by the window, and although his back was bent and his movements stiff, there was such a dignity to him, Sonja still saw him as the tall, imposing man in a customs uniform who had taken her and the huge shipment of drugs in her case to one side.

Sonja hadn't had much of an appetite, but once she started, she immediately felt hungry and ate the cutlets with gusto, along with the potatoes, onion gravy and salad, and finished by gnawing the bones.

'I'm frightened that I'm no longer needed,' she said in a low voice, dabbing at her lips with a napkin.

Bragi nodded and handed her a bowl of stewed rhubarb with cream. She put it away quickly, and finally felt that she was full. Bragi nodded towards the flasks of coffee at the far end of the dining room, so she fetched two mugs.

'Then it's your only opportunity to get out of this business,' Bragi said, sipping coffee through a lump of sugar that he held between his teeth. 'You're fortunate to get even one such opportunity.'

He was right. Somewhere in this situation was hidden a chance to get out, even though she couldn't see it right now. Or perhaps she didn't want to see it? She finished the coffee in her mug and put it down on the table. Bragi reached across and gently patted the back of her hand.

'There's a chance somewhere out there to extricate yourself from this vicious circle. You just need to want to grab it.'

Sonja swallowed the lump in her throat. He always saw through her. They understood each other. He was her conscience and she was the black stain on his.

88

The Grill Bar's dining room had long been one of Agla's favourite places. Its old-fashioned elegance, the chrome fittings and the star-speckled ceiling made her feel at home, and while in general she had nothing against change, there were some things that should remain unaltered. She ordered an alcohol-free cocktail, sipping it while she waited, and thought over the morning's events. She had been dressed up in fishing gear and about to head out of town towards Borgarfjörður when Elísa had appeared in the corridor outside her room at Vernd, in tears of despair. She had been asked to provide a urine sample. Agla had taken the beaker out of her hands and resolved things.

'There you go,' she said, back in the corridor, handing over the warm sample beaker. 'Nobody should be able to tell it's not yours.'

'Was it the amphetamine cook who helped you get me home yesterday?' Elísa had asked, and Agla smiled as she finally understood the big man's nickname. 'I don't remember much apart from you and the cook putting me to bed.'

'There's nothing to remember,' Agla said. 'We came and fetched you from a party.'

'Did I call you?'

'Yes,' Agla said. 'You called, so Kent came with me to collect you.'

She had no intention of explaining the real circumstances under which they had found Elísa. She seemed to be plagued by enough guilt as it was. Then she had leaned on Agla and wept in her arms. After the night's sleep Agla was free of the tension in her throat – her thoughts were clear, and she felt strangely contented with her arms around Elísa's trembling shoulders.

'Hello there, Agla!' Ingimar said warmly as he marched into the Grill Bar with William Tedd and another man Agla had never seen before at his heels.

'Mike Linane, Agla Margeirsdóttir. Agla, Mike,' Ingimar said.

Agla offered Mike a hand. His grip was soft and warm. This was a handsome older man, expensively dressed and with a beautiful smile. The chairman of the Meteorite Metals board. She knew he wouldn't have much to say this evening. She had often used members-for-hire herself to man the boards of various companies. For a while she had even put the janitor at the building she owned in Luxembourg on the boards of a few. All that was needed was to look good in a suit and to have a clean record. She hugged William and kissed him, French-style, three times on the cheeks. She hoped that he would forgive her for what she was about to do; he was the one man who came close to being a friend.

They had made themselves comfortable around the table when Jón joined them. The others appeared surprised by his appearance, and he seemed taken aback to see them too. Agla watched, admiring how they all pretended that nothing was wrong. She had told Ingimar that it was about Meteorite, but she had told Jón nothing. Once they were all seated, William ordered a bottle of wine, but Agla placed a hand over her glass, even though this was an evening to celebrate.

The waiter brought menus and with Ingimar and William discussing the eight-course option and Jón complaining that it was all too much, Agla decided to cut to the chase.

'I'm not going to be dining with you, gentlemen,' she said. 'I just wanted to inform you, face to face, that Meteorite Metals is under new ownership. It's always so unpleasant to get that kind of news over the phone.'

Jón stared at her inquiringly, and Ingimar raised an eyebrow. William sat expressionless, waiting to hear more, while Mike the chairman was still eyeing the menu hungrily. There was no doubt in her mind that they thought she'd brought them here because she wanted to be a part of their scheme, that they would haggle over dinner and at the end of the evening they would sell her a small stake in exchange for an exorbitant amount of money.

'What do you mean by new ownership?' Ingimar asked, shifting in his chair, obviously uncomfortable. Ingimar always coped badly with losing control.

'As of midnight I'm the main shareholder in Meteorite Metals. It's a pretty neat system you've cooked up there.'

'That's impossible!' Jón burst out. His eyes seemed about to pop out of his narrow face, but at the same time an understanding smile appeared on William's.

'Could Pierre's salmon fishing trip to Iceland have had anything to do with this?'

His smile now turned to a pained rictus.

'Yes. Pierre and I cast a few lines together today,' Agla said. 'Just about the time he landed a twenty-pounder, the bank offloaded its share in this scam. It was relieved to do so, as it's a pretty dubious business, what with stockpiling aluminium contravening all kinds of international regulations.'

The men sat in silence while Mike looked from one to the other, his face one big question.

'Enjoy your evening, gentlemen,' Agla said as she stood up. 'The bill is on me.'

She was almost out in the corridor when she turned; with a smile she walked back to the silent men around the table.

She leaned close to Ingimar's ear.

'I assume that María and I will have our ID numbers reinstated tomorrow morning,' she whispered to him.

89

It was the first time that Ingimar had used the safe word to stop *her* halfway through a flogging. They hadn't been going long enough for the endorphins to kick in with their rush of wellbeing. Instead he had been overflowing with stress and adrenaline, while the pain in his back was becoming unbearable. Although she had stopped the second he had used the safe word, a quarter of an hour had passed during which he had sat on the sofa and cried like a baby.

'I need painkillers,' he said, and she went to the kitchen, returning with a couple of tablets and a glass of water.

'If this is connected to me being busy when you called yesterday, you know I have a life outside of all this.'

Ingimar shook his head.

'No, no, no, my sweet. It's not about you. It's another problem that's biting my arse.'

'Tell me,' she ordered, arms folded as she stood in front of him.

'You know I need you to ... I don't know exactly how to put it: bring me down a peg or two.'

'To remind you what a worthless little worm you really are.'

'That's it.' Ingimar smiled. 'To put it in a nutshell, there's another woman who brought me down quite a few pegs this evening. Let's say she whipped me thoroughly in a piece of business.'

'That's just as well, maggot,' she said, and he nodded.

'Perhaps,' he said thoughtfully. 'Perhaps it serves me right. It may well be that it's healthy to not win every time.'

She sat at his side, stroked his hair and inspected his back.

'You're all right,' she said.

He got to his feet.

'I'll make the usual deposit,' he said.

'There's no need,' she said. 'You didn't get anything for your money.'

She held out his shirt to help him into it.

'No arguments,' he said, lifting a hand with one finger raised to indicate that he wouldn't listen to her protests. As if he was ready to accept charity from a skint student! This evening had been terrible enough already.

'Show your face again when your pride's getting too much for you,' she ordered. 'Worm.'

He smiled and kissed her cheek.

He would return when he was back to his usual self. He hoped he'd soon feel well enough to require her services again. Hopefully Agla hadn't ruined this for him as well.

90

'It's good to see you under rather more pleasant circumstances,' George Beck said.

Agla smiled. This was much more comfortable than having the glass screen between them up at Hólmsheiði. They had gone to the Jómfrú Scandinavian Kitchen on Lækjargata for Danish-style *smørrebrød*. George also paid full attention to the beer and schnapps on offer while they had talked through a whole range of subjects that had nothing to do with business, as if this was a premature celebration of their joint success.

'Well,' George said as the coffee arrived, indicating that it was time to turn to serious matters.

Agla was prepared. She took from her briefcase a sheet of paper with a short summary concerning Meteorite Metals and handed it to him.

'This is the bottleneck you've been looking for,' she said. 'This company is sitting on all of the LME-registered stock that hasn't been in circulation.'

'Stockpiling?'

'Not exactly,' Agla explained. 'There are restrictions on stockpiling, so what they have done is to restrict the flow to a trickle, cranking up the price that can be fixed through supply and demand – that's to say, they're limiting the amount of unregistered product on the market.'

George sighed.

'It's brilliant,' he said.

'True,' Agla said, and she had to agree. The scam had been on such a large scale and it had brought in so much cash, she couldn't deny it was a work of genius. 'And it's within legal limits, but only just,' she added.

'And who is behind all this?'

'That no longer matters. I have arranged to buy the company and I'm prepared to sell it for the right price.'

'Ah, I understand.' George smiled. 'So you're ready with the next move? I expected nothing less of you. And what might be your idea of the right price?'

Now it was Agla's turn to smile. She wrote a number on a serviette and pushed it across the table. George picked it up and peered at it. Then he brought it closer, his eyes half closing as he examined it, counting the zeroes. He put the serviette down, half opened his mouth and closed it again, shifted in his chair and cleared his throat.

'Wow.'

'Yes.' Agla's smile broadened. 'As you can imagine, I've had to pay out a substantial amount to buy the company, and while it's run at a colossal loss, there are individuals on both sides who are prepared to pay well to gain control of it: on one side are the large aluminium consumers such as your company; and on the other are those connected to aluminium producers who would be keen to restrict the flow even further.'

'I see.'

George got to his feet, took out his phone and went outside to the pavement. While he conferred with his people, Agla decided to use the time to take out her own phone and call William. There was a text message from Kent waiting for her on the screen: *Can't find her anywhere.*

Agla had asked him to search around for Elísa. This was no longer about getting her back to Vernd before the curfew. It was too late for that; she'd breached her probation conditions by failing to return to the hostel the previous evening. Now Agla was simply worried about her. She felt the ache welling up in her throat at the thought of Elísa lying helpless somewhere in dubious company and in an even more dubious condition.

She shook the feeling off and called William's number. He was cheerful in spite of his defeat, ready to start working towards a deal. Agla had always appreciated how quick he was at taking in the big picture.

'I'd be interested to get a figure – what you'd expect to receive for maintaining Meteorite's activity unchanged,' he said. 'We're talking a respectable slice of the cake.'

This was what Agla had wanted to hear.

'It's worth thinking about,' she said. 'But that slice would have to be very respectable, considering the size of the investment.'

'Aren't you happy, Agla?' William laughed. 'If I'd landed a deal like this one I'd be on the way to Las Vegas in a private jet. You have the whole thing in the palm of your hand.'

Agla smiled to herself. This was no idle description. He was just the type to head for a party in a private jet.

'I'm satisfied,' Agla replied. 'I have a few loose ends that need to be tied up, and I need to get rid of this ankle tag, then I'll join you for a night on the town.'

'Promise?' William asked.

'I promise,' Agla said.

'And you'll send me a figure?'

'I'll think it over.'

She would think it through in the unlikely event that George and his people didn't come on board. A deal with William and Ingimar was her Plan B.

'My people and I are amenable to reaching an agreement – one that we believe you'll be fully satisfied with,' George said as he returned. He looked relieved, and waved for the waiter to bring him another schnapps.

'I'm pleased to hear it,' Agla said.

In fact she hadn't been concerned at all; a consortium of one of the world's largest soft-drinks producers, a leading international aircraft manufacturer and a computer giant wouldn't hesitate to pay out money to ensure its access to vital raw material. She would happily knock half a billion krónur off the figure she had written on the serviette, and everyone would then feel they had come out a winner. This was one of the largest deals she had pulled off, and all without having to do much for it. But William had been right. She wasn't particularly happy.

91

María was deep in printing out annual reports and information about Meteorite, highlighting key points in yellow, when her computer pinged a warning that sounded like a virus alert. When she looked more closely, however, she saw that it was a piece of software that Marteinn had installed for her so that she could monitor websites she wanted to keep an eye on. She could instruct it to alert her whenever a particular word or phrase was posted.

This time it was from MarketWatch – a new mention of Meteorite Metals. She clicked the link and a news item opened, detailing trading in a majority shareholding in Meteorite and changes to the board of directors. María stared at the names of the two entities that had bought the Paris bank's holding in the company. These were names that she knew well, and had long been familiar with. This went all the way back to her time at the special prosecutor's office. Although at the time it had been difficult to prove who the owner was, she knew perfectly well that Agla owned both companies.

'Explain this to me,' she snapped into the phone the moment Agla answered. 'Explain to me how you've become the owner of a semi-bankrupt aluminium storage company. What the actual fuck?' Agla laughed as if it were funny and this only made María increasingly furious. 'Don't tell me you're working with Ingimar to corner the aluminium market?'

'Hey, take it easy. You don't think I wanted to dig into this purely for the investigative journalism? If all the soft drinks company had wanted was information, they would have simply employed a private eye, or an excellent journalist such as yourself. When a company like this brings in someone like me as a consultant, it means they want to see involvement.'

'And what then? Are you going to take over where that bastard Ingimar left off and sit there with all the world's aluminium stocks under your bed?'

'No, not at all, María. This is just a move in the game. I'm not contemplating involvement in any business, neither aluminium nor anything else.'

'Aha.' Now María understood. 'I imagine the soft drinks people will be prepared to buy Meteorite off you for a decent price?'

'Now you're learning!' Agla said. 'Send me an invoice for everything you've done, and don't be shy when it comes to the figure.'

'Fucking disgusting! Everything you touch is revolting!'

María's voice shook with rage. Suddenly the feeling she had long had about Agla, ever since she had cost her her job at the prosecutor's office, came bursting to the surface. The woman was simply poison. Everything she touched turned out badly for everyone except herself. María had been burned by her dealings with her, and now Agla was about to make some astronomical amount of money from an affair that had cost María untold pain and, possibly, Marteinn his life. But Agla would land on her feet like some infernal cat that nobody could ever stop.

María yelled with all the power she had in her. It was good to scream and be angry, it blanketed the powerlessness and the disappointment. Anger was as good as a painkiller for sorrow.

92

Ewa the warder was at reception and seemed genuinely pleased to see Agla again.

'How are you?' she asked, after looking her up and down.

'I'm just fine,' Agla said, placing her bag and coat in the storage locker. It was quite true: she was feeling good, and after the relief of knowing that Elísa was back in prison and not dead somewhere, she could finally allow herself to enjoy her triumph with the successful Meteorite deal. Less than an hour after she had heard that Elísa was back at Hólmsheiði, having broken her probation conditions, George had called to let her know that his company had agreed to co-operate with another large aluminium user and accept her original offer for Meteorite Metals. That meant an extra few hundred million krónur she hadn't been expecting.

'You know this has to be a window visit,' Ewa said apologetically, opening the door to the inner reception area. She asked Agla to wait a moment while she fetched a handheld scanner to check her. As the door closed behind Ewa, the door to the visiting area swung open and out came another prison officer, Sigurgeir, with a woman behind him.

For a moment time stood still as Agla watched the woman follow Sigurgeir the few steps from the door to the outer reception. Her hair was darker and she was taller than Agla remembered, but her quick movements and attractive face were at the same time both intimately familiar and strange. There was a scar on her chin that hadn't been there before. Agla stared at it as if it could in some way explain all the missing years.

'Sonja.'

She said no more, but it was enough to make Sonja glance up and stare at her in return.

'*Hæ,*' Sonja said, and there was an element of wonder in her voice.

Agla found herself unable to say another word, and even if her life had depended on it, she could not have defined the emotion that swelled inside her as she looked Sonja over. She wanted to go over and throw her arms around her, but the time that had been lost between them put that out of the question. They were no longer close and had become strangers.

She also longed to punch her.

'How are you?' Sonja asked, as if they were no more than casual acquaintances who met a couple of times a year to drink coffee and exchange superficial gossip. There was nothing in her answer that gave any inkling of why she had walked out and disappeared so soon after declaring her delight with the new house and with Agla.

Having whispered her love so often into Agla's ear, it now came down to 'how are you?'

Agla had no answer to her question. She turned away and knocked on the warders' door to hurry Ewa along, and when she turned back, Sigurgeir was locking the outer door behind Sonja.

'You know each other?' Sigurgeir asked.

Agla shook her head.

'No,' she said. 'Not really.'

Ewa appeared with what she referred to as her magic wand, ran it over Agla's body and read off the numbers.

'She's as clean as a whistle,' she pronounced, smiling like a proud parent, and Sigurgeir opened the door to the visitors' corridor, pointing her towards room number two.

Agla entered the room in a daze. But as she approached the glass she was wrenched from her thoughts, as if the earth's gravity had hauled her back to the ground. Elísa was sitting hunched in a chair behind the window, weeping.

'Shh, don't cry,' Agla said as she picked up the handset on her side. 'I'm not angry with you, sweetheart.'

She had no intention of adding to Elísa's guilt for having messed up her probation. She knew precisely how women felt when they were brought back to prison for the third or fourth time. They could dish out their own servings of self-reproach.

'I'm just deep in the shit,' Elísa said. 'The Boss gave me a massive bollocking just before you got here.'

'The Boss? The Boss came here? You mean the drugs Boss?'

'She said horrible things about what she would do if I opened my mouth. If I was going to grass, then I would have done it by now. I don't need a visit like that every time I get locked up.'

'She? You said "she"? Is the Boss a woman?'

Elísa stared into her lap and wiped her face with her sleeve.

'Just when was this Boss here?'

Elísa raised her head, a look of surprise on her tearful face, and Agla realised how sharp her voice had been.

'Just now,' Elísa said. 'She's just left. Didn't you see her?'

Black dots danced before Agla's eyes. She sat down hard in the chair, and for a moment she felt as if the blood had drained from her head and she was about to faint.

'Elísa,' she said, her words heavy with emphasis. 'Is Sonja the Boss?'

93

Anton listened to Radio Edda while he fixed up the cardboard box that surrounded the toolbox containing the bomb. The subject for discussion was the welfare system, and several callers were adamant that immigrants moving to Iceland and living on benefits were spongers. Karl, who was a frequent caller and who described himself as having 'a master's degree in life', came on the line, and at first there was a light-hearted discussion with the presenter. After all, he had called in so often that they knew each other well.

'What we can say is that Icelanders are buying their own terror threat by letting all these Muslims into the country and supporting them through the welfare system while they could be preparing terror attacks!'

Anton closed his eyes and took a couple of deep breaths. This kind of talk filled him with trepidation; but at the same time it was good to hear as it reminded him of why he was preparing this bomb. It was to make Iceland safer for Júlía; to make the world a safer place for her. He had promised her father that he would look after her, and judging by what he heard on Radio Edda, it was time for action. This kind of thing couldn't be allowed to continue unchecked.

He folded the box shut, not intending to tape it closed until he had put it in place and activated the bomb. He eased it onto the sack truck that had been Gunnar's final contribution; as he had completely forgotten that his family were all going to Spain as soon as school broke up, so instead of being there to help Anton carry the bomb, he had brought him the sack truck. As much as Gunnar was obsessed with explosions and always wanted to make as much noise as he could, Anton had the feeling that he was actually relieved that the forgotten summer holiday had come up.

'I'll be watching the news from Spain, my man!' he had said as Anton gritted his teeth and swore to himself. The only thing that would be more difficult to do without Gunnar's help was place the bomb where it was needed; but it wasn't impossible. He had decided that he would need to borrow his father's car.

The hard part was lifting the bomb into the boot, but it wasn't so heavy that he couldn't manage it – it just required a little effort. The drawback was that he would be longer getting the bomb in and out of the car. But there was no point sulking about Gunnar any longer. It had been Anton's own idea and, in truth, it was better for him to be alone at the finish. The responsibility for the explosion would be solely his.

It was as well that his father had an electric car, because it made no sound as he switched it on. He had lain in bed for forty minutes after he had heard his father turn in, waiting until he was certain that he was asleep. He had gone to bed later than Anton had hoped he would, but things were still on schedule.

He set off slowly, carefully looking about as he did so. Being picked up by the police for driving without a licence and with a big bomb in the boot would be no fun at all. But by keeping clear of main roads as much as possible and by threading his way along side streets through the Thingholt district and up into Norðurmýri, he was able to park the car safely in a gateway on Brautarholt where it was out of sight. He had printed out a false set of numbers on two large stickers and had stuck them onto the plates; from a distance they looked pretty convincing, so long as it didn't rain. If that happened, the ink would run and the stickers would turn to mush.

This was one of the security features in his grand plan. The false numbers were in fact those for an identical car, so if he were seen on a security camera somewhere, that would be the vehicle the police would start searching for.

The other security measure was to park in the next street but one. This was a cramped, quiet residential street where there were no companies with CCTV cameras. He put on his hat, then pulled up his hood, tugging it forwards over his forehead, and retrieved the sack truck from the back seat. It was harder to get the box containing the bomb from the boot, but he managed it eventually, placed it on the sack truck and tied it down with a couple of bungee cords he had taken from the garage at home.

There was no wind and the light was wonderfully blue, as it always was at night at this time of year. He wheeled the sack truck silently along the street. There was nobody about, although to be sure he stopped at the corner to listen out for any traffic. All he could hear was the distant whine of a motorcycle up on Laugavegur, so he hurried across the street and into the car park. He could feel a stab of anticipation and terror in his stomach, which only passed when he pushed the sack truck up past the building and around the back. There was a window there that he had planned to smash using the monkey wrench that was in the box, but there was no need for it. The window hadn't been properly hooked shut. He slid a hand through the gap to open it and a moment later he was inside.

He carefully opened the door into the corridor, peeping through the gap to be sure, but the place was dark and silent. He went to the back door and opened it, putting the doormat in the opening to stop it closing behind him while he fetched the sack truck with the bomb and rolled it inside and along the corridor.

Gunnar wouldn't be happy that he had left the sack truck behind, but he could buy him another one to replace the one he had borrowed from his cousin. It was old and battered and would be destroyed in the explosion, so it wouldn't be traceable, and it was safer not to have to take it back to the car. That reduced the likelihood of any passers-by paying him any attention.

Anton stopped the sack truck in the middle of the corridor, opened the box and the toolbox inside, and activated the bomb. Then he closed the hasp of the toolbox's lid and jogged out into the corridor.

He hurried away as soon as he was outside, not that there was any danger yet. It wasn't time for the explosion. He still had to go home and erase any traces left from when he'd put the bomb together. In the morning he would be back here, and he'd have the remote control with him.

94

The *Spotlight* team were interested and had struck a deal with María on the basis that the TV programme's editor agreed to buy her Meteorite story. They had sat into the night listening to every minor detail of the story, making notes and then calling the editor, waking him up in the process. He responded by saying that he was fully booked the following day but suggested a meeting at seven, before usual working hours, to go over the matter and finalise a contract.

María had told them the whole story, not omitting Agla's role in it. She was still angry, although maybe not as livid with Agla as she was with herself. She should have known that Agla would never have become involved in investigating someone else's misdeeds unless there was something in it for her. What María had failed to appreciate was how dearly it would cost her personally to take on this assignment on Agla's behalf. She thought over the whole investigation – the revolver's muzzle pressed hard against her cheek, the truck driver with his fist bunched around her wrist, the days in the dark cell, Marteinn's death. She had told the *Spotlight* team that she expected the payment for her work to reflect the effort that had gone into this. But payment wasn't the chief issue. She knew that she could go to Agla and get more from her for *not* using the story than the state broadcaster would pay for it. But if the TV bought the story and ran it, then foreign media would also latch on to it – an international conspiracy story always made great headlines – and that would give María the recognition she was looking for; the recognition that The Squirrel was a medium for genuine investigative journalism. On top of that, perhaps Icelanders would also wake up to the reality of what was happening to their natural resources.

She hadn't slept, instead spending the night lying awake and staring at the ceiling. Finally she got up, made herself some coffee and made her way to The Squirrel's office to collect all the paperwork connected to the story and the computer containing her own narrative, which she would hand over to the *Spotlight* team as soon as they had signed a contract. It was half past five; she didn't have to be at the state TV's offices until seven, so she still had plenty of time to tweak her story before she had to leave.

She parked behind the building. The spot was empty and although it was intended for deliveries, including to the grocery store next door, she often parked there when she was in a hurry. She fumbled in her bag for the keys as she walked towards the building, but when she got there she saw that the door was open and a doormat had been placed in the doorway. She checked her watch in surprise. It was early, but it looked like she wasn't the only one who was out and about at this hour. She hoped it wasn't Radio Edda's station manager as she had no time to spare to talk to him, but she could hardly be brusque with him after he had come to her aid when she had found Marteinn hanging in her office. She went inside, and looked quickly around but saw nothing untoward – only that someone must have been making a delivery to Radio Edda, as there was a sack truck with a box on it in the corridor.

95

Anton's heart felt as if it was about to burst as he jogged breathlessly over Skothús Bridge and turned along the path that ran along the lake and curved up towards Tjarnargata. He was dressed in tracksuit trousers and a windcheater, with the headphones of his iPod dangling around his neck, so it looked as if he was genuinely out for a run for the sake of his health.

He had run straight back through Norðurmýri and across Skólavörðuholt as soon as he had been able to make himself move. For a moment it had been as if the explosion had rooted him to the spot with terror, and while the pall of smoke dissipated and tongues of flame took hold of the sides of the building, he could no longer feel his own feet.

When he'd heard the wailing sirens he'd realised it was time to go. The fire brigade used cameras to film any bystanders at house fires, and he had no wish to be on their footage. He could hardly tear himself away, though. It was like trying to run in a swimming pool, and even the resistance of the air was a barrier to break through. He had walked with difficulty up the slope and when he was on Skipholt he remembered that he needed to get rid of the remote control, so he dropped it on the ground and stamped on it a few times until all that was left was a pile of plastic fragments and a tangle of wires. He picked up the plastic rubbish and stuffed it in his pocket, then suddenly felt his energy return as he began to run, not slowing down until he was on Fríkirkjuvegur, where he stuffed the remnants of the remote in a bin and jogged on in the direction of the bridge.

When he reached his house, he gingerly opened the door. His whole plan had been delayed. He hadn't managed to clear up the bomb-making stuff in the basement, and was later getting home than he had intended.

All the same, he had managed to set the bomb off before seven, before anyone who worked there had arrived. He listened carefully and heard nothing that indicated his father was up, so he slipped off his shoes and tiptoed upstairs to his room. He lay in bed wearing his sweaty running gear and switched on his computer. The news simply stated that the Reykjavík fire service had been called out to attend a large explosion.

Although he was already hot, when he heard his father moving about he pulled the duvet up to his throat. In fact, since school had broken up he had stopped coming in to wake him in the mornings, but to be safe, Anton decided to pretend to be asleep, just in case his father should look in. But he heard him go down the stairs and run through his usual routine. First he heard the snap of the letterbox as his father took the newspaper, and then heard water running, followed by the coffee machine at work. A moment later there were footsteps on the stairs and he heard the shower running in the guest bathroom.

He scrolled through a few websites; some of them already had pictures. He peered at one, looking hard at the scarred building. It seemed to be holding itself up by force of habit alone: a large portion of the lower wall looked to have disintegrated. When he had stood nearby with the remote in his hand, he had shut his eyes, expecting to hear a bang. He had anticipated quite a loud explosion but hadn't been ready for the ground to shake under his feet and for windows in the surrounding buildings to be shattered by the blast. He had never imagined just how powerful the explosion was going to be.

96

The glint in her eye had gone, replaced by a kind of hardness that Agla hadn't seen before. Kent had easily been able to get hold of Sonja's phone number, and to Agla's surprise, she had agreed to meet for coffee. Now they sat in worn armchairs by the window in Iða Zimsen's coffee shop and awkwardly looked each other over.

'The town's going crazy today,' Sonja said.

It took Agla a moment to realise that she meant the explosion. She hadn't been able to concentrate on anything since they had run into each other at the prison the day before, so today's lurid headlines had passed her by.

'Coffee? Latte or espresso, or something?' Agla asked and was about to stand up when Sonja stopped her.

'Agla, I owe you an explanation,' she said, leaning forwards in her chair. The steely look in her eye gave way to a softness that at one time would have melted Agla's heart. 'When I left it wasn't because I wanted to; there were circumstances beyond my control. I was forced to go to London, and although it might not be easy to accept, it was better for you that we broke off all contact.'

'You don't need to sugar-coat anything. I know you're the Boss.'

Agla was taken by surprise – it seemed her longstanding need for an explanation had vanished. Now that she sat opposite Sonja, she no longer wanted to hear her side of the story.

'Oh.' Sonja looked disappointed and frowned sadly. Agla was familiar enough with her mannerisms to know that she was searching for the right words. 'If you know that,' she said, haltingly, 'then you'll be aware that the business I got caught up in isn't exactly easy. I wasn't making the decisions and would never have left you if I hadn't been forced to—'

'I'm not here to talk about us,' Agla said firmly, cutting her off mid-sentence. Instead of being soft, as she had expected to be, she found that inside she was as hard as stone. She was here for one reason and in truth there was nothing else she wanted from Sonja. 'I want to buy Elísa's freedom from you and your people.'

Sonja stared thoughtfully at her for a while.

'I understand,' she said. 'That's who you went to visit in prison yesterday?'

Agla nodded.

'Tell me how much you want for her,' she said.

Sonja sat up sharply, and as she did so, the hardness returned to her eyes.

'I don't know what you've heard from Elísa, but the truth is that her situation is mainly of her own making,' she said. 'And I doubt that you can save her from it.'

'I doubt it as well,' Agla said. 'But I intend to try. I want you to let her go, and for all the people under your control – which I understand is practically the whole of Reykjavík's drug trade – to put her off limits, so that she can't buy dope anywhere.'

'You're massively overestimating my influence,' Sonja said, and looked searchingly at Agla for a moment. 'Are you in love with her?'

Agla swallowed and shrugged. The last thing she wanted was to share confidences with Sonja.

'Perhaps,' she said.

'I see.' Sonja's eyes were still fixed on her, but her expression had become gentler. 'It's the least I can do for you,' she said. 'I'll pass the word around that Elísa is a grass. That's the best way to make sure nobody will have anything to do with her.' Sonja stood up and slipped into her coat. 'I'm relieved that you've found someone to love. I was hoping that you weren't still alone.'

97

The squawks of the seagulls drowned out her scream. As she had left the coffee house she'd signalled to Alex to keep his distance, and had then marched down to the quayside, where she stood and yelled with all her breath into the harbour. The tension that had been brewing inside her since Húni Thór had arrived, saying that he was taking the store, seemed to have boiled over as she sat opposite Agla in the coffee shop.

To begin with she had been relaxed and at ease, but there was something about Agla's movements that put her on edge, the way she laid a hand on her knee; without wanting to, Sonja recalled those fingers inside her, and her body responded with a racing heartbeat and a flush of heat.

Agla had changed. She came across as uncannily cold, which was a surprise as while she had always been stiff, she'd never been icy. Sonja had always sensed that there was some kind of inner turmoil Agla was constantly fighting to conquer. But now that was gone. There was no longer any tension between them. Maybe that was no surprise, now that Agla knew all about her. Anyone who knew who she was, who genuinely knew what she did, could only have one feeling towards her: fear.

Now, standing on the quayside and yelling, she was swamped by a wave of regret, but she didn't know if it was the pain of lost love that she should have experienced all those years ago when she left Agla and which had now returned with a vengeance, or if she was standing on the quayside mourning for herself, for the Sonja she had once been; the person she could have been.

'Now then, that's enough,' Alex said, taking hold of her shoulders, turning her around and leading her back up the dock and towards the town. Sonja dried her face with her sleeve and sniffed. Screaming had left her half choked with sobs.

'We might need to organise an escape route,' she said. 'If I don't find out how Húni Thór is going to bring the goods in, then I can't stop him, and once he has a large-scale transport route, then I'm no longer needed. And you know what Sebastian does with people who are surplus to requirements.'

'We'll draw up an escape plan,' he said. 'The question is, does Tómas come with us or not?'

Sonja gasped. She would either have to leave Tómas with his father, which was a risk, or take him with her on the run, which itself was extremely high risk. It was a position she had not expected to be in, at least not with this suddenness.

'Shh,' Alex said, opening the car door and guiding her to a seat. 'You'll find someone who knows something. And Sponge is running around asking questions. He has a way of persuading people to tell him what they know.'

His tone was soothing and relaxing, as it always was when she lost her temper. It didn't happen often, but when it did, she could trust Alex to remain calm.

'And if I don't find anyone who knows anything, and Húni Þór manages to ship in one go as much as it takes me months to send using mules? That means he has the whole thing in his hands. Fucking, fucking, fuck.'

'Take one hour at a time,' Alex said. 'One at a time.' He started the car and pulled away. 'Now we need to go to Tómas's friend's place and pick up the backpack he forgot there. He called me and asked me to collect it; but I reckon there'll be fewer questions if his mother knocks and asks for it, rather than a foreign bodyguard.'

Sonja knew that Alex had been relieved to be asked to run this errand, and that he was aware that having something other than her own problems to think about would calm her down.

'Which friend?'

'The one who was on the football course with him last summer. The one who lives by the lake on Tjarnargata.'

'Anton.'

'That's him. Anton.'

98

'Let's order the five-course menu,' Anton said, smiling as Júlía's eyes opened wide at the sight of the prices. She frowned as if to indicate that it was far too expensive. 'Anything you want,' he added. 'Money's no object.'

They had ordered Coke, and the waiter had brought fresh-baked bread and some green-brown paste made from olives that Júlía eagerly spread on her slice. This had to be the kind of thing she was used to at home. He had often been offered some strange spicy jams and chutneys in her house.

'You're sure?' she whispered. 'All this is three or four trips to the movies for us.'

Anton laughed. The evening had begun just as he had wanted it to. Júlía was almost shy of the smart, formal atmosphere and had undoubtedly never seen such expensive food before in her life. She wore a dress Anton hadn't seen before, which shimmered blue-green. He wore a shirt, with a tie that his father had knotted for him and a jacket that he had taken off and hung on the back of his chair, because he was hot and didn't want to be embarrassingly red in the face. The low-key sound of a piano tinkled in the background, there were real flowers on the table and candles flickering inside little lanterns. His father had chosen the perfect place for them.

The waiter returned and asked if they were ready to order. He was young, which Anton found a little disconcerting as it was obvious that he saw them as a pair of kids; Anton was concerned they wouldn't get the same level of service as the other guests. He would have preferred an older man or woman with a less casual manner; someone who showed more respect.

'Is there any pork in the paté?' Júlía asked, pointing to an item on the five-course menu, the reindeer paté.

'I'm not sure,' the waiter said. 'I'll check with the chef. Do you have an allergy?'

'No,' Júlía said apologetically. 'I just don't want to eat pork.'

The waiter left and was soon back at their table.

'There's no pork in the paté, just a little lard.'

Júlía looked at Anton questioningly.

'Lard is pork fat,' he said.

'There's no taste to it,' the waiter explained. 'There's just the taste of reindeer, and the lard is used because reindeer meat is so lean...' he continued, apparently ready with a lecture on making paté, but Anton felt a surge of irritation and lifted a finger to stop him.

'She's a Muslim and doesn't eat anything containing pork,' he said. Then realised that he had maybe said that a little too bluntly, as Júlía sank down in her chair. She always felt uncomfortable under such circumstances, and of all nights, this was not the one for her to have to listen to any kind of crap.

'We'd like to order from the five-course menu, and would appreciate it if the chef can provide something to replace the paté,' he said. 'Something that doesn't contain pork.'

99

Ingimar spent a long time under the shower, the hot water softening his skin before he shaved. His bristles were so tough that it made a difference if he allowed himself the time to have a good soak first. Normally, if he was at home in the evening, he would put on comfortable trousers and a T-shirt, but today he took his best suit from the wardrobe and selected a good shirt to go with it. He decided against a tie, leaving the shirt open at the neck, and then splashed himself liberally with aftershave. It stung, but the sting was refreshing. He brushed his teeth and patted down his hair as he inspected himself in the mirror.

Helping Anton prepare for the birthday meal with Júlía had put him in the mood. Everything he had explained to him about how he should groom himself and treat the lady had triggered his own desire to be somewhere with a drink in one hand and a beautiful woman on his arm. There was no point letting Agla destroy his zest for life.

His phone pinged and he swore as he read the message. His date had pulled out; something unexpected had come up at the last moment. The truth of it probably was that she had looked him up in the National Registry or somewhere to check on his age. That was one of the problems with Tinder, his usual charm didn't come across. He suddenly recalled another girl. He scrolled though his contacts, looking for her number. He had hung on to it even though he rarely liked to sleep with the same woman twice. This one was rather special though. She was young, gorgeous and had a daddy complex that left her with a weakness for older men. He punched in a message and had a reply within seconds: *Go fuck yourself Ingimar*.

'You look smart,' Rebekka said as he came down the stairs. 'Where are you off to?'

Ingimar went over to her and kissed her forehead. The wind had been taken out of his sails, and the moment he saw Rebekka all the energy drained from him, and he realised that he couldn't be bothered to go to some bar to pick up a woman.

'Nowhere. I'm staying here with you.'

Rebekka seemed to be taken by surprise. They had not touched for a long time and any kind of tenderness between them was a rarity. But she was quick to sidestep it.

'Isn't that jacket getting too small for you?' she said, and he waited for the expected insult. 'You great lummock.'

He tried to pull the jacket closed over his midriff, but couldn't. In any case, he always left the jacket open, so nobody would see that it didn't make any difference that it couldn't be buttoned up.

'We're neither of us at our best,' he said, and Rebekka looked nonplussed, before turning away, topping up her glass and taking another mouthful.

'Not me, at any rate,' she said, stretching with theatrical exaggeration. She wore creased pyjamas, no make-up and her hair was in disarray. 'It's a while since I was at my best,' she said and sat on a chair at the kitchen table.

'Would you like something to eat?' Ingimar asked. 'A couple of fried eggs or some toast?'

'Don't act as if you give a shit whether I eat anything or not. That kind of pretend concern gets on my tits.'

Ingimar sat opposite her at the table. He knew he could break down her defences by coming closer, by massaging her shoulders, whispering something to her to tell her that he still loved her, holding her close and stroking her hair. Then she would become docile; she'd spread her legs and would cry as she came, but in the morning she would start looking through his phone, asking what the hell he was doing on Tinder, scream and argue, swallow more pills and then settle back into a daze; and he couldn't be bothered with that either. He was worn out, tired of everything.

'It's not a pretence,' he said. 'I'm thinking of Anton. I'd prefer it if he doesn't have to bury his mother before he's out of his teens.'

'Oh, shut your face,' Rebekka retorted, then stood up and stormed out of the kitchen.

He was about to follow and shout something up the stairs at her, when a ring at the doorbell stopped him in his tracks.

100

Anton's arm rested around Júlía's shoulders as they strolled away from the restaurant. The air was cool, but without a breath of wind, and the slopes of Mount Esja across the bay glowed pink in the bright evening light.

'Where are we going?' she asked, and Anton smiled.

'We'll walk a little way further, then uphill and then I have something to show you. Are you cold?' he asked and he straightened her scarf, taking care not to pull her shining black hair. The meal at the restaurant had been a success in spite of their initial awkwardness, and the waiter had done everything he could for them. Although he had been a little too cheerful for Anton's liking, it was obvious that Júlía had enjoyed his funny asides, and the icing on the cake had been when he brought their dessert with sparkling candles, and sang 'Happy Birthday' for her, solo and slightly off-key. This was turning into what it was supposed be: the best evening of their lives.

They just needed to turn the next corner and the explosion site would be in front of them. Anton had to stop himself hurrying ahead and pulling her along with him. He had waited so long for this.

'Look at all the police cars down there,' he said when they turned the corner. 'They've been there since this morning.'

'I know,' Júlía said. 'Radio Edda was blown up.'

'Now they won't be able to keep on damaging the community by preaching hate against immigrants,' Anton said, reaching into his pocket and handing Júlía the envelope. He could see that she wasn't joining the dots, and her expression was even more perplexed as she tore it open. He had printed the day's best news image from the

internet on the front of the card. It showed the scorched building and
the Radio Edda sign, with its *Iceland for Icelanders* slogan, broken on
the pavement.

'There you are,' he said. 'That's your birthday present.'

'What do you mean?' Júlía still didn't seem to be making the connection, so he smiled and explained it for her.

'I blew up Radio Edda. For you.'

To begin with Júlía laughed, and then shook her head.

'Tell me you're joking,' she said. 'This is a joke, isn't it? You'd never
do anything like this?'

'Now they've learned their lesson,' Anton said. 'The rest of the media
will think twice before they start spouting hatred against Muslims and
all that prejudice.'

Júlía took a couple of steps back, collided with a lamp post, stum-
bled and then sat down on the stone kerb that separated the car park
from the pavement. He was about to sit down next to her when she put
out a hand to stop him.

'Now you're going to have to tell me that this is some disgustingly
unfunny joke,' she said. 'Before I start to cry, Anton.'

She stared down at the shattered and scorched building, her face
expressionless, as if carved in stone. This wasn't the reaction that Anton
had expected. He had expected disbelief, but not on this scale.

'We've talked about this so many times,' he said. 'That crowd from
Radio Edda are the ones who make it so difficult for people like you
and your family to live here. We've been through this so often, Júlía.
The situation gets worse all the time – they even haul out lawyers and
university professors to say that Muslims are dangerous. They're trying
to brainwash people into hating you.'

'Was it really you who planted the bomb in the radio station?'

Now the tears were flowing down Júlía's cheeks.

Anton melted inside, stepped towards her, spreading his arms wide,
ready to wrap them around her. But Júlía swatted away his outstretched
hands and quickly scrambled to her feet.

'I thought you were the best boy in the world, and my parents are always saying how lucky I am to have met such a good boy, who's so different to all the other Icelandic guys. But there's a murderer inside you!'

Anton went towards her, his thoughts in turmoil. This wasn't the way it had been supposed to be.

'I'm no murderer, Júlía. I would never kill anyone. I made sure to set it off when there was nobody there.'

'There *was* someone there,' Júlía snapped back. 'Someone was injured. They said on the news that someone's in hospital! You're an idiot, Anton! You're the biggest idiot I've ever met!'

'But you told me yourself that something needed to be done about all this,' he said, conscious that all the sincerity had gone from his voice. He was shocked at the news that there had been someone in the building. Now he was confused, and all his convictions, which had sounded so logical and reasonable, had been dashed. 'I told your father that I would look after you,' he said. 'And this will change society and make it better. For you.'

'Don't you dare say that you did this for me or my dad. When Dad says you should look after me, he means keeping other boys away!' Now Júlía's voice had risen to a yell, with all the power her lungs could put into it. 'Why do you think we came here from Syria? To be somewhere people argue normally or go downtown with a placard if they're pissed off about something. We fled Syria to escape from people like you. To get away from bombs.'

101

'Come in,' Anton's father said. 'Anton's out so I'll have a look in his room. Do you remember what the backpack looks like?' he asked, his foot on the first step of the stairs.

'It's black, with a Puma logo, as far as I remember,' Sonja said, looking around.

It was a beautiful house, with an old-fashioned interior, panelling halfway up each wall and white window frames. She heard Anton's father upstairs in the bedroom and took a couple of steps into the living room, looking around her. The furniture was all antique, beautifully made and polished, and family photographs stood on the mantelpiece. She moved closer to the row of pictures and peered at one of them. In it a young man in a traditional woollen sweater stood on a quay, a big ship behind him. She recognised the look of the man, but decided she had to be wrong. Glancing over the other pictures, she noticed another that attracted her attention: a family sitting on a sofa. It had to have been taken at Christmas, as on the table in front of them was an Advent wreath with four flickering candles. Anton's father sat on the sofa and next to him was a woman who had to be his wife, as between them sat a little boy, presumably Anton, of around two years old. Next to the couple were two girls in their teens, an adult woman, and then *him*. Sonja leaned closer and squinted at the picture, hoping to see him more clearly. It was quite an old picture and he had changed, but there was no doubt who it was.

'Is that Húni Thór?' she asked as Anton's father came into the living room, Tómas's backpack in his hand.

'I should say so!' he said. 'He's my sister's boy. You know him?'

'Slightly,' Sonja said. 'That's to say our paths crossed a long time ago. And I used to see him on TV sometimes when he was in parliament.'

Anton's father took the picture down from the mantelpiece.

'That's my sister,' he said, pointing at the woman next to Húni Thór in the picture. 'She was a single parent with the two girls and him, and the boy was out of control. So I more or less took him under my wing and made a man of him. Pushed him through navigation college and then helped him find his feet in business.' There was a note of pride in his voice. 'This is him with the first boat he skippered,' he added, pointing at the picture Sonja had noticed first.

'Was he at sea for long?' Sonja asked, for want of anything better to say while she stared at the photograph.

'No. That's the thing with Húni Thór. He doesn't stick with anything for long. He was a few years at sea, then two terms in parliament, but that didn't suit him. He seems to have done well in business, though.'

'What sort of business did he go into?' Sonja asked. But when she saw the look on Anton's father's face she immediately regretted her question. It was clear Húni Thór's uncle was aware that there was something shady about his nephew's business activities, although Sonja doubted that he knew exactly what kind of business Húni Thór found most profitable; a business that she was also involved in.

'I guess he's much the same as me,' he said, handing her the backpack. 'Does what works out best, depending on the circumstances.'

Sonja thanked him for fetching the bag, and Anton's father showed her to the door.

'I forgot to ask your name. I know we've met before, when the boys were playing football together, but it's completely escaped my memory.'

He extended a hand and she took it firmly.

'Sonja,' she said.

'Ingimar,' he said and smiled again. His discomfort following her awkward question about Húni Thór's business was gone. 'Tell you what,' he added. 'Maybe you and Tómas would like to come down to the dock to see my new boat being delivered? I'll give you a guided tour.'

Sonja smiled apologetically, unsure whether Ingimar was flirting with her; he had held on to her hand for longer than necessary and was now gazing straight into her eyes. She wondered how to decline courteously.

'Anton will be going to sea for the first time this summer and he'd enjoy showing Tómas around the boat. And you'll be able to say hello to Húni Thór as well, as you're old friends.'

'Say hello to Húni Thór?' Sonja looked at him questioningly. 'Will he be on board?'

'Yes, he's steaming it across from Fraserburgh for me.'

Ingimar picked up a copy of that morning's paper and showed it to Sonja. She stared at it transfixed. She had seen the front page in two or three places already that day but hadn't taken a close look at it; pictures of ships weren't something that sparked her interest.

'We'll be fishing for langoustine, and I'll be taking every second trip this summer myself, with Anton as part of the crew. It's a twenty-metre boat, steel hull...'

Sonja no longer heard what Ingimar was saying, and his voice faded into the background as he rambled on about the boat, the trawl gear, langoustine fishing and the sea in general while she read the news article. A fishing company owned by Húni Thór, and presumably also by his uncle, Ingimar, had bought a trawler from Scotland, according to the article, and Húni Thór was the skipper who was bringing it over to Iceland following a refit. At the end was a quote from Húni Thór Gunnarsson, 'former parliamentary star and entrepreneur', who described the boat in glowing terms. He seemed to be displaying the flair that had served him so well through the years.

Sonja put the newspaper down on the sideboard and told Ingimar that she and Tómas might well take up his offer to look over the boat if they had time, although during such a short visit to Iceland there was naturally a great deal to do, with plenty of people to visit and errands to run.

She tripped quickly down the steps and sat in the car next to Alex. She took out her phone, punched in 800 5005 and as soon as the police confidential hotline responded she began to speak.

'You need to take a good look at the boat that's on the front cover of *Fréttablaðið* today: *Anton RE*. It's due to arrive in Iceland the day after tomorrow and on board is the largest shipment you've ever seen. Coke, Es, speed, steroids.'

She ended the call and took the battery out of her phone. Alex looked at her questioningly. He understood no more than a few words of Icelandic, but he could see that Sonja looked relieved.

Messing up the occasional shipment was never appreciated, but Sebastian would never forgive Húni Thór for losing the whole of the store in one go. This would put Húni Thór out of the game and her back in a key position. The knot of tension that had been growing and hardening in her belly over the last few days had vanished, and now she gazed along Tjarnargata and admired how beautiful the dark-green shrubs on the bank of the lake looked even this early in the summer.

102

Agla had waited with her phone in her hand all evening, but when it finally rang she was so startled, she dropped it and it bounced onto the floor and under the sofa. On her knees, she groped for it, finally found it and answered.

'What are you up to?' Elísa asked. 'Right now. What are you doing?'

'I'm in my dressing gown, on my knees on the floor crawling around to find my phone under the sofa.'

Elísa laughed.

'I wish I was there with you,' she said. 'So I could laugh at you.'

'I wish you were as well,' Agla said. 'But I have the feeling you're best off at Hólmsheiði for the moment.'

'Yeah, I know. I'm getting treatment for the withdrawal symptoms,' Elísa said. 'I have an AA meeting tomorrow and again the next day. I'm going to be at every one from now on.'

'That's good, sweetheart.'

'Am I your sweetheart?' Elísa giggled quietly and Agla imagined her standing hunched against the white-painted wall by the wing pay-phone, and immediately felt a strong wave of desire.

'You're my sweetheart,' Agla whispered. 'And now you're mine. You're free of the Boss and all of that crowd.'

'I'm free of them at least for as long as I'm in here,' Elísa said. 'The problems start when you're let out and old friends start to call, you know. Of course you're fond of them and don't want to lose them, and all that. But before you know it you're back in the shit and doing all sorts of stupid stuff.'

There was a desperation in Elísa's voice, so Agla hushed her.

'It won't be like that next time,' she said. 'I've fixed things with Sonja. With the Boss. You'll be left completely alone.'

'How did you do that?' Elísa suddenly sounded agitated. 'I owe one of the guys who works for the Boss and promised to do something for him instead, and those debts don't disappear, even after a couple of years. You don't know how all this works, Agla.'

'Don't worry about all that. You're safe. The Boss doesn't own you any longer. You're mine.'

'That's if you want me now,' Elísa said and burst into sobs. 'I've no idea how it happened, but I've just been told my blood test says I'm pregnant.'

103

His father was sitting in the living room, watching TV when Anton came home. He dropped onto the sofa next to him, kicked off his shoes and loosened his tie.

'Well, then,' his father said, with the habitual artificial cheerfulness Anton knew he switched on in order to appear buoyant when things had been difficult. More than likely his mother had been more than usually unpleasant to him this evening. 'How's things with the younger generation? How was your evening? And the meal?'

'The meal was fine,' Anton muttered.

'Good to hear,' his father said. 'I told them to look after you, and let them know that it's Júlía's birthday. Did they make something out of that?'

His father switched channels, as the ten o'clock news bulletin was about to start.

'They brought ice cream and sparklers and stuff, and the waiter sang for her,' Anton said, and his heart ached. Two hours ago they had sat in the restaurant, happy and satisfied. Júlía had gazed at Anton as she did sometimes, with a tenderness in those brown eyes that made him feel there could be nobody happier than he was.

'Hey, what's the matter?'

His father turned down the TV and turned to Anton.

'Nothing,' Anton said, yet wanted his father to keep asking, because there was so much that had gone wrong.

'I can see something's up,' his father said. 'Spill the beans, young man.'

'Umm.'

He didn't know what he could tell his father without saying too much.

'What happened, my boy?'

Now his father had switched to the gentle voice, and Anton felt himself give way. The tears forced their way out and he buried his face in his hands.

'We split up,' he gasped.

His father stared at him in amazement.

'What? And tonight of all nights? My poor lad.' His father shifted closer, put an arm around Anton's shoulder and pulled him close. 'There, there, my boy,' he crooned, patting his back as if he were a small child who needed to be burped. 'There, there.'

Gradually his words and the patted rhythm on his back drew him in. It had been years since he had grown out of curling up in his father's arms, but this time he let himself lie against his shoulder, in the security of his bulky body, while the ten o'clock news bulletin, devoted solely to the explosion, rolled across the screen.

104

'It's all wrecked. All the information I had gathered, everything I had written, all the links and the screenshots and everything I had ready for you has been blown up. Not that any of it fucking matters.'

María knew that she was still sedated because she felt like she was floating on a white cloud, although she could see clearly enough that it was a hospital bed she was lying in. But her feeling was correct: she didn't care about all that stuff, all the missed opportunities and ideas of some kind of justice. She was just relieved to be alive – relieved that she was going to be fine.

'We have the timeline of events that you let us have, and to be honest, the explosion doesn't do the story any harm.' The guy from the *Spotlight* team, whose name María couldn't remember, seemed keener than ever. 'Even though important documents have been lost, some of that can be retrieved and as this is linked to the explosion, we'd be guaranteed record viewing figures. Everyone wants to know about it.'

'But it's not connected to the explosion,' María said, realising she was unable to speak clearly. 'The police said Radio Edda was the target, and The Squirrel had been, you know, collateral damage.'

'That's not what my sources in the police are saying. They suspect that The Squirrel was what they wanted to blow up, precisely because of your coverage of this scandal. The same source said they've managed to trace the vehicle used to place the bomb, and it won't be long before there's news of an arrest that will take people very much by surprise. It seems it's also linked to a massive drugs operation. That's what I've been hearing.'

María shrugged and closed her eyes for a moment. She was too tired to keep track of what the *Spotlight* guy was saying. He was mixing things up, just as Marteinn used to when he saw conspiracy everywhere. When she opened her eyes, he was still talking; now it was about how media across the Nordic countries wanted to buy her work, so she shut her eyes again. She just didn't care. She heard him continue to murmur steadily, and then she heard the nurse come in and tell him that she was tired and needed to rest, and he ought to come tomorrow or the next day.

'Bye, bye,' she said, or at least that was what she thought she said. She was so desperately worn out, she couldn't be bothered to open her eyes, let alone raise a hand to wave him goodbye. She allowed herself to sink back into the stupor she had been in, between spells of wakefulness, ever since she had walked along the corridor, past the sack truck with the box on it, and had been about to open The Squirrel's door. She'd realised then that she needed the toilet, so she turned and went back along the corridor to the horrible, stiff iron door that turned out to have been an ancient fire door that Radio Edda's manager had at some point decided to have fitted there as a cost-saving exercise. Never again would she complain that she had such a small bladder. Her modest bladder had quite literally saved her life.

105

Ingimar coughed and blinked hard, but could see nothing through the smoke except the pattern on the Spanish rug right in front of his eyes. He could feel the handcuffs behind his back, then one of the police officers crouched behind him, hauling his hands high so that he was completely helpless and pain shot through his shoulders.

He had no notion of how all this had happened. He had dozed off on the sofa with Anton, and a moment later he found himself here on the floor in handcuffs. He had the impression that all of the police officers were in black, wore helmets and were armed; this had to be the Special Unit.

'Anton,' he tried to call, but his voice was drowned out by the shouts and noise of the police team. Somewhere in the din and the smoke he was sure he could hear Anton's voice calling, '*Dad!*'

'Anton! Anton!' he shouted, before it dawned on him that he might have more success calling to the policemen so that they might treat the boy more gently than they had him. 'The boy's only fifteen,' he yelled. 'He's fifteen!'

The police officer behind him shoved his knee harder into his lower back until his vision began to darken. When he was again able to concentrate, the smoke had mostly dissipated from the living room and the noise level had dropped enough for him to make out words.

'Ingimar Magnússon you are hereby under arrest for terrorism. You are not obliged to answer questions about the matter on which you are charged. You have the right to a lawyer, and the police are obliged to respect your wishes in appointing legal representation. On arrival at a police station you will be given a sheet of information establishing these points, which you are obliged to sign.'

Ingimar stared at the feet of the police officer giving this speech, and then craned his neck to see Anton. As soon as he saw him, he felt the fear overwhelm him. Anton sat in a chair in front of him, a burly police officer training a weapon on him. Anton stared back at his father and as their eyes met, the tears began to roll down the boy's cheeks. The look on his face was the one he'd had as a little boy when he had done something seriously naughty.

Terrorism meant the explosion yesterday. There was no other explanation. Anton nodded, as if he was reading his father's thoughts.

'Dad...' he gasped as two police officers hauled Ingimar to his feet. But Ingimar managed to hush the boy, frowning so that Anton understood that he was telling him to keep quiet. He was silent.

If anyone had asked him how he would have reacted if his son had caused a huge amount of damage by setting off a bomb, almost killing someone in the process, he would have said that there would be no end to his fury. But now, standing in the living room in handcuffs and watching Anton in tears, he felt himself overwhelmed by a need to protect him. There wasn't anything he wouldn't do for the boy, not a thing. He would accept any kind of endless punishment if it would spare Anton.

'I'll sort this out,' he whispered to Anton as he was led out. 'I'll sort it all out.'

He was swept down the steps between two police officers, who held his upper arms so tightly that his feet barely touched the ground.

'This is all some misunderstanding,' he said to the young officer who placed a hand on his head and folded him into a seat in the patrol car.

'People like you,' the young man snarled. 'You think you can get away with anything. But now we've nailed you.'

He shut the door behind Ingimar and sat in the front seat as the bald policeman in the driver's seat started the engine. He twisted around to reverse, and looked into Ingimar's eyes.

'"*Soon they'll come; soon my ships will come to harbour*", eh?'

It was clear from the police officer's grin that he thought he was being clever, quoting poetry, but Ingimar failed to understand the connection. More than likely it was the usual Icelandic spite aimed at anyone who did well for himself; and of course his new boat had been in the news recently.

August 2017

106

According to the radio, it was the warmest day of the summer, and Agla could feel it, standing in the shade of the church wall. She took off her jacket so she wouldn't sweat.

William laughed.

'You're nervous,' he said.

Agla shook her head.

'No,' she said, taking the hand sanitiser from her bag and rubbing some into her palms.

'That's the third time you've disinfected your hands,' William laughed. 'You really are nervous.'

Hearing footsteps in the gravel, they looked up and saw María coming towards them. Her limp was obvious, but otherwise she looked well. Agla left William to enjoy his third cigarette by the church wall and went towards her.

'Thank you for coming,' she said, offering María her hand.

'I was surprised to get your invitation,' María said, breathless from the walk from the car park and through the cluster of old buildings that formed the Árbær Museum. 'Didn't you see the *Spotlight* documentary?'

'Sure,' Agla said, 'It's not as if I had any reputation to lose, so it could hardly do me any harm. It's worse for poor Ingimar.'

'I don't feel sorry for him,' María said. 'Who would have imagined he was smuggling drugs as well?'

'He was fitted up by his nephew,' Agla said. 'That's what my sources at Hólmsheiði say, and they're reliable.'

'Serves him right, all the same. I hope he rots behind bars,' María said, her mind clearly made up. 'But congratulations!' she added in a happier tone, leaning forwards to kiss Agla's cheek.

'Thanks,' Agla said. 'And congratulations on the new job. *Berlingske Tidende*, isn't it? Not bad at all.'

'It's great. There wasn't much left of The Squirrel, and I'm overjoyed to be leaving this miserable, corrupt island run by a lousy old boys' network.'

They were at the church doors now. Agla introduced María to William, who immediately started to flirt, much to María's displeasure. She seemed to have instantly worked out who he was – she had studied him in detail for the *Spotlight* documentary – but William was obviously yet to make the connection.

What was so strange was that when Elísa had asked if there were any of her family she would like to invite, there was nobody who came to mind, and after thinking it over, Agla had decided that on a day like this she preferred to have around her the people who really knew her. She didn't care that these people might not like her, as long as they knew the real Agla. So she mentioned María and William, and Elvar the lawyer. Elísa happily wrote their names on the sheet of paper, in a column marked *Agla's friends*. The column marked *Elísa's friends* was packed with names and could have been longer, but the whole crowd was unlikely to appear. Only a few people could be seen in the church. Elísa's father was there, sitting on the front pew, along with her brother.

'There'll be coffee and pancakes afterwards in the café,' Agla said, again helping herself to hand sanitiser. Her palms were sweating badly.

'Very Icelandic,' William said. 'Except there's no alcohol.'

He was quite right that it was all very much according to tradition. She would have been satisfied with a visit to the Sheriff's representative at the prison, but as far as Elísa was concerned, the only option was this old-fashioned little church, with herself in national dress.

'And can Elísa stay for the coffee afterwards?' María asked.

Agla nodded.

'Yes, she has two hours' parole, with an escort.'

'You didn't want to wait?' María asked. 'I mean until she's released?'

It was an awkward question that Agla didn't want to answer, but considering it was María, who already knew everything about her, she went ahead.

'No. We're doing it now because she's pregnant.'

'Oh.' There was no mistaking that this was not the answer María had expected.

'We don't know who the father is, so Elísa wants me to be mum. Or rather, the other mum. She'll have the baby with her to start with, and then I'll take it while she finishes her sentence. I know nothing about children, but it'll work out.'

'Of course it will,' María said, placing a hand on her back. 'But what's in it for you?' she asked. 'You once told me that you never do anything unless somehow or other there was something in it for you. That means love as well? Not just nuts-and-bolts stuff?'

Agla smiled.

'People change,' she said. 'I've extricated myself from a lot of business. Even you wouldn't find me linked to anything shady now.'

María's eyes widened.

'That's a big change!' she said. 'What came over you?'

'Love,' Agla said. 'That's what's in it for me.'

As the words passed her lips, she saw the car approach around the corner of the workshop, one of the old buildings that had become part of the museum. She had expected it would come from the other direction, but it was just like Elísa to arrive from where she was least expected. William hurried into the church to let the priest know, and Agla put on her jacket.

Ewa, Sigurgeir and Guðrún all got out of the car. It wasn't something Agla had thought about, but now it looked as if Elísa was some kind of highly dangerous gangster who deserved an escort of three warders. Agla had made sure to invite the three prison staff they both knew, in the hope that it might make visiting Elísa smoother – a wedding softened every heart. Elísa stepped out of the car, a broad smile on her face, and Agla again dropped a silent word of thanks for this beautiful August day.

Elísa's hair had been simply done, hanging loose and with a dianthus in it, and the national costume suited her perfectly. Agla had tried to buy it, but the old woman in the hire shop had flatly refused to sell. One day she would have a traditional costume made for Elísa, who had said that these were the smartest clothes she had ever seen.

'*Hæ*,' Elísa said, and kissed her.

'*Hæ*,' Agla said. 'You're beautiful.'

'You too,' Elísa said, and Agla felt a moment's discomfort. She had done nothing special; she had simply bought herself a new suit. These were the only clothes she felt at home in. But she had been to the hairdresser to get her hair and make-up fixed so that she would look respectable for the pictures that Elísa had been adamant ought to be taken so the child could look at them one day; and to show the girls at Hólmsheiði too, of course.

'Are you happy?' Agla whispered to her.

Elísa skipped in excitement.

'Shit, Agla. Just a bit. It's so beautiful here, and I love the Árbær Museum, and you, and the church and everything. It's just what it should be.'

'Ready?' William asked, standing in the church doorway.

Agla buttoned her jacket and took Elísa's hand. As the doors opened, they walked together down the church aisle, which echoed with the ABBA song they had agreed was the one that would be played at their wedding.

'*Take a chance on me.*'

Acknowledgements

Getting a book that was first written in the ancient and archaic Icelandic language into the hands of an English reader is not a simple task. It takes many people, each a specialist in their own field, whereas the writer's role during this process is mostly to watch in awe and excitement.

I feel very lucky that my work has reached the English-speaking world and there are quite a few people I want to thank for making this happen.

The person who has been key to making my story available in English is, of course, my translator, Quentin Bates, one of the 340,000 speakers of the Icelandic language. My warmest thanks go to him; our collaboration has been a joy.

I also want to thank my publisher, Karen Sullivan, and her wonderful team at Orenda Books. I feel very privileged that my books are part of the catalogue of such an amazing independent publisher who has such a good eye for quality. Every writer needs to feel they have their publisher's support, and I can say I have always felt cherished at Orenda.

Editing a translated book is no easy task and sometimes requires assuming the role of diplomat, a position my editor, West Camel, has managed superbly. I want to thank him for all of his support, kindness and help.

I also want to thank Mark Swan for the striking cover designs for *Snare*, *Trap* and now *Cage*, which make my books stand out on the shelf. I am one writer who is very proud to have her books judged by their covers.

Thank you also to all the journalists and bloggers who have taken the time to read and write about the previous two books. It is very comforting to know that *Cage* will be welcomed and given a fair chance to prove itself by such a book-loving crowd.

Finally my thanks go to the readers who have stuck with my story throughout the trilogy, who have rooted for the characters, questioned their motives and enjoyed the ride. I hope you find *Cage* a satisfying end to the tale.